BILLY BRAZIL

A Novella

Emilio DeGrazia

Minnesota Voices Project Number 50

New Rivers Press 1992

Library of Congress Catalog Card Number 91-61255
ISBN 0-89823-130-2
Edited by C. W. Truesdale
Editorial Assistance by Paul J. Hintz
Cover artwork and design by Paul Burmeister
Inside artwork by Earl Potvin
Book Design and Typesetting by Peregrine Publications

The author wishes to express his thanks to several people—among them Dr. Kristi Lane,
Carol Slade, Jack and Lynn Nankivil, Elizabeth Colapietro, Karen and Dick Hastings,
Seymour Byman, Katie Maehr, Paul J. Hintz, and Jack and Jean Ervin—who made
thoughtful suggestions that were useful at various stages of revision. Many thanks also
to Susan Roberts, Bill Truesdale, and Monica DeGrazia for their especially careful and
caring critical comments.

The publication of *Billy Brazil* has been made possible by grants from the Jerome Foundation and the Metropolitan Regional Arts Council (from an appropriation by the Minnesota Legislature). Additional support has been provided by the Arts Development Fund
of the United Arts Council, the First Bank System Foundation, Liberty State Bank, the
Star Tribune/Cowles Media Company, the Tennant Company Foundation, and the National Endowment for the Arts (with funds appropriated by the Congress of the United
States). New Rivers Press also wishes to acknowledge the Minnesota Non-Profits Assistance
Fund for its invaluable support.
New Rivers Press books are distributed by

The Talman Company   Bookslinger
150 Fifth Avenue   2402 University Avenue West
New York, NY 10011   Saint Paul, MN 55114

Billy Brazil has been manufactured in the United States of America for New Rivers Press,
420 N. 5th Street/Suite 910, Minneapolis, MN 55401 in a first edition of 2,000 copies.

This Book is Dedicated to
Kevin O'Brien
And to the Memory of
Don Lund

One

BILLY BRAND distinguished himself on the very first day. "My proper Christian name," he said as Professor Holmay called the roll, "is William Allan Brand. Call me Billy, please sir."

For two weeks Billy said nothing more. Then Holmay asked the whole class, "What would you have done with someone like Bartleby?"

Holmay had a habit of waiting for his words to circulate in the room, as if their sound were a breeze clearing the air. After fifteen years of teaching he was still impressed by the deep tone of his voice, and now and then even surprised by a sense of urgency that seemed to return from an unmemorized past. Once upon a time his words had been full of urgency. "I am a professor," he used to say, "because I have something to profess." What he professed, in those days when he thought of his as a voice crying in the wilderness, was that words had the power to save souls and societies.

Carol Munson, shy and alert, finally replied. "I'm not sure, but Bartleby stood up for his beliefs."

Holmay paused, suddenly wary; Carol Munson knew something he didn't know. "What's this story all about?"

"Nothing," said Lance Walcott from the back row. "It's about a guy who ends up working in a lawyer's office. But he doesn't want to work and doesn't want to pay rent. He just sits there like he's stoned, staring at a wall. Bartleby was weird."

"So what was his problem?" Holmay asked, shifting his attention to Carol Munson.

"I'm not really sure," she said as she lowered her eyes. "It isn't anything you can put your finger on."

"What would you have done with Bartleby, Lance?"

"I would throw him out in the street where he belongs."

Carol Munson was shaking her head. "No, that wouldn't be right. But I'm not sure what I would have done."

Holmay surveyed the room, eyes shying away as his approached, confusion ashamed of itself. Only Billy was looking up, his eyes alert as if suddenly everything had become clear to him.

Holmay glanced at the clock. Eighteen minutes after nine. Twenty-five more minutes more of this.

"So what is this crazy story really all about?"

A blond-faced boy spoke from the middle of the room, his words turning like an engine that would not start. Yes, Holmay nodded, yes, yes. That's your opinion, yes, and your opinion is of course all yours, your idea, and your idea is a thought, notion, belief, interpretation, impression, feeling, absurdity, fact. Your fact. Does anyone else agree? From left to right a few hands in the air, eager to have their say, the room filling with more words—opinions, ideas, thoughts, notions, beliefs, interpretations, impressions, feelings, absurdities—and he nodding yes, yes, keep them talking. Words to grease the wheels of the clock.

"Class dismissed," he said after stealing one last glance at the clock.

He stood at the door smiling as they filed out, a sense of failure and loathing within. He had endured another hour and had delivered his own ten-minutes-worth of words, pausing just often enough for the students to scribble them down, words not really his, occupying a space in the room as apart from himself as the faces waiting for him to say something that mattered to them. All those faces strangers to him.

Billy was waiting for him in the hall. "Dr. Holmay...I mean...that was something in there."

"Then why didn't you add your two-cents-worth?"

"Because I was...I think the story was great, sir. I just couldn't stop seeing it all. And then when you explained it everything was just so clear."

"Everything?"

"And I was just wondering, Dr. Holmay, sir, just how you do it...how you see everything like that. If I could do it too."

"There aren't many jobs left in this business anymore."

"I mean...do you think I would...qualify?"

Before Holmay could reply, Billy turned his head away, his eyes following something in the corridor.

"Come to my office tomorrow and we'll talk."

"Do you think so?" Billy said, still absently looking away.

2

When Holmay walked to his office door he could not resist looking back. Billy, still standing in the middle of the hall, was staring at him. Holmay quickly nodded and fumbled to find the key to his door. When he closed it behind himself he could still feel Billy's presence on the other side.

Two

When Matthew Holmay was sixteen years old he made up his mind about human nature. "Man must be basically good," he scribbled in a spiral notebook containing a few dates and names for a world history class, "because we all have the power to sympathize. Nobody teaches us how, so it has to be inborn. It survives in all of us, no matter how bad we are and no matter how hard the world is on us. From this comes all good. All evil comes from putting it down."

Holmay kept the notebook in an old trunk full of yearbooks, clippings, love letters, and photographs. From time to time he threw a few things out, but the notebook always remained. When he was nostalgic he went to the trunk and reread the words, recalling with embarrassment his boyhood blunders and crude victories. But he was always proud of the boy who had written these words, and believed he had never improved on them, had come to no explanation more convincing, simple, or heartfelt.

At the age of twenty-nine he became Dr. Holmay, Ph.D., Assistant Professor of English at Center State University in a midwestern town. He was married the same year in the First Presbyterian Church, a white-steepled stone building across from the university gymnasium. His fiancée Cynthia was persuaded to have the marriage ceremony there even though she was a Roman Catholic, "with a small c." Holmay liked the Presbyterians. Though they tended to vote Republican, they at least had no clear theology and were only serious about church a few hours

4

a month; therefore they were easier to get along with than true-believers of any sort. Few Presbyterians knew anything about Knox, Calvin, predestination, or the doctrine of election, Original Sin rearing its ugly head in their minds mainly when they had sexual thoughts. And because they preached a gospel of social responsibility, they gave thousands to the United Way. So Holmay concluded that if he had to get married in a church, it might as well be a Presbyterian one.

The divorce was finalized eight years later, two years after a daughter, Evelyn, came along. The split was clean and sharp, in part because the lines were so agreeably drawn. He wanted Evelyn and the old house, and Cynthia wanted some things, some dignity, and a chance to start over again. It took little time once Cynthia had the courage to mention "divorce," for they had enough respect and good sense to let the details fall equitably into place. She would have to endure the censure and guilt that fall on mothers who forsake their children to pursue their own lives and careers; he would have to take on the daily responsibility of raising a little girl mainly by himself. Cynthia, who found her husband more tolerable than her suspicions that he was having affairs, knew he was getting the better end of the deal. The house would be paid off and he would remarry in a year or two, once he realized that raising a child required more than a bedtime story every night. So he would get someone else's help, while she would be a woman, divorced, bearing the added stigma of her decision to defect. Within eighteen months she was married again, this time to a middle-aged man with two teenaged sons. "He's a wonderful guy," she wrote from her new Minneapolis home, "and I must admit he reminds me of you. But him I can trust."

After Cynthia's departure Holmay's love-life never took off. He could still turn a few heads, but eyes did not invite the way they did when he was a married man. I'm getting older, he thought. It's as simple as that. No, said another voice. It's because you're not married any more. You were a perfectly safe rental then. Now you're an expensive property for sale, and how many women do you know willing to make payments for life these days? And Evelyn, not for sale at any price, would have to be part of any deal.

He spent long minutes staring at his books, outward and visible signs of his once-upon-a-time faith that they, and he, had something to say. And when he stood in front of a class he found young eyes staring at him as if he were babbling in Latin or Greek. Books were a bother, the eyes seemed to say. Whatever in the world did he see in them?

Other eyes were watching him too. Harold Richards, department head, took him under his wing one late afternoon. "I can't recommend you for promotion quite yet," he said, "because we've got to have something to show for it."

A book.

"It's all a game," was all he could think to say in response.

He began showing up a few minutes late, vaguely uncertain of himself, unable to find the right opening words. Once, suddenly and irrelevantly, he confessed that he was tired of exposing himself in front of the class. Everyone laughed, thinking he was telling some sort of dirty joke. He left the room ashamed of himself. Defunct. How could he compete with video, computers, and rock-and-roll? He who could not find the right words, had nothing to say, no book. Yes, he was becoming defunct.

When Cynthia had driven away with the U-Haul he watched from an upstairs window until she disappeared around the corner. Then he sat on his bed for over an hour, waiting for her footsteps on the stairs, her form in the bedroom door, her announcement that she had returned. He waited and waited, ashamed of the sense of relief overtaking him as he realized that she would not come back. Evelyn, not even two and a half, was asleep in her room. When she woke she would ask where her mother was, and he would tell her she had taken a long, long trip. His words would make no sense to her, but the time would come when the little girl would awaken in the night and cry because her mother was gone. Her crying would be full of outrage and pain, and his hours of silence full of guilt. Eventually he would make everything up to her, but for now he would have to find the right words.

So he had no book. So his teaching was slipping, his passion for the Big Questions about literature, life, culture and classrooms becoming even less than narrowly academic. He had Evelyn instead. So here was a chance for some sort of new life, new commitment and mission. The times were right. Divorce was not an unpardonable sin, and a woman's right to a life of her own was an established, if begrudged, social fact. For a father to gain custody was rare and fashionably correct, and such a father had much to gain from Presbyterians willing to grant a woman a divorce from her husband but not her child. He could be forgiven almost anything—even an indiscretion with a student—for having endured a woman who could do a thing like that.

Of course he said the right things, turned blame conveniently on himself, his efforts to make Cynthia look good too often feeling like gestures calculated to remind his friends of the minor nobility he had acquired in becoming sole parent to that lovely child. There was something in it for him, call it liberation chic.

There was another kind of uneasiness, more intellectual. Every explanation he could imagine for "what went wrong with the marriage" was not quite right. In fact, he did not know what went wrong. He, of course, had his reasons, and Cynthia had hers, but the reasons never added up in his mind, never came out even or pointed to a conclusion as inevitable as the decision to get a divorce. The divorce itself was a signal of professional failure. Would a man possessed by "something to profess" fail in a basically personal way? He never required himself to be a saint, but he wanted to be counted among the world's decent men. Would he count, especially when he couldn't trust his own explanations for the divorce? What did he really know about his divorce? Only that he and Cynthia lost interest in each other, that he was turned off, then lured away. The reasons, however many there were at any time of day or night, were never good enough. He knew some sociology, psychology, history and myth, and he and Cynthia never argued about money, religion, or politics. What, then, could it have been—fate, accident,

6

divine intervention? He clearly remembered one night in bed: Cynthia, clean as she always was, did not smell right to him. And their sex life was dying a slow death. So maybe it was "chemistry" that did their marriage in.

That explanation would not do. Though it had its way of insinuating itself into his mind, he fought it off. For if life's choices were the function of chemistry, was anyone anything more than its slave?

The question nagged him as he became more and more the father. Was it merely "blood" that made the devotion flow from him, at the expense of all the other passions in his life? Would a stranger-child, some orphan rescued from the streets, be able to generate the same intensity of devotion he gave to her? Evelyn. The naming had been special to him, the man of words. He held out for the name Eve, but Cynthia insisted it was too obvious, would embarrass a girl growing up. Cynthia was right again, so they negotiated toward Evelyn. But the very hour that Cynthia drove away from them both he had his way again, at least in his mind. Evelyn was his little Eve, and whether it was "blood" or "chemistry" or some vague virtue stirring his devotion to her, he resolved right then and there to be a God the Father to his girl, one more enlightened and benign than the tyrant who had pulled his cruel Garden trick.

Every day he changed the sheets on her bed and did a load of wash, with deliberate carelessness mingling his clothes with hers, as if the mixing of their smells in the wash would make it impossible for them to get out of each other's blood. He carefully screened each babysitter, looking for the small necessary enthusiasms. When Evelyn was three he cut office hours short to drive her home from Montessori School, and he spent late afternoons in playgrounds and parks, a book, mainly unread, always under his arm. She became a finicky eater and he indulged her tastes, and after a half-hour nap, sometimes begun at the kitchen table over a bowl of soup, she came alive until well after ten. She hopped rides on his back and rolled on the floor, trying to wrestle him down. Then just before bed, while she curled up under his arm, he read to her until she fell asleep. On tables and chairs he threw his own papers and books. They kept getting lost or left behind.

Except for the midnight hour, spent with a book the way a spent man feels obligated to pillow talk, he usually had two hours to himself, time to wash dishes, vacuum, rake leaves, wipe countertops—the small work of hands. It saved him, this work, from the nagging sense that he was wasting his life. He objected again and again to the nagging. No, he was not wasting his life. He was still a better teacher than most, and someday, someday, what he had to profess would find its way into a book. Could not a father's love for his daughter, expressed through faithful cultivation of daily necessary routine, be a work of some art? He glowed when he saw his sink, floor and countertops shine.

Then there was the house itself, the big Victorian thing with two living rooms, a den, five bedrooms upstairs and a spacious porch. Built in 1873, its stone foundation thicker than fortress walls, its high windows and gables expressed a sad altitude, as if mournng the loss of a genteel innocence. A house abandoned for

7

two years, waiting in rain and snow, for restoration, dignity, new life. He and Cynthia had eyed it more than once, and as the excitement was abandoning their sexual lives they clung to each other more closely at night, dreaming of the big old house. Finally they went to a bank. Together they would renew the exterior, reshingle the roof, paint the outside. Then they would move inside, do each room downstairs one at a time, and move up.

The danger of the house drew them close. When they walked out of the bank with their unimaginable thousands of dollars, their names still fresh on the dotted lines of the mortgage agreement, they stopped to embrace each other the way they once-upon-a-time did outside the Presbyterian church on their wedding day. The old green paint had to go, so the first summer they scraped and scraped until their hands moved back and forth in their sleep. Once the new white paint was on, the back porch, slanted haven for pigeons and squirrels, was next. Then came the wiring, walls and floors, the oak trim covered with layers of paint. One day, while he was stripping the mantle, Cynthia announced her pregnancy, and the mantle wasn't finished until Evelyn was two. When Cynthia drove the U-Haul away he had a mess in three spare rooms, the basement and garage, and some plumbing still undone.

With some contempt he resorted to how-to books, by trial and error learning to hammer and saw. Framing and drywall were easier than decoding allegories and metaphors. He grew confident, then arrogant, about the work he did on the house. "With my own two hands," he told even those who did not ask. "I did it all myself. And someday I'll get the whole thing done."

Still he felt the uneasiness. While the house became the talk of the neighborhood, and as Evelyn developed into a bright and lovely girl, he was betraying his books. Sooner than he imagined Evelyn disappeared around the corner the first time, and then she crossed the street on her own. Too soon she would be a teenage girl, then gone to some college far away. Then would his work of art be done? What then?

So when Billy spoke up in class and met him afterwards to say thanks, Professor Matthew Holmay felt a tingle of renewal. His work on the house and on Evelyn was incomplete but nothing to be ashamed about. He did what was required of both at the time, and as both required less he would take a new interest in his real work, the Billy Brands, those really interested in words and the life of the mind, those still trying to save souls and the messed-up world.

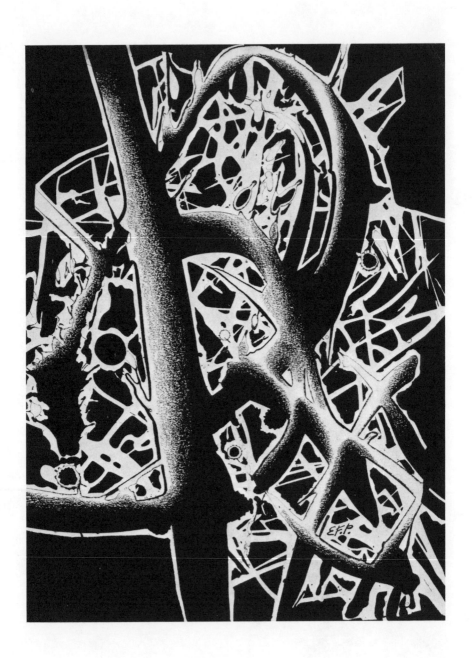

Three

ONE TIME, before Evelyn was three weeks old, Holmay woke up in the middle of the night.

"What's wrong?" Cynthia asked.

"I must have been dreaming," he said. "I was in a beautiful garden all alone, and under some bright green leaves I found a wonderful egg. I picked the egg up and it was still warm, and I was looking around for you. I was carrying it home, but tripped on the curb and dropped the egg. I got it all over my pants."

"Then what?"

"I woke up."

"It was a Freudian slip," she said as she rolled over and went back to sleep.

It was more, and less, than that. What stayed with Holmay was the terror of dropping the egg, the helpless despair of seeing it crushed, ruined. The first time he had lifted Evelyn up she felt like the dead robin he had found on his lawn as a boy, a fluff braced by a kitelike skeleton. His hands were too awkward and strong for her. He would fumble and let her fall, and no one would be able to put her together again.

Uneasily, he grew more careless with her. He swung her in circles and looped her over and around his back. His chest was her trampoline and his arms and legs her monkey bars. When she rode on his shoulders like a queen on an elephant's back, he kept an eye out for any sudden loss of balance, any small inclination to laugh and let herself go. He began seeing sharp corners everywhere, and was always on guard, ready to rescue her from a fall. When she was in another room he felt compelled to check on her every minute or two. Staircases were carefully fenced off and hard objects put away.

As she grew older he stood at the window worrying. She would turn the corner, wander lost in strange neighborhoods and never return. She would step off a curb and, right before his eyes, an oversexed car, drunk on rock-and-roll, would blast her to kingdom come. No, No, No, his heart screamed whenever he saw this happening to her. Please let it be me instead. He would tear the driver away from the car, punch and kick wildly at him, and at the same time he would use his body as a blanket to cover his little girl, keep the warmth of her life from evaporating out of time and space.

The subject in class one day came around to capital punishment. "What would *you* do," one of the hard-nosed boys said, "if somebody raped and murdered *your* little girl?"

Holmay had his answer prepared. If anyone hurt Evelyn he would want to kill that person with his own two hands, but what he *wanted* and what he *ought* to do were entirely different things. Revenge was not justice. It was never really right. He did not believe in violence, and no, he did not own a gun.

Easy words from a man whose daughter was safely in school, who had never personally known the victim of a violent crime. If anyone dared touch his little girl, he would shred that man's flesh with his fingernails and teeth.

❋ ❋ ❋

Billy, sitting on the floor next to Holmay's office door, was lost in his book. Holmay was late as usual. "I thought maybe you'd change your mind overnight," he said as he opened the door and showed Billy to a seat.

"Oh no," Billy replied. "Once I make up my mind, I never change it again."

What Holmay inspected for the very first time were Billy's long skinny hands, the thin moustache that seemed no more than a shadow on his face, and the straight black hair, too carefully trimmed and too short. Except for these peculiar features and the fact that Billy seemed too neatly dressed, he looked ordinary enough.

"You asked yesterday about studying literature here."

"Yes, what I would have to do to qualify."

"Well, you don't need to apply formally. Whether you pass your introductory courses will determine that."

"But I thought you were looking, sir, for a certain type."

"In a sense, of course, . . . I mean ideally we are. We're looking for people who really know how to read." Holmay caught himself in time. "Just what makes you want to get into this? Do you want to teach?"

"No, sir. I mean yes, sir. I don't think I would be be cut out for teaching, sir, unless I could do what you're doing. Do you know what I mean, sir?"

"If you mean that you're aware that jobs for college professors are scarce, then I know what you mean."

"Yes, sir. There's something really great about what you do with the stories we read. That's what I really like."

Holmay leaned away from Billy and rummaged on his desk for a stray tissue. Now and then, whenever a student sang his praises to his face, he was caught between wariness and embarrassment. Such students usually wanted a few words boosting their confidence, sometimes a grade, but he was never comfortable receiving praise.

"When students are interested and say bright things, it makes my job easy." He handed Billy a sheet listing the required courses.

Billy did not look at the sheet. "Maybe I'd like to get a master's degree someday too."

"It's something to think about."

A silence filled the small room as Billy looked up at him.

"Do you have any questions about the requirements?"

"Oh, sir, yes. But no, no, not really no. I...just wondered if there was anything else you wanted to know...I mean about me."

Holmay glanced at his watch without moving anything more than his eyes.

"Am I taking up too much of your time, sir?"

"Not at all. Yes, tell me about yourself."

Billy crossed his legs and shrank into his chair. For a long moment he looked the way he did in class—a stare, at once vacant and full, past Holmay, beyond the window at his back, beyond even the sky itself.

"I...I'm from Romersville, sir, you know, about twenty miles from here. I have a room of my own, in my house. I drive here every day with Stu Johnston. Do you know Stu Johnston, sir?"

"No."

"I want to study literature because...since I began reading books...I don't know, sir, but I just feel like I find myself there, right there...like that book by Thoreau, *Walden*. You know that book, where you're just in that cabin in the woods and nobody is bothering you and you're at peace with yourself and your thoughts, and you can just see yourself there."

Holmay smiled warmly at Billy, a small town boy, innocent, finding himself in books and therefore probably unpopular, a youth groping, as Holmay himself had groped in the dark, looking, as he had done, to the tangle of written words to help him make sense of life.

"But you know, sir," Billy suddenly said, "there's one thing I don't understand."

"What's that?"

"You say you never heard of Stu Johnston. I mean...why would you say that? Everybody in Romersville knows him, and he knows you."

"I've never been to Romersville, and I never had him in one of my classes."

Billy stared out the window. Then, as if talking aloud to himself, he said, "Ah yes, please sir, lots of times I wonder if he's lying to me."

Holmay smiled at Billy's words, and Billy looked away.

After Billy excused himself Holmay sat back and watched as Billy trundled down the corridor. What a strange bird, Holmay thought, somewhat amused by the strange mix of Billy's neatness and irrelevancies. He had seen enough carelessness in the majority of students—in their papers, talk and clothes— to welcome any sign showing respect for anything other than a sloppy blue-jeaned conformity. And irrelevancies, like stars in the galaxy, appeared everywhere in meandering written assignments. He had read hundreds, thousands, of student themes, most of them confirming a suspicion his heart refused to believe: that the ordinary mind, however full of bright flashes, was normally incapable of coherence, logic and clarity. Ah Freud, Holmay sighed. What a can of worms he opened for us. And therefore Ah Billy Brand, cursed by desire to sort the worms out and to make them stand at attention in rows so they could be counted and named. That boy, he concluded, is just how I used to be. Is maybe how I should be again.

A hand appeared around the corner and rapped twice on his open door. "Professor Holmay," said a mocking voice, "I didn't know we were having a test today."

Frances Drummond, woman, Assistant Professor, unmarried, intelligent, plain-looking and thick in the hips, peeked around the corner.

"I see you just had a visitor from another planet."

"Yes, his name is Billy Brand."

"William Allan Brand."

"You know him?"

"Not in the least," she said.

"He wants to become one of us."

Her eyes opened wide in mock horror. "But he already *is* one of us."

"He's a bit different."

"You're too generous. He's strange."

"I take it you *do* know this boy?"

"Yes," she said, lowering her voice. "He was in my drama course for six whole weeks. Never missed a day. Never said a word. Never turned in a written word."

"What's so strange about that?"

She closed the door. "He did talk to me. He called me up at home, told me how much he was getting out of it. *Et cetera.* Of course, he never turned in any work, even though he also told me, to use your words, that he wanted to become one of *us.*"

"So you think he's just trying to butter me up for a grade?"

"Grade? He never got a grade from me. He dropped out."

"Did you ask him why?"

"I know why," she said. "He quit coming right after I told him to stop calling me at home."

"Frances, you broke his heart. The poor kid's in love with you."

She shook off his irony. "No, that's not true and I'm sure of it. Matt, he followed me home one night. I saw him standing next to the tree right outside my house. I ignored him, put him out of my mind for two hours until I turned the lights out to go to sleep. And then on a whim I looked out the window and he was still there, in the same spot, looking not at my house but off somewhere else, somewhere really far away."

"I'm sure you just broke his poor longing literary heart."

"And I'm telling you I was scared the whole night."

"He was waiting outside in the cold for your love."

"Okay then, wise guy. Maybe now you're lucky enough to have him in love with you."

✳ ✳ ✳

That night, with Evelyn snuggled under his arm, he refused to let Frances intrude on his thoughts. No, he concluded, I've never done her wrong. It was bedtime story time, ritual devoted to filling Evelyn's last hour with the sound of words. The ritual had evolved its own form: At first she would giggle and squirm, but then she would curl up close to him until the story was done or her eyes began to fade. He would read on after she was asleep, then tuck the blanket neatly under her chin and turn off the light.

She had heard "Monkey Palace" twice before, so it was she who recited the first lines: "*Once upon a time there was a king with twin sons, John and Anthony, but because the king didn't know which of the two was born first, nobody knew who would inherit the crown.*"

She pulled the blanket in close and fixed her eyes on the ceiling. "Now you read."

"*The king wanted to be completely fair, so he required his sons to seek a wife, and the one whose bride brought him the rarest gift would inherit the crown. So the twins mounted their horses and galloped off. Within three days John happened on a lovely duke's daughter who gave him a tiny sealed box to take to the king. Anthony, entering a pathless forest through which he had to cut his way with his sword, suddenly came to a glittering palace of marble and gold. Knocking on the gate, he was met by a monkey exactly as tall as himself, and when he entered he found there a monkey world, all of them dressed in finery, all of them bowing his way. He was led to a sumptuous table in a dining room, and there he dined with monkeys in capes and plumed hats. After dinner he was led by torchlight to a bedchamber, where he was left alone for the night.*

"*He was awakened by a voice in the dark calling his name from the other side of the bed. 'If you promise to marry me,' the voice said, 'I will provide the rarest gift in the world.'*

"*In the morning the wedding carriage was prepared. It had a monkey coachman in front and two monkey footmen on the back, and inside, bedecked with jewels and ostrich plumes, was Anthony's monkey-bride. When the carriage arrived in the royal city, people pressed in close to get a glimpse of the prince's new wife, and a loud*

15

cry of laughter followed the carriage to the royal palace. 'Young Prince Anthony has found his better half,' everyone laughed until tears rolled. 'May they be fruitful and multiply.'

"The next morning both princes presented their wives to the king. From the tiny sealed box offered to the king by John's bride flew a live baby bird with a walnut in its beak and a tassle of gold inside the walnut shell. All eyes were amazed at the wonderful sight. Anthony's wife also provided a very small box, and it too had a baby bird inside. But in this bird's beak was a lizard, and in the lizard's mouth was a hazelnut containing a tablecloth embroidered by a thousand hands. And as soon as the tablecloth was spread in front of the king the monkey-wife turned into the most beautiful maiden in the world. 'By marrying me,' the maiden said, 'Anthony has delivered me and my people from an evil spell. Therefore Prince John can inherit his father's crown and Anthony can be king of all my liberated lands, and our two kingdoms can live in peace, love and harmony.'

"So the king," Holmay concluded, *"bade everyone to join hands, and they lived happily every after."*

Evelyn, her eyes heavy with sleep, looked up at her father's face and gave him a skeptical smile. "I like that one," she said as she pulled her blue blanket over her shoulder and curled her body closer to him, "but I wish Mommy would come live with us."

He folded the sheet over the blanket covering her. Then he planted a kiss on her forehead, whispered his goodnight, and turned off the light. It was stuffy in the room, so he went to the window and drew open the drapes. The window, painted shut years ago, he forced with the palms of his hands until he felt a small breeze coming through.

Then below, standing still next to the streetlight on the corner, he saw a human form looking up at his house. He strained to see into the shadows crossing each other in the yellow light, and once the notion occurred to him he could not imagine anyone else.

"Why, it's Billy," he said to himself.

Four

By THE TIME Holmay got to the front porch, no one was visible. He lingered a moment, holding his breath so he could hear small sounds in the night air. Had he seen anyone at all? Over the treetops the whistle of the Gopher Steelworks called an end to the evening shift, and two blocks away on Gower Boulevard cars took off after the lights turned green. Finally he turned his back, and for the first time since he had moved into his big old house, he locked the front door.

When Frances Drummond passed by his office the next morning she avoided his eyes. He read the gesture immediately. After a six-month truce, Frances had once again declared war on him. In the past four years they had been at war at least three times, and possibly more often than that, all the battles waged with the heavy artillery of silence and the sniping of a few carefully-aimed words.

He did not have to ask what it was this time, for it was the same old vague thing. Something he said or didn't say. The same old vague thing that came and went like the weather but always stayed the same. He was a man, divorced, a used car, but still somewhat shiny and usable. She was unmarried, in her thirties, more bright than he, willing to sacrifice romance in exchange for a marriage that offered companionship. So the thought crossed their minds every time their paths crossed, and they knew each other's mind. Once, but just once, he had asked her out for a drink. For weeks afterward her silence asked him what she had done wrong, but he could not explain that there was only one rub: she was not pretty enough, and too thick in the hips.

The explanation stopped there. He could think of better ones—he did not want to risk failing at another marriage, he wanted no distractions from his new little love, his Evelyn, and he wasn't in the mood just now to take on another responsibility—but the truth he couldn't get around was simply and basically the shape of her body. Frances Drummond in a beautiful body would have made a perfect second wife.

He knew better. What did he do every day in class but explain the need to look beyond appearances, to find value in the hints hiding behind the surfaces of language? Frances Drummond's hips made a hypocrite of him, and her silence, a run-on sentence almost too dreary to endure, forced him into his own sullenness. How honest could he ever be with her, or, to pose the problem academically, with student-disciples who had a right to honest answers from him? Could he ever come right out and say that love was, for him, a question of anatomy, which, reduced to its lowest common denominator, was a matter of chemistry? That this was one secret the great literature of the world did not reveal? And if this unlovely fact were true, what could Professor Holmay in good conscience profess? Nothing but his sordid personal truth—that a love could be made or unmade by the size of a woman's nose or hips. So maybe some things were better left unsaid. In class he would call on Lance Walcott and let Lance tell the unlovely truth: Why waste time with somebody who doesn't turn you on?

✳ ✳ ✳

Billy appeared at his office door. "Can we have that talk now, sir?"

"If you're clear-headed enough to make any sense," Holmay said as he motioned him toward the chair next to his desk.

"What do you mean, sir?"

"People aren't clear-headed when they stay up all night."

Billy looked away, his eyes ignoring Holmay's words.

"What were you doing outside my house last night?"

"Was it me you saw?" Billy asked, suddenly confused.

"I saw you standing there, right by my house."

"Yes, you're maybe right. I was out last night. I was taking a walk. I do a lot of thinking that way, sir, and last night I just couldn't turn the thinking cap off. Do you know what I mean, sir?"

"You weren't walking, Billy. You were standing there."

"That could have been somebody else, sir. But yes, yes, maybe he did stop by your house. I was thinking so fast I wanted someone to talk to, sir. Do you know what I mean? I thought maybe you'd want to talk to me. I saw the lights on. But then I said no, he doesn't want to talk to you. He's too busy right now. Maybe you'd come out and see somebody there, but you turned off all the lights in the room upstairs."

"So you just wanted to talk?"

"Yes. I have a lot of thoughts, a lot of thoughts. I walked and walked last night."

"So let's talk."

Billy wiped his brow. "Bartleby. I...I don't know about him. But...I'm sure. I read it three times yesterday...and this morning again. So I...haven't completely made up my mind. Why Bartleby suddenly decides...It was on Wall Street where he worked and I think that's symbolism, like the brick wall he faced and the room he was in that was inside another room. Was that symbolism too?"

"Yes, Billy, symbolism."

"And you have to wonder how the symbolism would be different nowadays for someone like him because we live in the nuclear age, and that's a wall too."

"Yes, that's right," Holmay said professorially. "The first part of our century was an age of irony and steel. Now we count on a balance of terror to keep us safe and sane."

"And Bartleby was against money and materialism, but there's something I don't really understand."

"What's that?"

Billy's face tensed as the thought formed in his mind. "Did he maybe commit suicide? Maybe just let it happen? And he's also Jesus Christ and that's what I don't get, unless Jesus Christ committed suicide too. I asked Lance Walcott about that after class."

"And what did he say?"

"He said, 'Sure, sure, Jesus pounded the nails into his own hands.'"

"Well," Holmay grinned, "that's just Lance being Lance. What did you say back to him?"

Billy lifted his head and spoke in clear tones. "I told him it all depends on how you look at it. There could be a world where when they pound nails in your hands it's like putting a gun to your head and pulling the trigger. There could be a world like that."

"In literature anything is possible, I suppose."

"Yes," Billy said enthusiastically, thrusting his hand toward Holmay for a handshake.

Bewildered, Holmay was paralyzed for a moment by the gesture. "I think we can shake on that," he said as he took Billy's hand.

They settled back in their chairs, both slightly embarrassed by the act.

"Do you think, sir," Billy began again, "that I'm cut out for it...?"

"For what?"

"To be a professor."

"Why should you think you're not? It seems you're learning how to read—symbolism, between the lines, that kind of thing."

"The sad thing, Dr. Holmay, is that there's so many who can't possibly imagine Christ nailing himself to the cross."

"As it were."

"As it were." Billy smiled.

"If you mean that there are unimaginative people, I would agree with you."

"I mean just that, sir—the vast majority, sir. They just don't read, don't see how literature opens the world up for them. I'm not like them. It just means so much to me. Will you be my mentor, sir?"

Holmay smiled. "You just study hard, Billy, and you'll find me looking over your shoulder now and then."

Billy stood and thrust out his hand again. "Thanks, sir. Thanks an awful lot."

After Billy left Holmay sat back in his chair, the tingle of Billy's hand-shake still warming his hand. William Allan Brand. What a strange bright bird he was, like an odd character in a book. His mind teeming with thoughts, trying to make sense of life. Difficult questions, all the impossible ones, haunting him all night, keeping him from sleep. No Lance Walcott here: no practical, soulless type. Holmay remembered himself as an eighteen-year-old. He too sleepless at night, the Big Questions hounding him as he passed house after house, in one of which was sleeping the Perfect Beautiful Girl. Had he not allowed himself to become too much like Lance—jaded, indifferent, unimaginative? Was there not a Billy Brand still alive in him, a small core of himself trying to be reborn, longing to have something to profess? Maybe he needed Billy more than Billy needed him.

* * *

Billy was not in class the next three days, his chair crowded out of the way by others on each side. Holmay had made up his mind to come right out with it. On a slip of paper attached to his lectures he had written himself a note: "Ask Billy where he's been."

From the corner of his eye he again saw Annette George watching him as he shuffled his papers and gathered the courage to begin. He hadn't noticed her until the end of the first week, mainly because he was always afraid of his students at first, looking not at them but out at himself standing in front of the room full of eyes watching him. Then one day name and face came together like a sudden revelation, and he had to move his eyes quickly away. She had a clear-skinned face with delicate features deepened by clear blue eyes, and her auburn hair fell naturally down to her shoulders. She was one of the elect, chosen by accident of birth to show how lovely the female form could be, and she was no more than nineteen years old.

She had never looked at him this way before. She had glanced up now and then, seeing him quickly shift his eyes away, and was vaguely smart enough to recognize the power she had over men. So when she looked point-blank at him, he was scared and confused. He fumbled with his notes, pretending to put them in order, and he forgot entirely about Billy Brand.

Halfway through the hour he asked Annette the question he would have wanted Billy to answer silently to himself. For the first time he singled her out.

"Given the ending of *Huckleberry Finn*, Miss George, does Twain seem to think that Huck is able to rise above the forces of social conditioning?"

While the question hung in the air Holmay applauded himself. The question made a student of Annette; he was giving to her what he had intended only for Billy Brand. And therefore she now had a chance to be in a class all by herself.

She lowered her eyes and shrank, unable to utter a word.

"He could have done anything he wanted," Lance broke in from the back of the room. "Huck Finn wanted to go out west to see the sights and start a new career, so he did. There was freedom out west. What was there to hold him back? In America people are free to do whatever they want to do."

Annette blushed like a damsel just rescued from distress.

Holmay found Billy after lunch. Half-hidden behind an ancient oak next to the library on the campus lawn, Billy offered no resistance to Holmay's gaze.

"Oh hello, Dr. Holmay, sir."

"I missed you in class."

Billy stood straight up as Holmay approached. "Dr. Holmay, I'd like to present to you Wendy Corrigan."

A girl's face, round and bland except for the curl in her smile, appeared on the other side of the tree. She had a wide white skirt spread like a blanket around herself, and in her fingers she twisted the stem of a yellow marigold. From her place at the foot of the trunk she extended her hand to Holmay.

"Nice to meet you."

"You must be Billy's excuse for missing class."

"It was her idea," Billy said accusingly. "It really was her idea, sir."

"But you went along with it, silly," she chimed.

"But I said I had to go to class."

"And you also said it was another real nice day. And you stay up all night, silly boy."

"I can't help that," Billy snapped back. "Did I miss anything, sir?"

"Maybe you did. That's for you to decide."

"I don't want you to hold it against me, sir. Is there something I can do to make it up to you?"

"Do me a favor. Quit calling me 'sir'."

"Oh yes, Dr. Holmay."

"And do me another favor."

Billy glanced at Wendy as if to ask permission of her.

"Go ahead," she said. "Just ask. Billy's no monster."

"Do you think you can get to bed earlier from now on?"

Wendy smirked and turned away.

"What do you mean?"

"It would be better for you to catch up on your sleep than to walk the streets in the middle of the night. That's what I mean."

"Didn't you go straight home after you left me off?" Wendy tried to look shocked.

"I can't sleep," Billy said. "I just can't sleep. I just have a lot of thinking to do."

Holmay threw Wendy a wink. "Okay. He's all yours now. I trust I'm leaving him in good hands."

As he walked away Holmay threw them another glance. While Billy stood with his hands in his pockets, Wendy reached up to offer him the marigold. When Holmay glanced again, nothing was visible but a part of Wendy's white skirt at the foot of the tree.

Ah young love, Holmay said to himself as he climbed the library steps. That country bumpkin Billy-boy's in love.

Five

EVELYN WAS THE princess her father locked in the tower that night. Only the man who killed Orgo, the two-headed monster ravaging travelers, would earn the right to marry her. And any man who failed would lose his head. So when the peasant boy Pepe resolved to save his mother from poverty, Evelyn thought the princess should marry him. While Evelyn yawned, Pepe set out on foot to find Orgo. He traveled first through the winding wood, then into the thicket at the foot of the mountain where he was assaulted by snakes, poisonous toads, eyeless ravens, and jackals, all of which he fended off with his shepherd's staff. When he escaped the thicket he came to a bridge presided over by an ancient man with almond-colored skin. The old man tried to bar his way, but a sudden wind blew the old man aside. From the bridge Pepe descended into a town where he met an old crone, who laughed when he told her of his quest. "Take these two hazelnuts," she said, "and follow the road to the left. There Orgo will find you, but he will keep you waiting forty days and forty nights. By that time you will be so weak that you will be an easy prey for him. Therefore at the end of that time crack both of these nuts and eat them to regain your strength." So Pepe waited forty days, and as the sun was going down on the last he heard a roar in the trees to his left. Out stepped Orgo, a long scaly tail swishing impatiently behind, globs of flesh hanging from the short claws attached to his breast, his two heads moiling around one another, one more eager than the other to get at him. Quickly

Pepe broke open the hazelnuts, and while the loud evil laughter of the crone flew overhead, he saw what he had in his hands. One was a perfect hazelnut, whole in his hand, but the other was rotten and full of worms. Quickly he ate the one nut, but he threw the other away in disgust, and just as quickly he felt a surge of strength. The monster attacked almost before Pepe had a chance to raise his stick, and the mountainsides echoed with the sound of the battle that lasted three hours. At last Pepe's strength gave out. "Jesu Maria!" he called out as with one mighty desperate blow he lopped off one of Orgo's two heads. Then he staggered, fell down, and swooned, and Orgo, full of mad fury, devoured Pepe whole.

Evelyn knew immediately that the old crone was Orgo's mother, the man on the bridge his father. But she could not guess that the Prince of France would come riding by, discover the gorged and weary Orgo by the side of the road, and lop off his other head with his sword. And she was satisfied when he continued onward to the tower where the princess was imprisoned, took one look at her lovely face, and married her in the cathedral the very next day.

"So they lived happily ever after," Evelyn said as she allowed her eyes to close.

"They certainly did," Holmay lied as he tucked the blanket under her chin.

He turned off the light and went to his room. This was his hour, the one time in his day that had no claim on him. He lay down in his bed and opened his book, words passing before him like birds high in an overcast sky, his mind now and then following a few in their haphazard flight. Pages turned like years before his eyes as weariness slowly worked its way upward from his feet and legs. Finally he let his eyes close, angry with himself for not removing his clothes and turning off the light.

The knocking on his front door came out of a dream. He had followed a lovely dark lady down strange city streets and suddenly she had turned and with a toss of her hair beckoned him to enter the door into which she disappeared. When he came to the door he found it closed.

"Who in the hell would it be at this time of night?" he asked himself as he tried to rub the sleep away from his face. There were long pauses between the knocks, as if the person on the porch was uneasily balancing his misgivings with his determination to get in.

Billy, wearing a white shirt and loose tie, did not look up or speak when Holmay opened the door.

"You need to talk," Holmay said as he let him in.

He led Billy to the small round kitchen table and showed him a chair. To make himself feel at ease he put on a potful of hot water for coffee or tea.

"Coffee?"

Billy shook his head no.

"Tea?"

"I don't think it's good for me, sir."

"A beer?"

"No, thank you. I don't drink."

Holmay turned off the fire on the stove, got himself a beer and sat down at the table, the window at his back.

"You'll have to do the talking, Billy. At least to start."

Billy looked past him without shifting his eyes, and Holmay had an urge to turn around to see what he was looking at.

"Is it Wendy?"

Billy nodded.

"Are you in trouble with her?"

"What do you mean?"

"She's not pregnant?"

"What kind of person do you think I am?" Billy scratched his collarbone, leaving red marks behind.

"You'll have to do the talking, Billy."

"In class you talk about love. Everything we read...you keep talking about it...and I might add, sir, that you find sex where I don't think there's any at all, but then you find love too right next to the sex. And one day you said that's the point of all books, passion—that all great writers have that and it's what makes them write their books. But then you find sex in all the poems and stories, and I don't see where you get all that."

"So that's what you want to talk about—love and sex?"

Billy went right on. "And one day you said writing was sex—that all great writers had sex when they wrote."

"I don't think that's really what I said." Holmay drew back. "Or that's certainly not what I meant."

"You said that no great author could keep sex out of his work. Only a pervert would do that."

"What I think I said, Billy, is that writing is an erotic activity, that writing is *like* having sex, that both stem from a common creative urge."

"I just don't think that's right, sir, and you're probably going to flunk me...and that's why Dr. Drummond doesn't like me and I just had to get away from her."

"You're not working hard to get away from me, Billy. You're sitting in my home at midnight."

"You talk about passion. There's the body and there's the spirit, the soul. And Wendy, she says she loves me, but I sometimes don't know any more if she's telling me the truth or being like Dr. Drummond."

"What is it about Wendy?"

"Dr. Drummond looks at me like she doesn't like me at all. And now Wendy wants me to go home with her next weekend."

"Sounds perfectly normal to me."

"I don't know why she wants me to do that. Her father would probably kill me, and what could I say to him, how could I look him in the eye? And Wendy would just stand there and introduce us like there's nothing wrong. And the thing is we love each other, Wendy and I. I told her tonight and she cried and told me she loved me too."

Holmay suppressed a yawn.

"And doesn't she realize what her father's trying to do? I asked her exactly that. Once he gets to know me he'll just do me in, and that's why he's forcing me to go home with her."

"What do you mean?"

"Just like he forced her. So why shouldn't he try to do me in too?"

"I don't know what you're talking about."

"We talked for six hours today. We told each other everything. We said it had to be that way if we were really in love and were going to get married someday. She told me about her mother and father, sir. She told me about her father. He had sex with her when she was seven years old."

His eyes found Holmay's and would not let them go.

"I love her," Billy said, "very, very much."

Holmay finished his beer and threw his head back. Dejection came over him as he looked at Billy. Young love. Contemporary young love. Billy, a farmer's son, a boy who wore a white shirt and tie when he went out to talk to his girlfriend, who believed in the existence of spirit and soul, courtship, truth, marriage, fidelity. Who discovered incest this night.

"It's something that will test your love, Billy. If your love can survive the hardest tests, it will maybe become the strongest love." Holmay saw himself at the window once more, watching as Cynthia pulled away from the house with her load of furniture.

"And my father would kill me. If he knew where I was going, he would kill me."

"Does he have to know everything?"

"My father would kill me. He brought me up strict. If I did something wrong, I had to pay for it. I know. So I know right from wrong. I learned the right way because he had a whip and he wasn't afraid to use it on me." Billy smiled for the first time, revealing teeth that seemed too small, too far apart. Then he fixed his eyes beyond Holmay again, who realized that Billy might have been staring at something looking in the window at them.

To break the spell he stood up. "Well, I appreciate your coming to visit me."

"I was scared, sir."

"Especially then we need to talk to each other. That's when we need each other most."

While Billy sat Holmay filled the room with words. He too had been in love. He too had been confused by it. There was something ridiculous about it all, but things had a way of working themselves out. Billy's problem was complex, but it was not like an H-bomb that at any minute could go off and end the world. He and Wendy would have to be careful and reasonable, and maybe they both would have to move away from home. Because there came a time in a young man's life when he had to leave his parents behind. There was nothing really to feel guilty about or fear, and everything, blah, blah, blah, would work out in the end.

Billy sat unmoved, his eyes fixed out the window.

"It's late, Billy. You'll have to go."

Finally Billy pushed his chair back and walked to the door.

Holmay performed his final duty as he reached to open the door. "I want to assure you, Billy, that I will hold your words in strictest confidence. And you should know that I'm flattered that you had enough faith in me to stop here when you felt the need to talk."

"I don't think you understand, sir."

"Understand *what?*"

"That I was scared. That's why I stopped."

"We all get scared."

"Someone was following me."

"Following you? Are you sure?"

"Whoever it was won't bother me after seeing me come to your door."

Billy stood looking out into the night.

"Well, you'd better be on your way. I have to look in on my daughter upstairs."

"She's a very pretty girl."

"That she is," Holmay said. "Did you see her on campus with me yesterday?"

"No, I watched her walk home from school last week."

Six

How DOES A man explain a simple heart? When Felicité was betrayed in love; when she watched helplessly as the children she loved more than a mother could, Theodore and Virginia, were stolen from her by death; when the woman to whom she had devoted a lifetime of faithful servitude, this woman incapable of seeing beyond herself to utter a word of gratitude, finally gave up the ghost and abandoned Felicité to a final solitude; and when even Lulu died—Lulu the green parrot, the jaded dove gracing Felicité's life even when dead and stuffed, mounted like an icon on an altar, it too decaying into a ragged thing of dust and worms—when Lulu died was Felicité not betrayed and abandoned again; or was there still another betrayal and abandonment, one more final and terrible than all, the moment when, as Felicité offered up her last breath as a final prayer to the God to whom she had remained true from beginning to end, He revealed himself as Lulu herself, no more and no less than the green parrot stuffed with rotting rags?

How explain to a roomful of people not yet twenty years old that Felicité's simple heart provided her happiness despite a lifetime of servitude, betrayal and abandonment?

Perhaps.

"I don't see how you could call an old bag like that happy," Lance said to make everyone laugh.

"Her name in French means 'Happiness,'" Holmay announced, feeling a bit like a magician pulling a rabbit from a hat.

"But how do you know she was really happy?" Lance said. "How do you know that writer what's-his-name wasn't a wise-guy? It didn't seem to me like she got anything out of life but a lot of work and troubles, and then she just dies."

"That parrot was really weird," said a girl's voice from the other side of the room.

Then for the first time Annette George spoke. "Do you think there's some connection between the old woman and that sort of step-daughter named Virginia? I mean...they were both...pure when they died."

Yes, yes, Holmay nodded. Purity, a virginity of heart maintained to the end.

"I mean..." Annette went on, "she never got married or had sex. That's why I agree with Lance."

Lance ran his hand through his hair and settled back in his chair, as if sure he had Annette where he wanted her.

"Maybe happiness is up to the individual," said Lori Mullins.

Then for a second time during the term Billy spoke, not clearing his throat or averting his gaze from what seemed not the wall in front of him but the stone, mortar or wood inside all surfaces and beyond the reach of human eyes.

"Of course she was happy. She had the peak of all human life—love. She gave it to everyone, and she gave it with no expectation of return, and even when God, in the form of the rotting green parrot, failed her, she even forgave God...because she tried so hard to do the right thing all the time."

So clear, precise, and simple were Billy's words that the others fell silent. Holmay let the words speak for themselves. At the end of the hour the students filed quietly out.

Since the time he had visited Holmay's house late at night, Billy had kept a distance. At first he disappeared for three days, and Holmay, hoping to stay clear of him, said nothing when he appeared in class again. Then he began seeing Billy and Wendy everywhere. In a cafeteria they sat at a small corner table, their heads bent over the same tray. They spent hours on the library steps and warm afternoons under the old oak. While out on an afternoon jog through the park, Holmay saw them strolling with flowers in their hands, and once, on the grass just outside the auditorium, he saw Billy reading to her.

The matter seemed settled. Billy had survived the midnight crisis and seemed well on his way to managing the torments of young love. True, his problems were special, for few had to deal with skeletons as ugly as incest in a lover's closet. But if a young man could understand a simple heart, he would cope with a twisted one. He and Wendy would make it—or they would not. They would do as other lovers do, flail away at flaws the way people do when their passion gets used to its routines. They would get married or they would not, and their marriage would survive or it would not. In any event, they seemed capable of carrying on, and despite Billy's idiosyncracies, normal enough.

In the shade of the old oak even Billy's oddness seemed to disappear. What was one to think of all the outward and visible signs that Billy was, in fact, a strange sort of boy? His personal habits and clothes set him apart—the plain white shirt he wore every day, and the hair, clipped unevenly and too short, and the thin moustache that never seemed to grow. These details alone kept him apart from the Lance Walcotts of the world, always cocky in the back row. Then there was Billy's peculiar habit of sitting upright, as if paying too much attention, while his eyes focused on nothing visible, the insides of concrete and stone. And the unevenness of his speech, its fits and starts; his dense innocence interrrupted by flashes of coherent intelligence such as his statement about Felicité. And the more bizarre events: his standing alone under the streetlight, his midnight visit, his explanation—no explanation at all—that he was afraid, was being followed until he entered his professor's house?

The mind has its ways of playing its tricks, Holmay concluded as he saw Billy and Wendy again and again under their old oak, and its ways of making everything turn out right. Billy would be just fine. There were other projects in life to worry about.

Such as the unfinished rooms in the house. One in particular, the downstairs bedroom, had nagged him since Cynthia left. She had asked him to paint the walls and strip the woodwork of its thick layers of paint, but he had resisted the chore. They were comfortable enough and he had more important things to do. If he wanted a promotion he would have to write a book. Didn't she understand that someday he would have to get started on that? Her silence and her eyes registered her sarcastic response. He was kidding himself. He would never write a book, "Just as you will never learn what it means to be a mature male," she said to his face.

He closed the door of the room after she left, leaving it empty and bare, and for more than two years he passed the door on the way to the kitchen without giving it a second thought. One day it occurred to him: why not finish the room, make it into his own private place, a study full of his favorite books furnished precisely in his own way, a place to retreat on long winter nights to write his damned book.

Inspired, he spent weeks scraping the old paint from the wood, happy to discover fine oak underneath. He patched the cracks in the walls, sanded the woodwork carefully by hand, then watched with wonder as he oiled it, the rich grain lurking inside the wood rising to meet the eye. One night, with Evelyn already asleep, he stepped back from his work and realized that only the walls needed paint. But still no book to write. So he closed the door and left the room undone.

To see Billy in love made him feel good. When he saw Billy reading to Wendy he became restless to read a new book, scribble a few lines of poetry, cut wood for the fireplace, work with his hands. He opened the door to the room again, left it open for three days, then bought a gallon of paint.

It was finished on a rainy Friday afternoon just before the middle of the term. On Sunday night he could not fall asleep. Though he had an old dresser in the basement and a bed in the garage, the room would need carpeting, bookcases and a desk. He added up the cost in his mind. This would be a very good room for some student, some boy who maybe would mow the lawn, study hard. Or maybe, just maybe, if the circumstances were just right, some girl—if she were the first to knock on the door and willing to look after Evelyn now and then, or if she were truly desperate for a place, was certain she could deal maturely with the unusual circumstances, and if, perhaps, she was as lovely as Annette George.

As he resolved to hang the ROOM FOR RENT sign out, he fell asleep.

The next morning Billy was standing in front of his office door.

"I won't be taking the exam," he announced as he showed himself to a chair next to Holmay's desk. "I can see no reason why my knowledge of the labyrinthine works we've studied this term should be reduced to the scribblings produced in an hour's time. Those exams are no real measure of a man."

"What is their purpose, then?"

"To get even with us."

"I'm sorry. I can't see it that way."

"You just prove my point."

Billy's insolence, an insubordination common to students trying to bull their way to better grades, took Holmay by surprise.

"Surely you don't expect special treatment from me?"

"Surely you don't think I'm just one more of *them?*" he shot back.

"In one sense you are, young man."

"Is that what you think? I'm no better than *them?*"

Billy sat straight in his chair, rigid as if his whole body, neck and head were one muscle flexed. His eyes had that look in them again, a stare able to penetrate stone.

"What's the matter, Billy?" Holmay said softly.

Billy did not move or flinch.

"Billy, what's the matter?"

Holmay waited again for a reply, and, just before he had a chance to make good on his resolve to raise his voice and recite the university policy on exams, Billy, as if talking to the wall, began:

"Wendy's the one who will get hurt by this. Wendy doesn't deserve someone like me. She deserves someone who knows less than I know, someone who doesn't see the way all things relate, interconnect."

Billy paused, looked at Holmay, his shoulders suddenly slumped into a question mark. "Do you know what I mean?"

Holmay nodded.

"It's my father who doesn't want me seeing her," he said almost inaudibly, lowering his head. "I know now he's the one. And she hasn't done one thing wrong, but my father knows everything about her, like he's her father too. And when I get home late he's waiting for me and he asks me where I've been and I know he still has the strap, and he calls me a filthy pig. That's the kind of Christian he is. So you want me to take this exam, and you don't even see it's all the same thing."

"I'm not your father, Billy."

Billy sat up straight again, deep lines of sadness visible on his face. "I knew you would use that argument. I just knew you would."

"You know, Billy, you're maybe the smartest student in the class."

Billy sat unmoved.

"Just take the exam. I'm sure you'll do fine."

"How do you know I'm the smartest student in the class?"

"By what you say. . .I can tell. . .I think you really. . .*understand* what you read."

"Then why are you making me take the test?"

"Because it's the rule."

"Rules?"

"Rules," Holmay said.

"You're doing it because you have to? Is that it? You have to do it to me. Is that the point of it all?"

Holmay nodded.

"Then I know what I have to do," Billy said, gathering his books. "I've got to talk to Wendy first. Then I have to get out. I just have to get out. And do you know why, Dr. Holmay? Because I know you've been wondering about me. I can see it in your eyes. I know you wonder about why I showed up that night at the door. And I told you but I never explained. I never told you who was following me."

He suddenly stood up and looked directly at Holmay. "Do you know *now?*"

Holmay had to turn away.

"My father beats me. It was my father following me that night. I saw him in the shadows. . .like he was flying from the shadow of one tree to the next and his eyes are the eyes of cats." Billy suddenly laughed.

"I'll see you at eleven o'clock for the exam," Holmay said.

Billy gave him a sideways glance as he walked away.

And failed to appear for the exam. A sudden downpour kept Holmay from meeting Evelyn at home after school the way he usually did, so he closed his office door and began reading exams. By the time his eyes began to tire, it was almost five o'clock. He gathered his papers and hurried home.

The front door was wide open, the way Evelyn usually left it when she arrived home from school. Holmay was struck by the ROOM FOR RENT sign he had nailed next to the mailbox that morning, for it occurred to him that he had failed to write his office phone number on the sign. He called for Evelyn as he entered, but there was no response. Then he called again. Maybe she had gone to a neighbor's to play.

Billy, with Evelyn on his lap, was sitting at the kitchen table. Before them was spread an open book.

"Hi, Dad," Evelyn said without looking up from the book.

"What are you doing here, Billy?"

"He's reading to me from *Alice in Wonderland.*"

"You know, Dr. Holmay, it's really incredible. I'd never read any of this before. Don't you think it's great, Evelyn?"

Holmay lifted Evelyn off Billy's lap and gave her a bearhug.

"We got all the way to the part where Alice drinks the magic potion that makes her real big," Evelyn said.

"She's quite a character," Billy said.

"How long have you been here?"

"He was waiting for me on the porch when I got home from school."

"I saw the sign. I know you usually get home at three o'clock."

"How did you know that?"

"Isn't your last class over at two?"

"You didn't show up for the exam."

"I asked Billy to stay for dinner, Dad. Is that okay?"

Billy smiled at Evelyn. "It would be really nice, Dr. Holmay. I came here because this morning in your office you helped me decide."

"Decide what?"

"To get out. To just leave."

"Where are you going?" Evelyn asked.

Billy turned in his chair and faced Holmay.

"I want to rent your room. I have a little money saved, and I can do work around the house like rake the leaves and paint."

Evelyn looked up with hopeful eyes.

"I'm afraid you're too late. The room's already gone."

The words hit Billy in the face. "But you just put the sign up this morning. How could the room be taken so soon?"

"I got a call at the office right after you left."

Evelyn grabbed her father's arm. "But Dad, you didn't even give him a chance."

"You mean there's really no room for me?"

"Can he stay for dinner, Dad?"

Holmay thought fast. "I'm sorry, not tonight. I've made plans for us to have dinner with Miss Drummond tonight."

✳ ✳ ✳

He hadn't really made plans but Frances Drummond would say yes, yes, she would be delighted to go out for pizza that night. She didn't have a thing in the house and was looking for an excuse not to spend the evening reading another book. And yes, she would be only too glad to drive. "And what about your genius, William Allan Brand?" Frances would ask in the car. "How is he these days?" Holmay would make sure Evelyn did not hear. "Billy's a bit strange." "I told you so," Frances would say.

"Who'd you rent the room to?" Evelyn asked, tears in her eyes.

"You'll meet him later."

"Nobody could be as nice as Billy," she said as she ran out of the room.

Seven

JUST BEFORE midnight another knock on the door.

"This is going too far," Holmay said as he pushed himself out of bed and put on his robe. It was time to have some hard plain talk with Billy Brand.

He looked into the darkness surrounding the front porch, concentrating on the place where he had seen Billy under the streetlight.

"Hey Doc!"

Holmay could not find the voice.

"Hey Doc, I wanna rent your room."

On the bottom porch step a figure, struggling to stand upright, appeared, the air around him thick with the smell of beer and cigarettes. Lance Walcott made his way toward the door.

"I wanna rent your room, Doc."

Holmay looked around into the dark again, then signaled for Lance to come in. Lance staggered to a chair in the living room and fell into it.

"I gotta have a room, Doc."

"Don't you live in the dorm?"

"Just got my walking papers from there."

"What makes you think I'd want a rowdy living in my house? I have a nine-year-old daughter."

"Hey Doc, no trouble. Honest. This will be good for me. I'll study all the time. I'm getting it together now."

Holmay went to the window and looked out. The wind was blowing hard, the streetlights doing a shadow-dance on the lawn. No one out there. Holmay scanned the darkness again, then made up his mind.

"No booze, no noise, no cigarettes. Those are the rules here."

Lance threw his arms up in surrender. "Hey Doc. Hey man. No trouble, man. Promise. How much you gonna charge, Doc?"

Holmay pulled down the shade. "One hundred per month."

"That's okay, okay. Cheaper than the dorm, Doc. You got a deal." Lance tried to stand and extend a hand to shake on it, but he stumbled and fell back.

"You'd better sober up. I'll put some coffee on."

"Yuk. I hate that stuff."

"Then you'd better call a cab."

Lance let his head fall to one side, then he rolled his eyes toward Holmay. "Hey Doc, can I stay in my room tonight? They kicked me out, you know."

"If you screw up one time you're out. You understand? I've got a nine-year-old here. I'll throw you out on your ass. The first time you screw up."

"I dig, man."

"I'll get you a blanket. You sleep on the couch. And you'd better not throw up all over the place."

Holmay awoke the next morning to Evelyn standing over him.

"Who's that man sleeping downstairs?"

"Lance, Evelyn. He's going to rent the room—the man I mentioned yesterday."

"But what about Billy?"

"Billy was too late."

"But Billy was here first."

"I already promised Lance. A promise is a promise."

"You didn't even ask me."

"You'll like Lance. I'm sure you will. He'll work out, you'll see."

Again Billy did not appear for class, but Lance, groggy-eyed and shiftless, struggled through the hour.

"Go home and take a shower," Holmay instructed him after class. "And get your things from the dorm."

Billy was waiting for Holmay in the cafeteria as Holmay made his way down the line toward him. Unmoved, his head that of a proud matador refusing to look at his bull, Billy did not respond to Holmay's glances. He stared instead beyond Holmay, his eyes narrow and certain, as if fully aware that he had been betrayed. When Holmay got to the end of the line, prepared to pass right in front of him, Billy was gone.

* * *

Holmay made sure he was home early, waiting on the porch swing from which he could see the sidewalk Evelyn took home from school. By quarter past three

Evelyn did not appear, so he wandered to the corner for a better look. In the distance he saw a small child, but in a minute the child turned off and disappeared. He started walking toward the school, tracing the path he was sure Evelyn took. The janitor told him he had seen her, skipping the way she always did toward home, and yes, she was alone.

If she was not at school and not at home, then where was she? An insane terror suddenly took hold of his heart and pulled it down into his stomach.

He rushed back and began calling neighbors on the phone. No Evelyn anywhere, though Evelyn told Nancy, her best friend, that she wanted to go to the park today. Did she maybe go to the park? Did she ever go to the park? Did he know the Lorrimers, who had just moved into the neighborhood? The Lorrimers had a girl Evelyn's age. Evelyn was very good at making friends.

Holmay hurried to the Lorrimer house, trying to compose himself as he waited at the door.

Yes, he was glad to meet them, glad to have them in the neighborhood, but did they see his little girl?

And where did he work?

He was a professor. Yes, at the college. Yes, literature. Books. His job. Would they please ask their child if she had seen his Evelyn?

No, Susan didn't know anybody by that name, but she's shy, you know, and it will take a while to learn everyone's name. Would he and Evelyn like to come over some time, and it is sometimes a good thing, isn't it, when the father rather than the mother takes custody of a child after a divorce? So would the two of them like to come over some time?

Yes, no, because he's in a hurry right now. And thank you, thank you again and again and again, but can't they see he's in a hurry right now?

One day you'll see, Cynthia told him just days before she left, Evelyn will turn the corner. She'll be on her own, learning to fend for herself, and then before you know she'll be off to college or someplace else, gone for good.

So he made a habit of watching her from the porch, careful to keep her from straying away, tough when negotiating the boundary lines she widened each year, her absences, unauthorized and random, leading to resolves, more often than not carried out, to be more careful next time. Still she was a wisp blown here and there. She sat on the lawn digging for a worm, then was on the back porch rummaging through a bagful of old clothes. She would wander to the corner and stop, looking across the street and faraway down the sidewalk that converged like receding rails toward a future she one day would be gliding toward on her own. That time, he knew, would creep up on him. Some distant university, some chance for an exciting career, some trip to Mexico, California, London perhaps, some handsome youth trembling with excitement over his good luck in getting her to say yes—and the corner would have been turned. And he, father and bachelor, would be alone.

The terror visited him again at night, sometimes following him as he took strolls. The time he first picked her up, a bundle no bigger or heavier than a warm loaf of bread, he feared that his hands would fail, that they would suddenly give way and she would fall to the floor and break. One night before she was a year old she rolled off the bed onto the floor. His heart stood still while she looked up big-eyed at him and held her breath, her little fists coiling as if to strike out at him before she suddenly wailed like a big hungry cat. She's tougher than she looks, he kept telling himself each time she survived a fall, a bruise, a scratch, but still he saw vulnerability in her face and fawn-like legs.

He measured her smallness against the menace in the world. He could not pass up a newspaper headline, pausing to calculate how faraway or close, past or present the latest outrage was. The ease with which people died. Two hundred in a disaster here or there, two thousand in a small African war, ten thousand in a war not yet declared. Other men's daughters dead by the dozens, their throats slashed in suburban homes, their bodies stuffed into the trunks of cars, their brains blown out by lovers, madmen, strangers still free to walk the streets.

What would you do to someone who did *that* to your daughter? he heard Lance Walcott ask again.

I'd kill him, Holmay vowed as he started toward the park.

* * *

Willoughby Park, which stretched for a mile and a half along the river on the eastern side of town, was named after the general whose main accomplishment was an Indian treaty that opened the territory to speculators luring settlers farther west. Along with tennis courts and a swimming pool, the park had play and picnic areas hidden away in coves that followed the river's twists and turns. At its center was a rose garden surrounding a fountain presided over by a statue of General Willoughby, whose farsightedness was memorialized by the way his hand shielded the sun as he gazed west toward the future of America, and by the words on the pedestal: "That the Wilderness May Know Christ's Truth."

As Holmay entered the park from its Walnut Street approach, he did not know which way to turn. Evelyn liked best the playground areas with swings, monkey bars, and slides, but there were at least six such areas scattered throughout the park, a few of them in the wooded stretches along the river bank. He headed toward the rose garden, looking for a sign of her. Two elderly ladies, strolling arm-in-arm from one rose plant to the next, smiled as they approached.

"Have you seen a little girl?" he asked.

They gave each other a puzzled look.

"She's blond, blue eyes—about nine years old."

"There were some girls riding their bikes," the shortest one said. "Was your girl one of them?"

"No, thank you, no. She was on foot—maybe. . .with a boy about twenty years old."

"What did he say, Blanche? Did you hear what he said?"

38

He tried to smile and climbed onto the edge of the fountain to get a better view. To his left the tennis courts were already full. A few joggers and bikers were visible on the ridge overlooking the swimming pool, and some boys were tossing a football in an open space. He climbed higher, pulling himself up to the pedestal of the Willoughby statue and hanging on with one hand while he strained to make out every small figure that came into view. To his right the woods thickened and wound away from town with each bend in the river. There were always a few fishermen on the river bank, a few teenagers hiding with their cans of beer, lovers with nowhere to hide.

He bounded down from the pedestal, opened his shirt collar, and started running toward the trees, his heart racing in his chest. If he dares, he vowed again and again, if he dares to touch one hair of her, I will tear him apart with my hands. Two boys on the path ahead of him reared their bikes like horses and swerved to avoid him, laughing as they passed. Fuck you, Holmay said to himself as he slowed to a walk.

In the trees to his left he caught a glimpse of a blue dress. Blue. Evelyn in blue. He remembered her in blue.

The path turned sharply away. He followed it to the base of a big dead elm. Fifty feet ahead of him, on a rock overlooking the water, Billy sat looking downstream. Behind him, as if sneaking up for a surprise, Evelyn approached, her shoes in one hand, a bouquet of wildflowers in the other.

"Close your eyes, Billy," she said, "and I'll give you a big surprise."

Billy put one hand over his eyes and without turning around held the other over his head.

"What a lovely gift, Evelyn. These are autumn wildflowers, but all flowers, you know, mean spring and love." Billy moved over to make room for her.

As they sat Holmay could not make out anything more than Evelyn's laughter, a laughter he knew well from the times she could not contain her happiness. He debated with himself. He could barge in on them right away, catch them, as it were, in the act, and warn Billy away from her once and for all. But how would he explain to Evelyn? He had told her about strangers, and Billy, obviously, was no stranger to her. Maybe, if he waited for Billy to make the slightest move, even to take her by the hand, then he would have justification enough, could move in right away with all the proof he required. And how far would Billy go? What did he want from her? What sort of demons did Billy have inside of him? From his place behind the old elm Holmay would get a chance to see for himself.

Suddenly Evelyn got up and called for Billy to follow her. They walked away from the water and trees into an opening, Evelyn always a few feet ahead, calling Billy to hurry, catch up with her. Keeping out of view, Holmay watched as she led him to a playground area, requiring him to watch as she went through her routine on the monkey bars. Then she ran off to the swings, her squeals loud and sharp as she pumped herself higher and higher.

"Come on Billy! You can do it if you try!"

Billy, sitting cross-legged on the grass, watched her, shaking his head no, the wildflowers still in his hand.

"Try the giant slide, Billy!" she shouted as she leaped from the swing. She ran to him, tugged at his arm, tried to pull him up.

Billy would not get up, shook his head, no, no.

Evelyn squealed her way down the slide a dozen times, took another turn on the monkey bars, then ran small circles around Billy on the grass.

"Come on, Billy! I gotta go home now."

She led the way past the rose garden, Billy quickening his pace to keep up with her. When they came to Walnut Street Evelyn waited for Billy to catch up.

"Hurry up, slow poke! Daddy's gonna kill me!"

They walked down the shady side of the street, Evelyn looking up at him, chattering, laughing, Billy gesturing with his hands, Evelyn laughing even more. Holmay, too far back to make out their words, crossed over to their side of the street and closed the gap.

Just before Evelyn came to her street she tugged at Billy's sleeve and made him stop. She said something to him, her head upturned as if pleading, but he shook his head no, no. Then as naturally as she had taken her own father's hand a hundred, a thousand times before crossing a street, she reached out, took Billy's hand, and turned the corner toward home.

That rat, Holmay said to himself. That goddamned rat.

They were sitting together on the porch swing when he caught up to them.

"Where have you been? I've been looking everywhere for you."

"Billy took me to the park, Dad. I was with Billy all the time."

"Get up to your room right now. I've been looking everywhere for you."

Evelyn, her eyes beginning to fill with tears, ran into the house.

Jealousy. Sexual jealousy. That goddamned rat Billy had made him jealous of his own daughter, a nine-year-old who in a few years would walk hand-in-hand with many boys before turning the corner away from him for good. He glared at Billy, whose eyes, seeing beyond him the way they always did, betrayed neither innocence nor guilt.

"So what do you have to say for yourself?"

Billy gave a slight shrug.

"Do you always go for walks in the park with a nine-year-old—without asking permission of her parents?"

"She asked me to do it, sir."

"Do you do everything a nine-year-old says?"

"She said she wanted to go to the park. She said she would go alone if I did not go with her."

"And how does she come to ask *you* these things?"

"She was walking home from school, sir."

"You took that liberty with her."

"I took no liberty, sir. You are a man I respect and admire."

"To the point of worrying him sick."

"Because I want him to explain," Billy said, "what is wrong with me."

"What do you mean *wrong?*"

"Why you...*betrayed* me. Why I'm not good enough to live in your house."

Holmay's heart sank and the anger drained out of him. Billy Brand. Billy Boy. The boy who reads books, takes them into his heart, who falls in love with a young girl and has a child fall in love with him. Who always wears a plain white shirt. Whose hair is too short.

"I didn't...*betray* you, Billy."

There was a loud crash inside the house.

"Hey Doc, can you give me a hand with this bed?" Lance's voice carried through the open door.

Billy threw Holmay a glance.

"Hey Doc, I need a hand quick."

"Someone else got the room before you did. Lance Walcott was here first."

"Was he the first?" Billy asked as he suddenly got up. "I know about that. I know all about that."

He walked away holding his head high and proud.

Eight

THE SKY WAS too blue and the leaves too much ablaze with autumn's colors for lovers to resist. So only half the seats in Holmay's class were occupied. Billy's was not one of them for the third day in a row. With Annette George also gone, Holmay had only himself to impress.

"Nancy's terror. A black woman, an outsider in a white man's world. Slavery officially abolished, but Nancy still a slave. The contrast on the very first page between all things white—the bundle of laundry she carries on her head—and the blackness of her skin, her hands, yes, especially her hands. What did she do to deserve the wrath of Jesus? She had sex with a white man, and Jesus, her lover, found out. From that point on Nancy's terror grows. 'Jesus is waiting for me in the ditch,' she says to herself, and the only hope she has is the presence of the Compson children, who have no idea about what is going on. This poor woman, terrified, has nothing but children to hide behind."

He had them. They were certain now that the words they themselves had read made sense. But what really happened at the end, and what did it all mean?

"One question is unavoidable. *Was* Jesus really waiting for her in the ditch, and if he was would he have slit her throat?"

He paused, looking around the room for a response.

"The answer is in the story itself. Nancy thinks Jesus is in the ditch, though she fails to convince anyone else. And we, the readers, are never quite sure. So as her terror grows, so does ours. In the end we too fear for Nancy's life."

Jim Boyd, accounting major: "But does Jesus really kill her—I mean after the story ends?"

Holmay gave a sad little shake of his head. "We never really find out, do we? Does anything really happen after a story ends? Faulkner just leaves us there, wondering and terrorized. Just as he abandons Nancy, wondering and terrorized."

So logically it follows, Holmay said to himself, we the readers become Nancy. We become Nancy the 'nigger' laundry woman who screwed a white man for a dime and is waiting to collect her bloody reward.

"Do you see the connection?" he said, searching for eyes. "That's how Faulkner makes us feel for her."

Lori Mullins raised her hand. "But maybe she had it coming to her. I mean . . .in her day wasn't it wrong for a black girl to make love to a white man?"

"I suppose you could look at it that way too," Holmay said, suddenly depressed.

Billy was waiting in Holmay's office right after class, already in the chair next to Holmay's desk, his hands folded in his lap. Holmay ignored him and sat down, trying to let his silence say that Billy had his nerve. Billy waited him out.

"What can I do for you?"

Billy stared past him the way he usually did.

"You missed the exam, you have not turned in the paper due last week, and you've missed class again."

"Nancy's story," Billy began, ignoring Holmay's words, "is told by her hands, those poor parts of her that don't know how to use words. At the beginning her hands are strong—they hold all that laundry up, they keep her hanging onto the bars of the jailhouse when one slip, one sign of spiritual weakness, would have precipitated her fall—call it a fall from innocence, if you will, and certain death. Until she feels the presence of Jesus, until the full weight of her sin begins to fall on her, Nancy still has a grip on things. But then she begins to lose her hold. First her hands feel weak, wobbly—she drops things. Then they start to go limp— they dangle down. Then she loses all connection between body and mind—she puts her hand on the hot stove and doesn't feel the pain. By then her terror has taken possession of her flesh."

Billy, his hands still folded in his lap and his eyes locked into a faraway gaze, had delivered his words as if memorized. He sat unmoved as Holmay marveled at the clarity and coherence of Billy's analysis.

"That's very impressive," Holmay said. "Where did that come from?"

"From inside."

Holmay decided to see how well Billy could play his game.

"So what's the source of Nancy's terror? Why is her lover named, of all things, Jesus?"

"Because Jesus makes everything happen."

"Even if he doesn't exist?"

"Even if he's not in that ditch waiting with a knife or gun," Billy replied, "or anywhere else in the whole wide universe."

43

"So she's terrified by nothing?"

"Aren't we afraid of what we can't see, what's maybe not even there? And most afraid when something that's been around us all our lives suddenly seems strange?"

"So it's simply that—fear of the unknown?"

"No, of course not. Her fall into an existential void occurs because of the tear in the socio-political fabric. 'I ain't nothin' but a nigger,' she says."

"Meaning by that?"

"That she can't be held responsible for anything, even the entire ruin of her life. There's no one, no social worker or policeman or priest or judge or psychologist that can help her. She's completely niggerized, quote-unquote."

"Because she's incapable of letting them help her?"

"No," Billy said as he leaned forward, his eyes widening, "because nobody wants to help. And that, Dr. Holmay, is the secret cause of the tragedy."

He had concluded his case. He leaned back again, resumed his stare.

Holmay began shuffling papers on his desk. Billy had not memorized his words. There was an uncommon brilliance in him triggered, it seemed, by moments of self-confidence that swelled into arrogance. The stammering Billy—the Billy all heart, soul, and confusion—was the weak and vulnerable one. The intellectual one was perhaps intolerable. Holmay looked him right in the eye.

"Where in the hell have you been?"

"I've been reading Faulkner, sir. I read three of his novels and a couple dozen short stories. He approaches Melville, don't you think? Except, of course, *Moby-Dick*. Nothing touches that."

"You've finished that?"

"Two weeks ago."

"I'm going to flunk you, Billy."

"Alas, no justice in the world."

"There's some."

"Will you be flunking me because I don't know my 'stuff,' as the vulgar say?"

"I suspect you know your stuff. But you don't play by the rules."

"You will flunk me for being a nonconformist?"

"I'm not flunking you. I'm flunking your nonconformity."

"*Touché*. A distinction only somewhat nice."

"I could give you one more chance. Take the exam tomorrow and get the paper in by Monday. Do you want to play ball?"

"No."

"Your choice."

"Ah, choice, pretty word. Besides, it's too late. I already quit."

"What do you mean quit?"

"I dropped your course yesterday—officially."

"You're here to inform me or to insult me?"

"I'm here, Dr. Holmay, because I respect and admire you. In some other time or world the word love might be permissible. Oh, have no fear. It's not *that* kind

44

of love I mean, vulgar lust. I mean the other kind—the kind we find in the better books."

"I don't know what to say, Billy."

"What I want you to say is that we should let the past be—the ways we've, how shall I say, disappointed, flunked, each other since the time we…you…decided to call me by my first name."

"I didn't think you'd want it any other way."

"We forgive each other, then?"

Holmay struggled against Billy's logic, but could not hold it back.

"Yes, of course."

"Good," Billy said. "Then I think we should celebrate. I have a room, a room of my own now. It's with Mrs. Lupinski on the south side of town. She's a very nice lady and I do things for her. There's a nice yard and I'm going to put a garden in next spring. I can read there all day—and I'm going to start writing a book."

"A book?"

"Yes, a book. A book about my beliefs. That's what all the better books are about, isn't it?"

"That's wonderful, Billy. A book. Are you ready for a book?"

"Of course I'll have to return to classes someday soon. A person has to make his way in the world. I need money to be on my own, a job of some sort."

"What will you do?"

"I will be a professor someday—like you. The contact with students would be intellectually stimulating, and the pay I suppose will be adequate to support my writing of books."

Holmay nodded his approval.

"Now, as for Saturday night—we wonder, Wendy and I, and Mrs. Lupinski—whether you and Evelyn would like to come over for dinner. Wendy's teaching me to cook, but she's doing it all herself this time. So what do you think?"

The alarm went off again in Holmay's head. "Oh, I'm sorry, but Evelyn's going to spend the night with some friends."

Billy lifted an eyebrow in doubt. "Then you should be free that night."

Holmay could not think fast enough to lie again. "Yes, sure, I'd be glad to come."

"Then you could bring Evelyn over some other time?"

"Maybe some other time."

✳ ✳ ✳

Mrs. Lupinski's house was on Division Street across from the loading docks. Like all other houses in that section of town it was a squat four-room dwelling bordered by patches of lawn and a small yard behind. The houses on Division were unique because the old railroad tracks, still in use, ran along the street just a few paces from front doors. More than once the town council had discussed the possibility of demolishing the row, but each time the issue arose the homeowners there emerged and, one by one, made their way forward to plead

45

for their homes, often in broken English few could understand. Thus the houses, as broken as the people inside, survived the untiring traffic of trucks and trains.

Surrounding the patches of lawn in front of Mrs. Lupinski's house was an unpainted fence, at the base of which bloomed rows of marigolds. A small wooden porch leaned dangerously askew, but hanging down from hooks and nails were potfuls of flowers in autumn bloom. In the center of the window to the left of the door was a faded portrait of Our Lady, her eyes pleading and mournful as her hand revealed the Sacred Heart at the center of her chest.

Billy, standing behind Mrs. Lupinski as she let Holmay in, wore a big smile and plaid wool sportcoat to go with his white shirt and tie. Mrs. Lupinski, seventy, perhaps seventy-five years old, was a short, stooped woman with a white shawl over her shoulders, her face curling into wrinkles whenever she showed her kind, almost toothless grin. In the kitchen Wendy, a smile straining her lips, waved a hello as she peeked into the living room. The house was full of smells—the stale dusty odors of old age and of dank basement stones, and, strongest of all, the sharp smell of strange new soup.

Holmay took a seat on a lumpy sofa, with Mrs. Lupinski, grinning and silent, stooped like a servant in front of him.

"Would you like something to drink?" Billy asked.

"Why sure," Holmay replied, just to be agreeable.

"We have orange juice," Billy said.

"We got whiskey too," Mrs. Lupinski said.

"I think he'd want something else," Billy said. "I'll get you orange juice, Dr. Holmay."

Mrs. Lupinski grinned and sat down in her rocking chair.

Holmay got up and helped pull the kitchen table out from against the wall. He sat with his back tight against the refrigerator, his knees aching to spread out. The table was covered by a linen full of hand-embroidered flowers, and the silverware, showing green tarnish marks, had not been used since Mr. Lupinski's funeral.

"He is professor?" Mrs. Lupinski asked again and again from her rocking chair, shaking her head in disbelief

"Yes," Billy replied. "He is *Doctor* Holmay."

"He is *doctor?*"

"He is a professor of literature. He is a doctor of philosophy."

"Doctor," she said, shaking her head and laughing the way people do when they're ashamed.

"He is a doctor of the soul and mind, not the body, Mrs. Lupinski."

Wendy, excusing herself, went to the stove to stir the soup. For the first time Holmay saw that her breasts were full and firm and that behind her makeup was a pretty face with sly darting eyes.

"Billy, you're going too far," Holmay said with a little laugh. "I just teach English."

Wendy appeared over them holding the potful of soup. "Soup's on," she said, turning her nose up to show Holmay that the soup was not her fault. "Mrs. Lupinski's favorite soup."

"What kind of soup is it?" Holmay asked.

"Special for you," Mrs. Lupinski said. "Very good soup. It is blood soup, with carrots."

Holmay held his breath with each spoonful, saving a swallow of his orange juice for a final wash.

"There's nothing wrong with blood soup," Billy began as soon as he was sure Wendy was seated and listening. "At least it's an *honest* food."

Wendy lifted her left brow toward Holmay and put the spoon up to her lips again. Holmay tried a faint smile that Billy caught and did not like. Mrs. Lupinski, her spoon trembling, saw only her soup.

"We're all parasites, you know," Billy said.

Again Wendy lifted a brow.

"We eat each other—sooner or later we all do. I know because I grew up on a farm. I saw it there every day. I know what it's like to feed a steer from the time it can barely stand and then two years later shoot it in the brain. I know what it's like to drain all the blood out—I know. And I know what chicken blood tastes like too."

"Billy!"

"Because it was a waste of good life. The blood that flowed through that bird's heart—it just spilled on the ground. So one day I made up my mind to it. And I drank it before it could spill."

Holmay loosened his collar, and Mrs. Lupinski, pleased to have him feel at home, nodded and smiled.

"Can't you talk about something else, Billy?"

"I only did it once, but I only needed to do it once. And that's why I never could go along with Catholicism. Because they say you have to do it every Sunday."

"Billy, I'm Catholic," Wendy said. "What are you talking about?"

"You know what I'm talking about. I'm talking about the way you people do Communion."

"We don't even get to drink the wine."

"That's why it's not honest. That's why it's better to sit around this table and drink this soup. At least it's honest this way. At least the blood's really there."

Mrs. Lupinski looked up confused, her bowl empty.

"What good does the actual blood do for you?" Wendy made no effort to hide her disgust.

"Probably more nutritious than Pepsi," Holmay said without cracking a smile.

"We become part of each other," Billy went on. "That's what communion is. We commingle. We mix our spirits together...and we become *one*."

"But why the blood, Billy," Holmay inquired, assuming a pedagogical tone.

"Did you ever, Dr. Holmay, consider the mosquito? Think of it, the tiny troublesome mosquito. With one slap we wipe its existence away, but there is always another there to take its place—a hundred more, a thousand, a thousand million more. Did you ever consider that they feed the world. Bats, birds, fish, frogs—you name it and they feed on mosquitos. And who feeds on these larger

species, the birds and fish and frogs? Larger species do. And who feeds on them—
right up the line? We do—man. We give them a pinpoint of blood, and they give
us life in return. Millions of them do."

"Well, of course, biologically considered... "

"No, it's not just biological. It's spiritual. The process is an ancient and holy
one. It's a ritual. That's what Jesus meant when he shed his blood for us, and
that's why the priests lie when they say they're giving Communion and then they
use wine instead of blood... "

"And they drink it all down themselves," Wendy laughed.

"And why vampires... "

"Oh, now you're talking legend, myth... " Holmay broke in.

" ...why vampires need blood to live on. They actually did it, you know. People
actually sucked blood." Billy turned to face Holmay. "You know that, don't you?
You know there are recorded instances. Not just legend. Not just myth. Real *fact*."

"I really don't know much about...history," Holmay said.

Wendy got up and opened the oven door. "The roast is done," she said cheerily.

"But you see the significance of all this. We're all hosts and parasites. It's all a
big circle. Everything fits."

"And we're the hosts tonight," Wendy laughed.

"And blood is what we all have in common."

"Why," Holmay interrupted, "does it have to be blood?"

"Why not feelers," Wendy laughed, wiggling her fingers at him.

Billy sent a sharp glance her way. She ignored him and set the roast in front
of Holmay's plate.

"Blood carries the life. *The* life," Billy said for Holmay's benefit. "Definite article.
And I just know how I feel."

"You're going to feel better after having a slice of this roast beef," Wendy said.

"How I felt and how I feel."

"About what?"

"The blood. After I drank the blood I felt different all at once." Billy's eyes
widened as the experience grew in front of him. "I became...suddenly light, as
if I could almost fly. And it scared me, especially when I looked at my father,
and I remember, I remember now I just started to run and I ran like I never ran
before...as if I almost could fly. I didn't come back until dark, and I was still
afraid." He looked at the roast. "I was sure my father would kill me that night."

"And I'll bet he almost did," Wendy said, stroking the back of his neck.

"He did—with the strap," Billy said.

Mrs. Lupinski speared a potato with her fork and dropped it into Holmay's
soup. "Eat, eat, doctor," she smiled. "Is good for you, all this food."

Holmay picked at his food. Across the table from him Billy stopped chewing
and put down his fork, fixing his eyes on Holmay with a gaze full of intensity.

"We have to be perfectly honest," Billy said. "We really are, you know."

"Are what?" Wendy asked.

"Parasites."

Nine

HOLMAY HAD prepared his excuse carefully in advance. So by nine o'clock he was on his way out the door, already late, he lied, for his appointment to pick up Evelyn. Mrs. Lupinski, weariness clouding her eyes, waved her hanky as he backed out, while Wendy, smiling and sad, stood to one side. Billy, who had discovered Plato that week, followed Holmay all the way to the car with a stream of words about Goodness, Beauty and Truth.

Evelyn was asleep when he picked her up at the Lorrimers.

"Such a dear, dear child," the Lorrimers said, "and such a wonderful thing for you to be raising her all by your lonesome self."

Evelyn was harder to lift. He struggled to open the front door without losing her, but he managed with a final push to gather her in. For a moment he stood at the foot of the stairs, the hall light directly overhead, and he looked at her face. She had been a lovely baby, not the lump of flesh the others always were, and her loveliness had refined itself as she grew. Evelyn stirred in his arms, and as she turned her head away a crimson flush appeared along her neck. He kissed her there.

He lay awake thinking about Billy. The something wrong or something too right with him. The idealism about ideas and books. The strange notions about mosquitos and blood. The strange watch he seemed to keep over the house. The little love affair with Evelyn, the other with Wendy, who, except for the curse visited on her by her father when she was a child, seemed normal enough, maybe too normal for Billy. Billy. Abnormally polite and abnormally sober. Abnormally clear-headed at times, and yet...absurd. Something wrong or something too right.

A door slammed at the back of the house. Goddamned Lance had just announced his arrival. He had told Lance to use only the back door. Now he would have to tell him not to slam it every time. Would it matter what he said to Lance? Lance was probably drunk again.

So maybe Billy would have been better to have around. Why not Billy? At least Billy was intellectually alive, searching for ways to connect his actions and thoughts. And maybe he, The Professor, could have learned something from this earnest boy, student of life. What was Lance? The stuff of ordinary daily life, pizza and beer, efficient, arrogant and dull. In Florida a man was scheduled to die in the electric chair at seven in the morning. Someone would pull the switch and that someone would go home to his wife and kids and no one would think there was anything wrong with him. In small countries everywhere soldiers killed civilians by the hundreds, yet no one was declared insane. The globe itself was held hostage by a handful of men in charge of insanely powerful bombs, and the vast majority approved, even as they saw the balance of terror slipping away. Was there something mad about them? Lance? Normal Lance. Lance no doubt believed that a penny saved was a penny earned, that cleanliness was next to godliness, especially clean-shaven and uniformed cleanliness. And for Lance food came from supermarkets, and he deserved everything he got, and tomorrow things would be better than today, and God was a man, yes, a bearded old man sitting on a cloud, or else some sort of Jesus able to walk on water and then turn water into wine. Or beer, for Lance's convenience.

Lance. Did he believe in the Father Almighty, the Maker of Heaven and Earth, in Jesus Christ His only Son, who was crucified, died, and was buried? Of course, he would say. We're Americans, ain't we?

That He descended into hell, that He rose again on the third day, that He sitteth on the right hand of God?

Well...that's what The Book says, don't it?

That He shall come to judge the quick and the dead?

Sure as shit. That's what I believe.

And Lance will go to heaven someday?

Well, if there's a heaven, why not?

Was Lance more or less insane than a boy, trying to make sense of the senselessness of life, drinking the blood of a chicken, performing, as it were, a ceremony of atonement for the taking of a life?

Yet the giddiness Billy described, the light-headed desire to fly: Wasn't it proof that Billy was strange? A mad moment perhaps, induced by emotional stress. A crazy moment—an emotional high. And how many such moments had Billy experienced—how many more ceremonies had he performed, how many more secrets did he have locked behind his impenetrable stare?

No, Billy's weird, Holmay concluded. There's something about him. It's in his eyes.

✳ ✳ ✳

He saw nothing more of Billy for two weeks. He signed the necessary forms officially dropping Billy from his course and tried to put him out of his mind. Then Frances Drummond began making herself more visible. Instead of passing his office without blinking his way, she said hello, pausing to chat. She did not know why he asked her out for pizza, and was too politic to ask. All had gone well that night, and afterward Evelyn offered her opinion without being asked. "She's really nice, Dad."

He trusted Evelyn's opinion more than his own. Consciously, deliberately, relentlessly he tried to teach Evelyn to read—not words in a book, for teachers were doing well enough with that, but the signs of the times: the implication of a gesture or mannerism, the connotation of dress and hair, the tone of the spoken word, the syntax of shapes. He was surprised, alarmed sometimes, at how far afield from each other their interpretations were. Where he heard screams in music, she heard fun; where he saw a black snake burrowing into the heart of prairie grass, she saw only bright yellow stalks and a thick black rope, and certainly no train called Progress. She would come around, he told himself, in time. Her eye was innocent, untrained. More basically he believed that there were roughly zones within which consensus could be achieved. The facts in the world were facts, and two people looking at them long and clearly enough could eventually agree about what they were, if their hearts were inclined to agree. He tried to invoke this spirit in his classes every day. Here are the words, he said to his students, and here is how they add up to mean something humanly understandable. We no doubt will differ about details, but we will have no trouble discerning the basic truths. This is what it means to learn how to read.

He had little trouble having his way every time.

He knew he was skating on thin intellectual ice. He also knew that Evelyn was right in her assessment of Frances Drummond: "Dad, she's really nice." But he did not know if the conclusion resulted from a chance hit reflected off surfaces or if it revealed a deep intuitive sense lost to jaded adults. He wanted to believe the latter, though it spelled trouble itself. For one night, as Evelyn was barely able to keep herself awake, she said in words so innocent that they seemed to come right out of the blue, "Dad, why don't we ever see Billy any more? He's really nice."

One morning Frances Drummond dropped into his office to set the record clear.

"You shouldn't be the last to know," she said as she helped herself to the edge of the chair next to his desk.

"You mean that men from Mars have landed again?"

"The Promotion and Policy Committee meets at three."

"To decide our fates."

"It's fairly clear that they're pitting us against each other."

"You can have the promotion. I don't care that much."

"It means a lot of money, over the long haul."

"You deserve it more than I do."

"You've been here longer," she said.

"I don't have a book—not even close to starting one."

Frances sat back and carefully closed the door. "It's not just that, the money, the promotion. They may try to cut a position."

"I've heard some talk of that."

"Maybe you."

"They wouldn't dare."

Frances lowered her eyes. "It's been done before."

"Do I have any friends on the committee?"

"Halverson, Gadjecki, Roberts, and dear old Ella Mae—they're neutral. You know how stiff they are."

"Hoffstein?"

"Hoffstein called you an asshole. That's what Ella Mae said."

"An *asshole*? He really *used* the word?"

"Ella Mae did. *Asshole.*"

"He was projecting. He hopes I'm an asshole so he can stick it to me."

"Is he gay, do you think?"

"He's not gay. He's just trying to be gay. He's just plain nuts. Did you ever listen to what he says about practically every great writer under the sun? He sees assholes in every written word that's got an *o* in it."

Frances got up. "He's trying to get rid of you. He says you're *unproductive*."

"And stupid too?"

"Ella Mae said he used the word *dumb*."

"Fuck him."

"No thanks," Frances said. "But . . . I just want you to know I'll do what I can. I don't want to compete against you."

"Thanks," he said after she left. "Thanks for all the good news. You really made my day."

❊ ❊ ❊

He shrugged the bad news off. Frances would be promoted ahead of him, but he could live with that. She was at least half-finished with a book, and he had nothing to profess. Did this mean he was "unproductive"? If they tried to cut his position, he would be in for a long nasty fight, one that would divide people who brushed shoulders every day. If he had to fight he would, but not until the bitter end. He had classes to prepare, he announced to himself, as if the evaluation committee were present in the room.

When Wendy appeared on his porch just after dinner, he suddenly imagined that

Billy would be the one to deliver an oration to the committee on his behalf, "The Student's View of Professor Holmay." The fantasy fled after he took a closer look. Wendy, her blouse hanging out of her jeans and her hair disheveled, was choking back sobs.

"It's Billy," she said, "you've got to try talking to him."

Evelyn, standing behind him when he answered the door, drew herself back inside, close enough to hear without being seen.

"I'm afraid," Wendy began. "I just had to call it off with him."

"What happened?"

"Nothing happened," she said. "That's part of what was wrong." Her experienced eyes asked him if he knew what she meant.

"He's quite a puritan, isn't he?"

"He wouldn't let me...kiss him at first. I had to ask. Can you imagine that?"

"Your...family history must be very difficult for him."

"Oh God," she said. "But that wasn't my fault."

"What happened?"

"Nothing happened. We talked and talked—hours of nothing but talk. You saw us under the tree—and in the park that day. Hours of talk. And he's so smart, so full of ideas, really interesting ones. Then he would read to me, and he has some poems."

"You got tired of it all?"

"Not exactly, no. No." She threw her hair back to get it out of her face. "I tried to loosen him up. Do you know what I mean?"

"You tried...having fun with him."

"Yesterday, at the park. I pulled him over real close to me. I just wanted... "

" ...him to touch you."

"Yes."

"And."

"He got stiff. Then he wouldn't talk. He went back to Mrs. Lupinski's house without saying a word. Not one word. He just left me there."

She shook her head as if she could not believe her eyes.

"Then this morning I opened the door in the dorm to go down the hall to brush my teeth, and he was standing right in the door. Then he came into the room and he started talking and talking and talking."

"What did he say?"

"I don't know. Weird stuff. Stuff about gods and goddesses. Greek myths. Plato or whoever he is. He just went on and on, and he kept saying that the body was not the same as the soul. And finally I started crying, but he wouldn't sit down with me, and he wouldn't stop talking, talking, quoting books at me."

"Did he leave on his own?"

"I cried, couldn't stop. Then I yelled at him, told him to get out, I never wanted to see him again. Then the dormitory guard came by and he asked Billy how he got in. And they just stood there arguing until Billy turned around, called me a name, and walked out."

"What did he call you?"

"Lilith."

"Lilith? Do you know what that means?"

"No."

"It isn't all bad. She was very good to men. I wouldn't let it worry you."

She put her head down. "He made it sound like slut, whore, bitch, cunt. I've heard all those words before, Dr. Holmay."

He reached over to take hold of her hand, but as soon as he touched it she turned it over and wrapped her fingers around his. Holmay slowly pulled his hand away.

"Will you be okay?"

She nodded.

"And Billy?"

"I worry about him. I can't go on with him. I really can't. He's super-intelligent and he's really a good person, but he's not my type. I'm going to miss all his ideas and stuff, but I need more from a guy."

"Does he know that?"

"I told him that. I screamed at him. I told him I never wanted to see him again. And I mean it. I really do."

"Where is he now?"

"I don't know."

"Any ideas at all?"

From behind the door Evelyn appeared, glaring at Wendy.

"There's a rock that hangs over the river down at the park. Billy's there."

"How do you know?"

"That's where I would go," Evelyn said. "I can just see him there. Will you please go look, Dad? Just for me. What if Billy's really, really sad?"

"I'll stay with her here, Dr. Holmay, if you want to look. I really think Billy needs your help."

Evelyn gave Wendy a careful looking over. "Please, Dad, would you please go?"

* * *

Billy was staring upstream when Holmay approached, his legs crossed under him, his posture upright and head unmoved. Even when he saw Holmay he did not make a move, as if to move would be to betray his silent communication with some god visible to him beyond the trees.

"Billy," Holmay called softly to him.

Billy did not blink an eye.

"Billy, don't you want to talk?"

Holmay took a deep breath.

"Billy."

"Will there be anything else?"

"Wendy stopped by and told me you two were having . . . a lovers' quarrel, Billy."

"She doesn't want to see me any more."

"People sometimes say things, Billy. They don't always mean what they say."

Billy turned, uncrossed his legs and let them drape down over the edge of the rock. Holmay advanced, sat at the foot of the rock, and gazed at the water streaming by. "I just want to help you through this, if I can."

"What can you do for me?"

"I don't know exactly what I can do, but I'm older, Billy, and I've been through a lot of things, so maybe I can offer a different perspective on things."

"So tell me what you know."

"Well I can't just . . . "

"Why not? You are a Doctor of Philosophy. If you can't explain, who can?"

"Billy, I can only explain things from my point of view."

"Then go ahead, explain. I'll do the listening."

"Maybe what you have to realize Billy is that . . . "

. . . the course of true love never did run smooth. Strange things happen between men and women, especially when they think they're in love. Sometimes they think they're in love, when really they just feel the need to be loved. Opposites don't necessarily attract. Sometimes it's better to go slow in building a relationship, better to build brick by brick from the ground floor up, not expect love to be a sunburst of energy. And sometimes lovers fight with each other because they're together too much, because they only have each other to take their frustrations out on, and really they should spend more time apart, to develop their inner resources. Sometimes fights, explosions of anger and energy, are good, help clear the air, give people a chance to start over again. Lovers often don't have each other as friends, don't allow each other to have friends of their own. Sometimes they need to be less serious—need to play jokes on each other, roll in the grass, tickle each other, kiss and hug.

Billy shot a glance his way, warning him to stop.

"And sometimes, Billy, it's good for lovers to break up. It's always hard and it always feels like Heartbreak Hotel for a few days, a week, sometimes two, but some people just don't belong together all their lives, and the sooner they cut the tie the better it is for both of them."

"You were divorced, weren't you? So what went wrong?"

"That's personal."

"What did she do to you?"

"She didn't do anything to me, Billy. Sometimes things just go wrong."

"Did Wendy make you come looking for me?"

"No."

"Then how did you know I was here?"

"I thought you might have come to the park."

"Were you following me?"

"No."

"Then who was following me?"

"I don't know, Billy. I wasn't following you."

"That wasn't you by the flower garden?"

"No."

"Then who was it?"

"I don't know. How am I supposed to know?"

"I suppose you want to know what to tell Wendy?"

"She's worried about you."

He lifted his head again, stiffening his posture and looking into the trees. "Tell her about Enceladus."

"Who?"

"You already know about him. He was the child of a Titan god, and the Titan's father and mother were Heaven and Earth. Now Heaven and Earth, as you well know, don't mix, so their coupling was incestuous, and Enceladus was a Titan's child and so he was a doubly incestuous offspring."

"I'm not sure what to make of that, Billy."

"You know what it means," he said, fixing Holmay with his eyes. "You know. So you ask Wendy if that's what she wants things to come to again. You just ask her that."

Holmay sighed in defeat. "Come on, Billy. Let's walk back together."

Billy stiffened momentarily, then suddenly looked over his shoulder. "I think I'd better walk with you," he said, "because I don't think he's going to leave me alone."

"Who, Billy?"

"The man by the flower garden. The one who was following me." He jumped down from the rock. "Come on, let's get out of here."

He walked Billy to Mrs. Lupinski's house, neither of them exchanging more than a few words. In the window the old lady was visible, watering her plants. She waved her hanky when she saw them standing outside.

"Please come in," Billy said.

"I can't," Holmay said. "I really have to get back."

"It's that little girl of yours, isn't it? You really love her, don't you?"

"Yes, I do, Billy."

"I really love her too."

Holmay turned sharply and started walking away.

"Wait!" Billy called after him. "I really want to pay you back somehow. . . I mean for what you do for me. I mean. . . it's *love*, what you do."

Holmay shook his head sadly.

"Would you like to go to the woods with me someday—I mean hunting in the woods?"

"I don't hunt, Billy."

"I'll show you how, the way I used to when I was a kid."

"I don't think I would enjoy hunting, Billy. I've never had a gun."

"I've got three guns. You could use one of them."

"No," Holmay said as he walked away. "I don't believe in guns."

No, not guns.

No, no, no.

Ten

HOLMAY BEGAN making a point of locking the doors.

"No need for that," Lance complained, "not the back door anyway." He grinned stupidly. "I always lose keys—never could hang onto them. And besides, you've got me to be the night watchman in back."

He gave Lance two keys and told him to keep the back door locked. Then he took Evelyn aside.

"I want you never to go anywhere with any stranger, even some people you know. Billy is one of them."

"There's nothing wrong with Billy." Her tone was defiant and firm.

"That's for me to decide, not you."

"You can't tell me who to like."

"But I'm telling you to never go off with him the way you did that day. Never go off all by yourself with him."

"What if he wants to take me for a walk in the park?"

"No. You are to go nowhere with him."

"You never take me anywhere. That's why I wish I was living with Mom."

"And if Billy shows up at the door, you call me at once. You make him wait outside until I come to the door."

"Why? You always used to let him in."

"Because Billy seems nice and maybe really is, but sometimes he does strange things. And maybe someday he might hurt somebody like you or me."

Evelyn's eyes widened in disbelief. "You mean people he really *likes*? Billy would never hurt me."

"Yes, when things go really wrong. So you have to promise me you'll do as I say." He glared at her eyes filling with tears. "You *have* to promise me."

She looked away.

He took a hanky out and wiped her eyes.

"But what should I do if he comes to the house and I'm the only one home?"

"Tell him to wait outside, that you're not supposed to let anyone in. Then you go to the back door and run through the alley to the Lorrimer's. You call me from there and wait."

He made her promise and held her close.

* * *

He heard no more from Billy for more than two weeks. Then one day he returned to a note under his door. Billy's hand was tidy and clear:

> *Dear Dr. Holmay:*
> *The transpiring of certain matters personal has brought to immediate attention the necessity of securing gainful employment. My own pending destitution, coupled with the discomfort of my dear patron, Mrs. Lupinski (who has been under the weather of late) has required me to suspend the research for and writing of my book. The local civil authorities have been most uncooperative and threatening since informed of my residency in her dwelling and of her patronage of my work, in return for which I provide her some everyday services to ease her distress. They threaten us with a cessation of funds for everyday subsistence.*
> *Would you be so kind as to prepare for my use a letter of recommendation, one suitable for presentation to employers able to make use of my ability predilections? Specifically, I have in mind employment as a mail sorter in the post office. Such a position would provide hours suitable to my continuing care of Mrs. L. This employment would help, of course, to keep the hound from the door (as they say), and (ha, ha) keep me close to the world of letters.*
> *Please see to this matter at once, and I will happen by within the week to secure the letter from you.*
> *Your loyal student and loving friend,*
Billy
>
> *P.S. Sometimes I feel awful. I'll never forgive Plato for banishing the poet from his Republic.*

* * *

"Loyal student and loving friend." Holmay stared at the words, trying, with a sweep of memory, to recall what he had done to deserve such adoration. Clearly he had gone too far, come too personally close to Billy. The nameless father with the strap had driven Billy to find in his professor the understanding father absent from his life, just as in Evelyn Billy desired a sisterly love, and in Mrs. Lupinski, "patron," the mother always absent from his talk. All this was easy enough to see—easier than interpreting the stories discussed in class. But how could one account for the untidy details—Billy's lurking at his door, the wild leaps in logic, as if wires suddenly short-circuited and the result was a thin mental fire that seared away the difference between myth and reality, magic and metaphor, figurative and literal truth, perhaps sanity and, at least momentarily, madness?

Billy didn't fit in, didn't add up. There was no apparent evil about him anywhere, but he had three guns. He seemed too good for the rest of the world, but he had three guns. He was intellectually superior to most, but the guns gave him the capacity for...

Capacity for what? To slip into the mainstream and swim or sink like everyone else. To drift further away, eventually so far out that he became wholly lost to the world, then caged like an animal behind the walls of some institution far from sight. Or perhaps to live his life on the outer boundaries of the normal, a benign eccentric—mad poet, prophet, philosopher—perpetually testing, and perhaps usefully expanding, the parameters of the possible.

He needs a job, Holmay concluded, and he needs a letter from me. That should be easy enough, but Billy makes nothing easy. What could a professor write on behalf of a student who had not made it through a sophomore course in literature, and who, he well knew, had also dropped out of Frances Drummond's class. Billy had turned in no written work, had refused to take the exam. He could be witness to nothing more than Billy's character, and there was too much of that to capture in clear words.

Reluctantly he began to write.

> *To Whom It May Concern:*
> *It has been my ~~privilege~~ pleasure*
> *I have known Mr. William Allan Brand for almost two months now, both as his professor in a literature course and as an individual who has shared with him a number of personal conversations. Therefore I suspect I can witness to his qualities from a personal perspective.*
> *Mr. Brand strikes me as a person having remarkable qualities. Possessed of an unusually high intellectual capacity, he promises to develop into an individual who will realize his highest ambitions. He was an uncommonly diligent student, clearly outstanding among his peers but unfortunately pressed by extenuating circumstances to abandon his studies. Though shy, he is hard-working and self-motivated; above all, he is loyal. I would not hesitate to put him to good use.*

Holmay reread the letter carefully, smirking uncomfortably as he turned each word in his mind. He watched as his hand scribbled "Sincerely" on the page, then grabbed the letter off his desk and marched to his department office.

"Sylvia," he said to the secretary, "would you please type this up for me? Then please put it in an envelope and keep it here. A boy named William Brand will pick it up from you."

"Unsigned?" Sylvia asked.

"Just sign it for me."

Frances paused as Holmay was taping to his door a note instructing Billy to ask the secretary for the letter.

"Are you posting a manifesto?" she smiled.

"No, I've seen the handwriting on the wall. What you see here is the opening chapter of my book, the one that's going to get me promoted."

She squeezed his arm affectionately as she passed. "Come to my office a minute," she said. Her gesture did not go unnoticed by Professor Hoffstein standing down the hall.

❋ ❋ ❋

Harvey Gabriel Hoffstein was one of three full professors in the department. "He's full of shit—that's what he is," said Holmay as he closed the door to Frances's office audibly behind himself. "I don't see why he just doesn't come out and admit he's a homosexual."

"He's got four kids," Frances said, "and a wife."

"Did you ever see her? How do you know she exists?"

"Maybe she's like God. You don't really have to see her to believe she exists. I hear she's. . .leathery."

"She's the Marlboro Man, the Green Berets. That's what Gadjecki told me.

"Maybe she's nice."

"I wouldn't care if she looked like Patton. I know she can't help that. It's her taste in men I can't stand."

"Harvey."

"Harvey."

They both put their hands over their mouths to keep from laughing out loud.

"Did you ever read his book? *Devious Demiurges: A Study of Subversive Symbolic Strategies.* Everybody's gay, Fran. Everybody. Emily Dickinson's a lesbian. Robert Frost. Charles Dickens. Shakespeare. James Fennimore Cooper. John Bunyan. Whitman."

"Whitman for sure."

"Wordsworth."

"But not Coleridge."

"Shelley. Keats."

"Did you read the last chapters, the ones on the contemporary poets?" Frances suppressed another laugh.

"I quit after Keats."

"They're not really gay. They're just trying to be. It's one of their subversive symbolic strategies. They're searching for a new normality. That's what he says.

"Is that the chapter with the computerized study of the letter *o*?"

Frances nodded. "Actually, it's quite interesting."

It was too late for her to retract the remark, so they let it do its silent work.

"I've got some good news," she said.

"Nepal has the bomb?"

"I'm getting promoted."

"I'm glad of that," Holmay said, his words tight as knots.

"But you're not out of it yet. I had tea with Ella Mae yesterday. She said they were going to reconsider your case."

"Harvey Hoffstein, who called me an asshole, is going to look at my case again?"

"Do me a favor," she said, squeezing his arm. "Finish reading his book. Catch him in the coffee room and just talk to him a bit. I think he thinks you don't like him at all."

"I think he thinks I can't think."

"You can think, and you're also a real nice guy."

He left her sitting at her desk, sure she was about to cry.

※ ※ ※

For class that day he began with last things first. "Why would anybody want to sleep with a corpse?"

Lance was the first to leap in. "Is *that* what she did? I thought maybe there was something fishy going on."

Emily Grierson had been disappointed in love. She fancied herself a southern lady, so when she was betrayed by a suitor, a commoner himself from the North, her honor was violated. What could a lady do? For such a rat only one thing would do: poison. So he suddenly disappeared, and a few days later a foul smell began emanating from Emily's house. Her faithful Negro servant spread lime around the base of the house, and in time the smell went away. Then Emily closed off her attic room and appeared less and less frequently in public view. Her hair grew gray as the dust of death settled over her house. She died alone in the house, alone with her secret in the attic; alone, that is, except for the secret itself, the remains of her only love whose head had spent many years sharing a pillow with her.

"Sick," said Lori Mullin. "Really sick."

"I thought it was great," said a business major who had never said a word before in class. "I could just *see* it."

"But does the story add up to something?" Holmay pleaded. "Does it *mean* anything?"

Lori Mullin: "She was just crazy, that's all. Just sick."

Nick Ferraro: "Maybe it shows what love can make you do."

Annette George: "Yuk."

Lance Walcott: "I say yuk too."

Holmay looked around the room for other hands. He loved stories like this, difficult enough so that few understood, complex enough to allow overlapping explanations, coherent enough to be tidily pinned down. They made him look good in class.

"We might best explore the story," he began, "by considering the levels of meanings it projects. From a historical point of view we could see Emily as a type from the Old South, her betraying lover as the crude North. So what happens is a Civil War of sorts, a lovers' quarrel. In a lovers' quarrel there's a love-hate relationship. As the Old South, Emily doesn't want the changes the North is imposing on her, so she has to stop all change. In killing her lover she tries to kill change, the forces destroying her southern way of life, her ladyhood, and thereby stop time itself. When time stops, when her lover's dead, she's happy, but it's a dead happiness, as it were."

He paused, looked around. "Any questions?"

People shrank in their chairs, their silence accusing him of pulling another rabbit from his hat.

"Let's try another level—the psychological one. We ask: What kind of mind would literally—or figuratively—enjoy sleeping with the dead?"

"Yuk," Lance chimed.

"Are the dead active or passive?" Holmay asked.

"Passive."

"Ultimately passive, aren't they? Now what kind of person would be attracted to a passive lover? Someone strong or someone weak?"

"Strong," said Nick Ferraro.

"Weak," said Lori Mullin. "They want weak people so they can do whatever they want to them."

"I don't think that's true," said Lance.

"Why not?" Lori said, turning sharply to confront him. "Guys do that to women all the time."

Lance, caught completely off-guard, had nothing to say.

"The story, I suspect," Holmay broke in, "supports Ms. Mullin's view. Emily's desire to resist change is synonymous with a resistance to time and life themselves. There are serious defects in her, defects that can stand no serious challenges. Hence she retreats to her place away from the world, her attic, and to the only kind of lover who won't be able to win against her, that dead man in her room."

"That was brilliant," said Billy, who greeted Holmay with an outstretched hand right outside the classroom door. "Let me shake your hand." Holmay saw the snickers of those brushing past as Billy took his hand. "I heard every word you said—right through the door. I really miss being in there with you. I really do. But there's work to be done, isn't there, to keep death from having the last word."

"What do you mean?"

"We know, don't we, why we write—to keep death from having the last word."

"Or because we want fame and gain," Holmay mumbled.

"What's that?" Billy said. "Say that again."

"Nothing, nothing."

"And don't think I don't appreciate what you've done for me," he said, showing Holmay the letter he held in his hand. "This letter means a lot to me, Dr. Holmay. It's like a new lease on life. It's been hard, you know, really awful these past couple weeks. It's like a new lease on life."

"It's the least I could do."

"And do you really mean all these things in the letter? Do you really, really mean them?"

"They're in writing, Billy, in black and white. Now good luck to you."

"Thank you, sir. Thank you very, very much. I'll try to do my best by you, sir."

Eleven

THE FACT CHURNED in Holmay. Billy and guns. All the goodness in Billy, innocent and puritan to the core, was too good to be sensible. It was comforting to know that Billy hunted, that he did one thing other normal boys his age did, but was Billy's hunting more than wholesome outdoor exercise? Was it ritual of some strange sort? Billy not only entered the books he read, but twisted and turned until he got wrapped up, perhaps lost, in them. And if his life in turn became like a book, what twist or turn of what incredible plot would he read into it, and how fictional would the taking of real life be to him? Perhaps like a priest he had drunk his cup of blood and had ritualized its reality, so that for him to take more blood would be as easy as going to church.

No, Holmay concluded as he walked home from a Friday class, he could not stand idly by. He had to keep locking doors, even if the act was only symbolic, an unfortunate ritual performed by rote in any dead or dying community. Billy was too good to be. He had no good reason to fear Billy, but he had reason enough. Maybe he even had reason enough to buy a gun.

A gun. No, not a gun. He had never owned a gun. He did not believe in guns.

That night Evelyn fell asleep before he got halfway through their tale. Too wide awake to turn off his light, he pulled Hoffstein's book off the shelf and turned to the chapters he could not face more than six months earlier. He read a few pages and fell asleep.

When he awoke the next morning he found Evelyn standing over him, the telephone receiver dangling from a finger.

"It's Billy," she said.

"Billy? What does he want?"

"He wants us to come over, Dad."

"What for? What does he want now?"

"He's got a present for us."

"A present?"

"A surprise. He won't tell me what it is. He says I have to come over for it. He says Mrs. Lupinski's got breakfast all ready for us."

"I've got too much work to do."

"But we've *got* to go, Dad. You went without me last time. You said you would take me to Billy's the next time."

"I never said any such thing to you."

"You said it to Billy."

"When?"

"The time you were there. He asked if you would bring me next time."

"And how do you know what we talked about?"

Evelyn lowered her eyes. "He told me."

"When? I told you to come straight home from school."

"He calls me."

"When?"

"When I come home from school. He calls and we talk. He says a lot of interesting things. Can I go, Dad, please? Hurry, he's still on the phone. Billy says he has to pay you back for everything you do for him. *Please.*"

※ ※ ※

From her rocker Mrs. Lupinski waved her hanky and smiled as Billy let them in. Weaving its way through the room crowded with the odors of age and dust, the smell of frying bacon and hot coffee offered some relief from the low ceiling that pressed down on him the moment Holmay stepped into the house. It was ten-twenty, and the November sky was clear and cool. He set noon as the absolute deadline to be out the door.

"Billy, he paint the inside of the house," Mrs. Lupinski said out of the blue. "Nice, no?" She looked around, amazed at her own house, and waved her hanky at Billy as if he were a hero passing in parade.

Billy blushed.

"Billy very good boy, doctor. You good too. Very good doctor."

"When do I get my surprise, Billy?"

"She's all excited about this thing, Billy. She woke me out of a sound morning sleep to get it."

"Evelyn," Billy said, his eyes narrowing. "You told. You promised me you wouldn't tell. You *promised.*"

Evelyn glanced toward her father and shrank. "I'm sorry."

"She promised," Billy insisted. "Why did you break your promise? Why?"

"What did you promise?" Holmay asked.

"That I wouldn't tell about the surprise."

They looked at each other, Evelyn waiting for Billy to speak.

"Dad," she said, "Billy wanted to surprise you too."

"Billy is good boy," Mrs. Lupinski broke in, sighing heavily. "You see the leaves outside? Billy, he rake all the leaves. He change screens on porch, and put on storm windows. Winter, it is cold in house. Billy is good boy."

Her smile died as she concluded her speech. She put her head down, concentrating suddenly sad eyes on her hands folded in her lap.

Holmay kept an eye on Billy as he and Evelyn disappeared into the kitchen. They whispered as Billy tied an apron around his waist and played the cook, turning the bacon just in time and attending to the half-set table while the bacon fried. He was careful to wipe each plate with a white cloth, careful to fold each paper napkin into halves. He put a pot of water on to boil, scrubbing the grease off burners as he waited. He seemed somber as he worked, his face changing its expression only when Evelyn's steady stream of quiet talk was broken by a laughing fit.

Mrs. Lupinski, who appeared to be falling asleep, opened one eye. "Billy," she called to the other room. "It is the time."

Billy reached into the top cupboard over the stove and brought down a half-empty bottle of vodka.

"Billy," she said. "Half and half, like I say."

He filled a tumbler half-full of the hot water and topped it off with the vodka, holding the bottle away from himself as if it were a dangerous thing. Then he wrapped the tumbler in a fresh linen napkin and brought it to her.

"Billy is good boy," she said, pulling herself upright. "Thank you, Billy. Now maybe you make one for doctor. Doctor, you want one too? Is good for the blood. Very good for the blood. Make you very strong in the, what you call it, sex." Her wrinkles curled as she smiled, took a deep breath, and drank half a glassful of the brew.

Billy watched stolidly, then turned away. "No, Mrs. Lupinski, Dr. Holmay doesn't want any today. He is not a married man." He suddenly turned. "You don't have a...girlfriend, do you?" He seemed confused, as if the possibility had never occurred to him before. "Do you want some milk, Dr. Holmay? I'm sorry, I forgot to offer you anything. I'll get you some milk," he said as he turned toward the kitchen again.

"Billy," Mrs. Lupinski said with a note of pique in her voice, "the water is not enough hot. The water it must boil three minutes. Did you boil the water three minutes or no?"

She expected no response and gulped down the rest.

Billy, a woolen shawl draped over his arm, returned with the milk. Carefully he moved Mrs. Lupinski forward as he placed the shawl on her shoulders and folded it over her chest. Mrs. Lupinski weakly lifted one hand and waved her hanky as if to say farewell. "I sleep one hour now. You eat."

"The eggs are ready," Billy said from the kitchen door. "I hope you like scrambled eggs, Dr. Holmay. I really hope you do."

Evelyn was wearing her surprise when Holmay sat down to face Billy and his eggs. She was decked out in a thick wreath of flowers that reached to her knees, and on her head she wore a crown of red roses.

"The flowers," Billy explained as he buttered his toast, "are archetypal symbols of love, beauty, goodness, new life, and growth. I'm sure, Dr. Holmay, that it's all obvious to you. It was the best gift I could think of to offer Evelyn, because she means that to both of us. So my gift, my surprise," he said turning to Evelyn, "is from both of us, your father and me. Because your father's love is in me and I, who have prepared this surprise for you, am both agent and principal. And because you, Evelyn, reciprocate, you are so much a part of us that we are three, but really we are one."

Evelyn looked at her father, waiting for him to respond. "Oh, they're real nice flowers, Billy. Thanks."

"The flowers are..."

"I think, Billy, there's no need to get melodramatic about it," Holmay broke in. "I think you're making too much of it."

Billy stiffened, unable to respond.

"The flowers are really nice," Holmay said. "Thanks a lot."

"Don't you think, Dr. Holmay, that children can feel these energies—the energy of love, I mean, that flows from nature to man, from one heart to another...when there's openness...and sympathy?"

"Yes, Billy. But Evelyn's only nine. I don't think you can expect her to know what the word 'reciprocate' means."

"But I do, Dad. It means back and forth, going back and forth, back and forth, back and forth." She giggled. "And these are good eggs, Billy, real good."

Satisfied, Billy let the issue drop.

They were almost finished when Mrs. Lupinski stirred in her chair. Immediately Billy got up and, taking a jarful of water with him, went over to her. Gently he lifted her head, readjusted the shawl on her shoulders and wrapped a blanket around her legs. Then he stepped back from her, as if to pity and admire. Before returning to the table he watered three plants growing in plain clay pots.

"I am most grateful," he said as he poured more coffee in Holmay's cup. "She is one of three blessings in my life." He held up his glassful of milk as if to toast the other two.

"Do you see much of Wendy?" Holmay asked.

Billy scraped his chair on the floor as he pulled away from the table. Without response he walked to Mrs. Lupinski again and once more made sure of her shawl. He stood at the window a minute and looked out before returning to the table.

"Do *you* see Wendy?" he asked accusingly.

"No."

"Then why should I see her?"

Holmay turned quickly away from the implications of Billy's words. "It's not that I go out of my way not to see her," he said. "Wendy and I are...friends."

"Then you know something I don't."

"Like what?"

"I don't know. That's between Wendy and you."

Evelyn dismissed herself, pausing to give Mrs. Lupinski a long look before going out to examine the flowerpots on the porch.

"There's nothing between Wendy and me, Billy."

"She wasn't at your house that day when you came looking for me by the river?"

"Yes, but so what?"

"You don't think she was just using you?"

"For what?"

"For what, he asks." Billy addressed his words to the ceiling, as if Holmay had become a third party, third person singular, in a conversation Billy was having with someone looking down on them.

"For what?" Holmay asked again.

"To get even with me, that's what."

"I don't know what you're talking about."

"He says he doesn't know what I'm talking about. He says he knows nothing about what Wendy tried to do to me, and almost did. He says he knows nothing about how I spent night after night sick in my stomach, out in the streets, not able to sleep, eat, think, do anything. He knows nothing of the pain." Billy paused, ran his spread hands up and down his chest. "Like she had poisoned me. Like someone had stuck a pin into a doll for her, and she gave that person my name and said go to it, work your magic on him, get rid of him, make him go to hell, make him hurt and burn...in his head, his chest, his stomach, his arms and legs, everywhere..."

Holmay looked at his watch. "I'm sorry, Billy. I have to go."

"And now you just leave?"

"I don't think Wendy's a bad person. I can't listen to you say bad things about her."

"So," he said, "that's what you think? You don't think she would hurt me?"

"I think your situation hurt you, but she never deliberately hurt you."

"You don't know her, do you?"

"I can't care about her now. I think you two had a bad love affair. That's all I think for now."

"Affair," Billy said with disgust. "She said love."

"She made a mistake."

"You use her words now, the very same words. And she was the one who lied."

Holmay pulled away from the table.

"No, please Dr. Holmay," Billy said, taking hold of his arm and then releasing it again. "Please don't go yet."

"I won't stand for your badmouthing her. You're remarkably bright, but maybe you have a few blind spots too, and maybe these are caused, Billy, by an emotional innocence you will have to do something about."

Billy, struck dumb by the words, glanced over his shoulder. Finally, in a whisper full of confusion and helplessness, he spoke: "But what can I do?"

"I don't know, Billy. I don't know what to tell you about that. We all have troubles to work out."

"You," Billy whispered again, "haven't been through the hell I've been through."

"And maybe you haven't experienced her little hell, Billy, Wendy's little hell."

Billy said nothing.

"Maybe we can try to imagine someone else's hell."

"It hurts," Billy said again, using his hands. "It hurts everywhere, especially at night."

"I used to have some pain like yours, over a girl named Catherine."

"And your wife when she left?"

"Yes," Holmay lied.

"And what did you do?"

"Time has its way of healing us. Maybe it's stages we go through, natural stages of some sort. That's what I think. These feelings of hurt, rejection, pain are natural when a love relationship dies."

"Like an animal dying," Billy said, his eyes suddenly faraway.

"So we can eat," Holmay said without choosing his words.

Billy's eyes remained fixed. "So maybe it is all natural. Without contraries maybe there is no progression."

"Or something like that."

The screen slammed behind Evelyn. "Dad, let's go home. I'm bored."

"Yes, we have to go now."

Billy suddenly sprang up.

"Mrs. Lupinski, it's eleven-thirty. It's time to wake up now. I'm going to start running the water for your bath."

Mrs. Lupinski's face quivered, then she opened her eyes.

"What's Dad's surprise?" Evelyn said to Billy.

"Ah, that. I'll get to that as soon as I turn the bath water on."

He returned from the bedroom with a package wrapped in pink paper, a bow on top.

"This," he said, "is a token of my thanks...because you believe in me."

"Billy!" Mrs. Lupinski called from the chair. "Is water hot?"

"And I trust," Billy said, ignoring her, "that tomorrow marks the beginning of a new stage."

"What new stage, Billy?"

"A job. I'm going to get a job."

71

"Oh I hope you like your new job," Evelyn said. "Now open your surprise, Dad."

Holmay found a book inside, *Whitman's Complete Poetical Works.*

"Published in 1934," Billy said proudly. "You mentioned him three times in class. I don't understand all of it yet, but maybe someday."

"Thank you, Billy."

"Thank you, doctor," Mrs. Lupinski said as Holmay backed out the door. "You good doctor, and Billy he is very good boy."

Twelve

HOLMAY DID NOT have the strength to finish the last four pages of Hoffstein's book. He slouched down too far in the bed and the book was a weight so heavy on his chest he could not reach it with his eyes. He found himself in a strange hotel. A woman, dark-haired and lovely, was standing on the sidewalk below pretending to look in the window of a jewelry shop. Now and then she glanced up at him, but he had already made up his mind that she would have to make the first move. Then Hoffstein knocked on the door and burst in. Billy, silent on a chair at the foot of the bed, ignored Hoffstein and stared out the window at the rooftops of the city. "Which way did she go?" Hoffstein shouted at both of them. "Which way?" Below, the woman had disappeared. Hoffstein took one look at Billy and ran out of the room. "I'll get even with you for this," he shouted before slamming the door. "I'll get even with both of you." Then there was a baby's crying in another room. Evelyn, he thought, something is wrong with Evelyn. He tried the door to the other room, but the room was empty except for one wooden chair in a corner. And the hallway corridor was empty, but behind the closet door he found what he was looking for, a baby, no more than a year old, crying without stop. But it was not Evelyn. It was a baby boy. Horrified, he slammed the door and ran out of the room. Once in the streets below he ran and ran, ducking in and out of alleyways to confuse the man chasing him.

It was after four in the morning when Holmay had the strength to turn off the light next to his bed. It seemed no more than minutes before the alarm went off. A note from Billy was tucked under the morning paper on the porch.

> *I just wanted to thank you for coming over Saturday. I felt better after you left. I appreciate your words of wisdom very much. One thing I forgot to mention. I reapplied to the Probation Board for academic reinstatement. No doubt you will be contacted to support my case. (They must actually think there's a relationship between grades and learning. I will let you wise them up.) Until I resume my university studies, I will achieve suitable employment and pursue independently studies the world (as you well know) tragically deems merely esoteric and valueless.*
>
>

Thanks,
Billy

❋ ❋ ❋

In the faculty coffee room Hoffstein sat in his corner. He always wore the same brown corduroy jacket, indifferent to whether it matched his pants or shirts. He had other habits Holmay could not tolerate, including the practice of consuming, daily at nine-thirty sharp, a bagful of midget-sized powdered white donuts, the debris of which he always left behind like the frothy wake of a small ship. And he was big, especially around the waist, which seemed firm and upright, unlikely to cave in to any inclination to exercise. He sat alone, looking just slightly over the tops of other heads in the room, as if anticipating the arrival of a remarkable personage.

Holmay ventured too close, then decided to go all the way.

"Good morning."

Hoffstein tilted his head away.

"Good morning," Holmay said again.

Hoffstein blinked twice. "Will there be anything else?"

Holmay swallowed his pride with the last few cold drops of coffee in his cup. "Yes, I just wanted to mention that I finished your book last night."

"Oh really? You must have studied every word. It's been out for a year and a half."

"I had trouble getting through the charts, but I still enjoyed it."

"I'm floored," Hoffstein said. "I didn't write it to amuse anyone."

"Your thesis is interesting nevertheless."

"Interesting, you say? Rocks, you know, are interesting, and so are automobile engine parts to mechanics and baseball cards to a certain variety of child."

"Can I have one of your donuts?"

Hoffstein, his hand inside the plastic bag fingering the next donut, could not find words to respond. Slowly he drew a donut out and held it up for Holmay to take from his hand.

"Thanks. I really used to like these things when I was a kid. I used to help my mother make them, but I gave them up because they're fattening. And just yester-day I read an article in *Ladies Home Journal* saying they cause arteriosclerosis."

"I have heart enough," Hoffstein said.

"Besides, they make a mess."

"That's what we have janitors for. To clean up messes."

"Well, thanks for the donut anyway. Sometimes I can't help myself. I'd better go jog today and worry about my arteries afterward. I just wanted to say I en-joyed your book."

Holmay was about to walk away when Hoffstein, clutching the top of his donut bag as if it were the neck of a dead goose, called him back.

"What did you find so *interesting* about my book?"

Here comes the test, Holmay thought, the exam. The next minute or two might decide whether or not Hoffstein would vote for him. There was a stain circling the bottom of his coffee cup. He put the cup to his lips, swallowed hard, and decided to pass the exam, just to save himself the trouble of having to quarrel on and on.

"The thesis, as I said, was interesting: that the contemporary writer has given up all faith in the power of words to change society, that mass media, govern-ment control of information systems, and a culture based on distraction have, as it were, made writers socially and politically irrelevant. So all writers can really hope to do, in Western society anyway, is to influence personal life, notably sexual life, which is the one thing the government can't really control."

"Yes, but that's all obvious," Hoffstein said, groping for the opening to the plastic bag.

"And whereas literature used to be the way to express social deviancy, and thereby was the vehicle for expanding personal freedom, nowadays it's used to put deviancy back in line."

"Even the homosexuals," Hoffstein broke in, "even they don't really want to be queers. You just read all their stuff sometime, and you just look at it. What do you see? You see some homosexual walking hand-in-hand with another one, and one of them's dressed like a girl. And when you get two queer girls, one dresses like a man. Now how do you explain *that*, I say?"

"Statistically, I suppose."

Hoffstein grunted an I-told-you-so grunt. "And what do the statistics show every time?"

Holmay knew the question was coming next, so he was ready with his reply. "That underneath the rhetorical dress of language there's a devious desire to be normal, wholesome, mainstream. That the 'Culture of Disgust,' as you call it, is part of our unconscious national will toward normalcy, that it establishes a platform of departure toward a sort of uniformity necessary to the survival of law and order and the state."

"And this is of course what...?" Hoffstein led him on.

Good or bad? Holmay hadn't read the last few pages of the book. "It's brilliant, Dr. Hoffstein. I didn't know how to say it to you before today. But it's brilliant. That's what it is." Holmay smiled, satisfied with himself.

"I must go teach," Hoffstein said, wiping his hand on his pants as he stood. "Do you have a computer?"

"No."

"You must have one, you know, these days."

✳ ✳ ✳

"He's crazy," Holmay said to Frances after he was sure the door to her office was closed. "That man is bonkers."

Frances, cupping her hand over her mouth, suppressed a laugh. "But you were nice to him anyway?"

"Oh I was *so* nice. Except that I ate one of his donuts. It took some doing on his part, but he finally sacrificed one to me."

"Have you ever seen his wife?"

"I told you. She's his God. I'm not sure she really exists."

"Someone saw them in a church."

"Church? That man goes to a church?"

"A true believer to the core."

"Russian unorthodox."

"Guess again. Baptist."

"Oh my God. Do you know what he talks about in class all the time?"

"I've heard."

"He made his students count every *o* on three pages of Hawthorne and compare them with those on three pages of Emily Dickinson."

"It takes all kinds," she said. "We all have our. . .fantasies."

"For example?"

"You tell me yours and I'll tell your mine."

"I don't have any," Holmay said.

Frances's cheek twitched just before she spoke. "Then how come you don't date women?"

"Maybe for the same reason you don't date men," he shot back.

"I'm sorry," she said, lowering her voice. "There's been a lot of pressure on me."

"To finish the book."

She nodded.

"And it's getting done."

"Yes," she said. "But please don't blame me for that. I know what a good teacher you are. I hear the students talk. And I know you take extra time out for them—and for Evelyn."

"There's no book in me," he said. "I have nothing to say."

"You say a lot every day in class."

"The words diffuse and disappear among the random noises of the world."

"And I can still see Billy Brand up there almost every day lurking outside your door." She heaved a sigh and then laughed. "Crazy Billy Brand, wherever he is."

"You think he's crazy?"

"Like the rest of us."

"Harmless, then?"

She shrugged. "He used to give me the chills, but I prefer to think he's harmless enough in his crazy way."

On his way out he stopped short as a question occurred to him. "I never did finish Hoffstein's book, and I wonder about something."

"Yes?"

"Whether he thinks it's good or bad—I mean that this 'Culture of Disgust' he writes about is really helping to create a world full of normal people?"

"He thinks it's wonderful. He's all for law and order and the established state."

"Then is he really like the rest of us?"

"Funny you should ask," she sighed. "Maybe the question is whether or not we're really like *him*."

* * *

Frances Drummond's words troubled him that night. She had admitted to the presence of secret desires, and he was sure they were normal and harmless enough. But his own secret he could not explain, even to himself, because he had not had the courage to stare it in the face and unmask its presence in himself. He knew it had something to do with why his wife had abandoned him, but when he asked her—first for forgiveness of his sin and then for an explanation of why he would do such a thing—she would break down in tears and say that only he could know why he did what he did, that she couldn't explain it herself and therefore had to leave. Over the course of a spring he had had sex a few times with a student in his class, a lovely creature, inarticulate and blond, who stole his thirty-seven-year-old heart completely away from him, left him for whole afternoons paralyzed with the emotion called love, and who then confessed, on a rainy May Monday and in the presence of her high school sweetheart, that she was still seventeen years old, that she was sorry and would do nothing to jeopardize his career. The act itself, eventually not enough of a secret to anyone, was not the secret that bothered him. The secret had something to do with why he allowed himself to fall for the girl, and why he would not allow himself to go any further with Frances Drummond than to touch her arm in a friendly way.

He was on his way downstairs to lock the front door when the phone rang, the ringing itself Billy's voice, shrill this time, insistent, a violation of peace and calm.

"I didn't get the job," Billy said. "I didn't get the job. You knew that, didn't you? You *knew*."

Billy hung up on him before he could get a word in. Good, Holmay said to himself. He has no right to barge in on my life like this, no right to violate my peace. Frances was right—she used the word. Billy was crazy.

He locked the door, checked it twice to be sure, then went upstairs to bed.

But Billy kept turning in his mind, rolling in and out of his consciousness like a train going back and forth across a bridge. Why would Billy imagine that he, Holmay, already knew he wouldn't get the job? Did he reread the letter of recommendation, this time read everything between the lines? A semi-truck groaned down the street, turned the corner, paused, then moved on. Like an elephant, Holmay thought, a dumb brooding elephant lost in a world he did not make. Like Hoffstein and his powdered white sugar donuts and his round thick stomach and hide. The truck came up the street again and stopped at the corner, its air brakes wheezing their complaint.

He threw the covers off and stormed to the window to draw the blind. Then suddenly he remembered Billy again, the way he stood under the streetlight. He approached the window, stealing a look down at the street below. The streetlight danced back and forth in the breeze, but on the shadows crossing the concrete he saw no human form.

Another noise woke him a second time, this one unmistakably at the back door. His heart was already beating fast by the time he was sure, his head upright, all ears, in the dark. Then he heard noises again—a thrashing as if a cat had toppled some cans, and then a loud thump, as if someone had leaned a shoulder into the back door. He eased himself quietly out of bed, stood still a moment, terrified, wondering what to do. In the next room Evelyn tossed under her blanket and finally made herself comfortable again. Lance, he thought, that goddamned Lance. The sonofabitch is drunk again.

He stole downstairs, heard the thump again against the back door. He debated: should he turn on a light? Ahead of him he saw the small glow of a light, in back near the kitchen, Lance's room. He made his way quietly and stopped, terrified, to see in the slice of light coming from behind Lance's door slightly ajar Lance himself, sound asleep. Unmistakably there was a third thump against the door, someone leaning a shoulder into it.

He felt helpless. A gun. If he had a gun. He swept the kitchen counter with his hand, found a fork on a dirty plate, then cowered next to the door. Impulsively he acted. With one hand he yanked the door open and then ducked down.

There was a scream, a form falling over him.

"Oh God," she said as he flipped on the light. "You scared the living be-Jesus right out of my panties. I was trying to get in to say goodnight to Lance," said Annette George. "Now would you please put down that fucking fork."

Thirteen

SHE TOSSED her hair back.

"I'm sorry," he mumbled. "I thought you were someone else."

She offered him a hand and pulled herself to her feet, not taking her angry eyes from him.

"Don't you think you should look before you leap?"

He averted his eyes. Her hand was small and soft, like Evelyn's, and he could see that her breasts, faintly visible beneath a white sweatshirt, were firm. He had never touched her before, never been this close. He liked the churlish curl on her lips and was secretly pleased to find her smelling of cigarettes and beer.

"Here," she said, "my necklace is undone. Help me get the thing on again."

She turned her back to him and held the ends of the necklace with one hand. As he took them she looked back over her shoulder as if trying to make contact with his eyes. He fumbled nervously with the chain until the two ends finally clicked into place.

"What's the matter?" she said as she turned around. "Haven't you ever had to do that before?"

"What are you doing here?"

"I was downtown," she laughed, "and I got bored."

He chose his words carefully. "So what made you think you'd find excitement here?"

79

She picked a piece of lint off his shirt and flicked it away. "I somehow knew there'd be some sort of thrill waiting for me here, Mr. Professor, and I have to admit that so far you haven't been a bore." She tossed her hair back again and looked up at him, her eyes glazed and half-closed.

"You're stoned," he said. "You should get to bed."

"He wants me in bed," she laughed. "Did you hear that, Lance? He thinks I should go to bed."

Lance, wearing only a pair of old sweatpants, was trying to make his eyes adjust to the light. "Annie, you ninny. What time is it?"

"After midnight," Holmay said.

"The bars close at one," Annette said. "I think it's after one—that's my interpretation. Now what do you think, Mr. Professor?"

"Annie, shut up." Lance moved in and took hold of her arm. She laughed and threw her head back on his chest.

"I'm really sorry about this, Dr. Holmay. I hope she didn't wake you up."

"He thought I was some sort of crook," she laughed again. "Can you imagine that? And now he's probably going to report this to the dean, and my mother and father, and my priest."

"I'm not going to report this to anyone," Holmay said as he turned his back on them. "You're both eighteen years old. That makes you legally responsible for your behavior. Just keep the noise down and lock the door."

"Oh for sure," Lance said as Holmay left, "for sure."

On the way to his room he stopped to look in on Evelyn. She was curled up on one side of the bed, her face, turned toward the hallway light, tranquil and innocent. Her eyes seemed gently closed, as if the world of sleep and dreams was a quiet entertainment and the world outside all lawn and rolling hills. Her skin seemed soft and smooth in the dim light, her fingers small, somehow birdlike.

He looked at her a long minute, feeling vaguely helpless and defunct. A thought flew by like a swift shadow: Were he a boy, a twelve-year-old, he would be hopelessly in love with her.

He closed Evelyn's door halfway and was careful to shut his all the way. Below he heard Annette George's voice send forth a shrill laugh, but all was silent after that. He imagined that Lance had her clothes off, that she was playing cat and mouse with him, that she was laughing as he was trying to keep her from escaping the bed. What happened after that was none of his business, as long as they didn't wake Evelyn up.

He turned off the light but sat up in bed. In the dark he admitted the truth to himself: When he saw Annette on the kitchen floor, he wanted her right there, before either of them said one word. Then after he finished with her he would have opened the back door and pointed the way out, and she would have agreed to leave without saying a word, only her smile indicating that she was perfectly satisfied and that yes, some night soon, she would return. He did not have the courage to act, though he knew, by reading the look on her face with as much certainty as he read the words in a book, that she wanted him too. And when he failed to act he became contemptible—in his own eyes and in hers. He remembered his words: "So what made you think you'd find excitement here?" They told her what he wanted clearly enough. He wanted Annette, air-brained child not yet twenty, but not Frances Drummond, and not, after the second year of marriage, his wife.

It was Annette's hair, the deep auburn shine of it. And her breath and clothes smelling of beer and cigarettes. Her wild look, the sense of abandon, danger, surprise, the sassy carelessness that started the dull yearning in him—everything he hated in principle or feared in fact.

He tried to imagine Frances Drummond in Annette's place—Frances sprawled on the kitchen floor, her hair wild, a necklace falling off her blouse. Abandon, danger, surprise, sassy carelessness, her voice pleading with him, Fuck me, fuck me right here, now, on the floor, from behind.

And Cynthia he had met just that way—sixteen years ago on a hot August night, the two of them abandoned by chance on a wildlife walk through the woods, the cabin all theirs for a half-hour at most, neither of them bothering with preliminaries, and no talk until they began wiping away the sweat smeared onto their bodies from the dusty cabin bunk. Once upon a time, then, it could have been Cynthia on his kitchen floor. And, in fact, he and Cynthia had had their trysts on the floor. They had looked at each other and suddenly smiled the special smile, and in a moment their clothes were off. It had happened in the kitchen most of the time, but also in the dining room and bathroom, and once, he recalled, in the basement next to the water softener. The very last time it ever happened was in the new house, downstairs in the living roon. They had just signed the mortgage papers and had come to the house, its bare walls and floors, agreeing that the upstairs front bedroom, the one looking down on the street, would be big enough for a new king-sized bed, then seeing each other thinking the same thought and sinking to the floor without taking off their clothes.

That was the last time they let themselves go. After the movers brought the furniture in and the paperhangers flowered the walls, the interior decorators matched everything with their new carpets and drapes. Then Evelyn was born and their lives seemed furnished enough. When he left footprints on the deep pile of the new carpeting, he sometimes thought he was leaving a mess behind. Later he felt most comfortable where Evelyn played, for everywhere on the floors she left her trail of toys, crayons, and abandoned dolls.

Their "chemistry" had changed. At first they sniped through the camouflage of their silences with carefully aimed words, and later they apologized. The silences grew thick, softened now and then by looks that asked for forgiveness of sins neither could name. Evelyn, not yet two feet tall, laughed and talked to them equally, as if there were nothing in the world wrong.

"Let's face it," Cynthia told him on the night she announced her decision to leave, "the chemistry's all wrong." The chemistry. From that night the word hounded him the way few had during his career as a professional man of words. "Chemistry." It's no explanation, he told himself, of what went wrong. It's no more than a descriptive metaphor taken from a physical science alleging that their passion was molecular, that its breakdown had something to do with ions, electrons, neutrons, and that their ignorance of its workings took the matter completely out of their control.

He did not feel relieved of responsibility, though his unfaithfulness to Cynthia occurred long after their chemistry had soured. He still loved his wife, refusing to believe his fling did anyone harm. He still loved her—in his way, as he had heard other guilty husbands say. For two months there was the other woman in his life—not a woman but a teenaged girl, and worse yet a co-ed—and three, maybe four times they had sex. They had sex yes, because he was hungry for it, and they exchanged silly words, all of them sincere because the words came naturally, driven by emotions they did not feel morally obligated to control. Then at the end of two months the co-ed—her name was Nancy—called it off. She could not carry on any more with a man twice her age, and she wanted out. One day as he sat in his office trying to conjure her face he realized that he couldn't remember her last name. But he remembered that her waist was so small he almost could encircle it entirely with his hands.

Cynthia's waist when they first met. Not once did he ever try to encircle her waist with his hands, but he imagined it small. "I prefer slender women," he told her, hoping to put her at ease. "Then I'd better go on a diet," she replied. Her words confused him because he thought she already was already just right, everything about her so very right. He remembered reading in old novels that men were quite taken with slim ankles, and had paid no attention to ankles before. But when he saw Cynthia's he found them remarkably slim, and suddenly he began appreciating them. Her hands also seemed small. As they walked down the street he liked to close hers into a small fist and then wrap his around, as if her hand were a nugget no bigger than a walnut. After a while she made the fist herself and offered it to him whenever they went on walks. At night he liked to run his finger along her collarbone. It was smooth and slender; he wondered why it didn't suddenly snap whenever she exerted herself. Her breasts were small. She joked about them all the time but he liked them just the way they were. "I don't think you've got anything to feel inadequate about," he told her again and again. "I told you I prefer slender women, and frankly I like them short, like you. And I know a lot of men who see things exactly the way I do."

Then one day, after he had been married for over a year, he found himself standing next to her in a crowded elevator. He could hardly believe she was only an inch or two shorter than he. When he was sure she was unaware of him, he double-checked more than once. One day he asked her point-blank, "How tall are you?" "I'm five-nine," she said indifferently, "give or take an inch." He tried to joke: "Have you always been this tall?" "Since I was sixteen," she replied.

From that day on he started paying closer attention to parts. Her ankles were slim, but they had blue veins, some of them very small, that turned and twisted like scribblings in ink no one would ever be able to wash out. For the first time he saw hairs growing around the nipples of her breasts. "Where did these come from?" he asked as he fingered one. "From me," she replied, "from inside of me." "But why weren't they ever there before?" "Because you always close your eyes when you're thinking of me," she laughed, "and because I usually shave them off." Then he could tell how many days had passed before she shaved her legs, and he saw, with disbelief and revulsion, that she also had hair growing along her upper lip.

The more he studied her the bigger she seemed. The waist once so small and light in his hands seemed wide, as if her skin were thickening into a hide. Whenever he held her close, flesh from her stomach and back seemed to droop into his hands. After she got her hair cut short her shoulders also seemed hunched, muscular. One day, as they were walking down the street, she reached over to take his hand. Instinctively he curled it into a small fist. From then on her hand seemed heavy and big; he wanted to be rid of the responsibility of holding it.

He watched other changes with curiosity, as if he were a doctor following the course of a mysterious disease. Her fingers seemed bony, the joints swollen, especially in winter time. He took up jogging and coaxed her along, but no matter how slowly he ran she always seemed to drag behind. He gave her time to regain her shape after Evelyn was born, but her stomach and breasts sagged as if deflated beyond repair. Toward the end, when there was no hope left, she cried every night for a week. He pitied her and he pitied himself, but he never could expel from his mind the idea that her eyes, swollen from tears and lack of sleep, were intolerably large.

Only in the dark, when he was securely alone and facing facts that required him to be perfectly honest with himself, did he ever admit that these small strictly physical matters did more to turn him off than anything she ever did or said. He never had the courage to breathe a word to her. What could he have said? That she no longer seemed like the same woman he once knew, that she had suddenly grown too tall? That her stomach, with its flap of loose skin, seemed repulsive to him? That when he kissed her he wanted her lips to be smooth and firm the way they were when she was young? That gradually, from the time he first started looking closely at her, she was turning into a stranger he had no desire to touch?

It's not chemistry, he told himself as he slipped down under the covers and pulled his blanket under his chin. But if not chemistry, what? Could she have been so invisible to him at the beginning, or he so blinded by love, that the changes he observed occurred only in his mind? Were they the workings of a subtle naturalism, the human body's way of regulating its own reproductive processes? They had, after all, produced their child, and maybe Nature, in its infinite cunning, was giving them good reason to lay off. But what of those who produced a dozen children and still hungered for more? And why, no more than a half-hour ago, did he want to fuck Annette George on the floor?

He turned over on his side and put the pillow over his head. No, he concluded, it was all my fault. There was nothing wrong, nothing different, about Cynthia. All those changes—the way she seemed to get tall and fat, all the hair, the swollen joints—all were in my mind.

The knock on his bedroom door was so tentative and soft that he wasn't sure he heard anything at all. Only when he saw the hall light on through the crack in the door did he respond.

"Who's there?" he whispered.

Annette George, wearing only the sweatshirt that fell loosely to her knees, came halfway into the room.

"I hope I'm not disturbing you, Mr. Professor."

He could not tell if she had any panties on.

"What can I do for you?"

"Do you have a few minutes...to talk?"

"About what?"

She took a step forward. "I...was wondering... "

He looked away from her.

"Can I close the door?"

"I have a daughter in the next room."

"Yes, we don't want to wake her up. I don't want to disturb... "

"Please keep your voice down."

"Should I close the door?" she asked, tossing her hair.

"What's on your mind?"

She smiled and closed the door halfway. "Oh nothing."

"Out with it."

She took another step forward. "I...was wondering."

"About what?"

"About how to get a good grade in your course. I thought you maybe could explain it to me."

"You're smart enough to figure that out by yourself."

"Actually," she smiled, "I'm pretty smart. But there's some things I just don't get."

"So you want to learn?"

"From my professor."

"Tonight?"

"Yes."

His heart was racing so fast he was afraid to speak. The toss of the hair persuaded him. She was vulgar and smart—knew exactly what she wanted. She was no fool with words—knew how to use innuendo and ambiguity to make her intentions clear enough. All he would have to do is nod, move over on the bed, then go halfway toward her with a hand. She would do the rest, swiftly, wordlessly, wildly. And once the madness took hold it would be her wildness and wordlessness that he would enjoy, the inarticulate abandon packaged in the tight-fitting body and lovely face, the auburn hair that he would see best when he closed his eyes. How beautiful she was and how vulgar, how smart and stupid at once. And for the first time he saw what it was that most attracted him—the cleverness yes and the beauty too, but most of all it was her vulgarity.

Yes, he said to himself, why not? If she wants to fall into bed, why not? Afterwards she would not want pillow talk. She would have experienced her little triumph over him and passed her little test of self. She would go quietly and merrily on her way, having scored first on Lance and then on a higher-up. The next day, sober and respectable again, she would feel enough shame to know she should hold her tongue and act her proper part, and this acting would keep her in control, a control she would not want to lose. No, there would be no dangerous strings attached to a careless fling like this.

"So what do you want to learn from me?" he asked.

"You're so smart, Mr. Professor. I want you to teach me everything you know."

"About life?"

She smiled. "Why not? What's wrong with that? Teachers love learning, don't they? They're supposed to love to teach and their students are supposed to love to learn. Aren't they supposed to love their students too?"

She spoke the words with no mockery in her voice, her tone all innocence, full of the earnestness he had tried to express and require in class. She was a vulgar child. What she had just said Evelyn could have said to Billy when they were alone.

Billy. What would Billy think of this scene?

"And you'd do anything to get a good grade?" he asked.

"Oh yes," she replied, her voice tightening.

Billy outside, standing under the streetlight, looking up.

"*Anything?* . . .Would you even *study?*"

"What do you mean?"

"I mean I think you should get out of here and leave me alone."

Fourteen

THE NEXT MORNING Annette's hair looked shiny and full, her face aglow with the soft blush of a girl who had had a long restful sleep. She entered the classroom after him and walked directly to her seat, lowering her eyes as if too shy to look at anyone face to face. Holmay shot a brief glance at her, but she was turning pages in her book. Then Lance, smirking like a satisfied cat, appeared in the door. He took the empty seat right behind Annette and slouched down with his feet on the back of her chair.

"The final exam," Holmay announced, "will be two weeks from now. I know that some of you are already deeply concerned about the exam, so I think it best to make myself clear right away. It will be mainly an essay exam requiring you to compare and contrast the works we've read this term. But it will not be enough to merely compare and contrast. I will want you to make connections—and explain the significance of the connections you see."

"What do you mean by *significance?*"

Holmay was afraid someone would ask. "These stories were written for important purposes. I want you to think about these purposes."

"How much will the exam count toward the final grade?"

Holmay saw Annette look up, suddenly interested.

"Fifty percent, more or less," he replied. "And there will be an objective part to the exam as well. I'll ask you to define some terms, make some multiple choices, and fill in some blanks. This way I'll really be able to find out what you know. If you want a passing grade, you'll have to study and think. And there will be no cheating on this test."

When Lance met Annette at the end of the hour, he was still smirking. He took her hand and drew her in close, sure that Holmay would see, and as they walked away they tossed a private joke over their shoulder at him. They had him and he knew it, and he felt dirty and undignified. Before he fell asleep the night before he had heard them snickering, his name rising up the staircase with the laughter and slipping into his bedroom through the crack in the door that Annette had left ajar. He knew she did not leave the house, for he heard other sounds until sleep finally came over him. When he was awakened the next morning at six by the sound of the back door slamming shut, he went down to find Lance alone in his bed, sound asleep. As he stood in the clear morning air he knew they had succeeded in invading his privacy. He had left Annette a small opening— his words, his eyes, maybe even his hands betraying his weakness to her—and she read the signs. Then she had enough courage to go all the way, even completely out of bounds, and enough nerve to have fun with Lance under his roof even after he tried to humiliate her.

It was carelessness, Holmay concluded as he sat at his desk. Annette and Lance were careless because they lacked the intelligence and sensitivity, the proper upbringing to care about the moral implications of their actions. And they were perfectly, normally, two-faced: they were model citizens the very next day, dealing with the ordinary problems of life in an ordinary way. But his own carelessness was of another kind. He was intelligent and sensitive, well-educated, and he cared about morality. Therefore, he concluded again, his failure was a more complex carelessness—a slip, a natural (or was it unnatural?) letting go, but one he put a stop to in time.

Lance and Annette were kids; he would have to be tough on them. In the meantime, he would have to get his own act together. He told himself again that he had done the right thing by turning Annette away from his bed.

He returned home to find a note taped to his front door.

> *I have been trying to reach you since 2 o'clock.*
> *It's important. Call me right away.*
> > Love,
> > Billy

Billy. No, not Billy again.

He tore the note up and flung the shreds into the wastebasket. No, he would not call Billy. He had a right to refuse.

"Evelyn," he called upstairs. "I'm home."

"Hi, Dad," she called back. "What are we having for dinner tonight?"

A scheme entered his mind. Billy would be sure to call, so he would be out of the house. "How would you like to go to Connersville for pizza tonight?"

"All the way to Connersville? Why all that way?"

"Just to get away—you know, just for a change."

"Just you and me?"

"Yes, just the two of us."

"Oh," she said with disappointment.

"What's the matter? Don't you want to go?"

"I want to go, but I was just thinking. . .you know. Billy called. . .and I was just thinking. . . "

"No. If we go, we go alone. Just you and me."

She said nothing in reply.

"So get ready. We're leaving right away."

In the car Evelyn told him that she did not sleep well the night before, that she thought she heard voices in the house, that she tried to wake up, find out who was in her room, that she felt as if she was actually wandering around in her own room, looking in her closet and under her bed, even behind the curtains and outside the window because maybe there was someone on the roof, but she couldn't get her eyes open so she really couldn't see who was there. And then she heard a door slam and suddenly the voices stopped, and finally, finally she fell asleep.

"A dream," he said. "It was all a dream."

"It was like a movie, Dad."

"Who did you think it was in the house?"

She shrugged and turned her head away.

Suddenly his mind flared. "Was it Billy?"

"No, Dad. If it was Billy I wouldn't have been afraid."

"Are you trying to tell me that if there was someone lurking in our house at night, you wouldn't be afraid?"

"Why should I be afraid of Billy?"

"Billy's strange."

"Billy's not strange. He's nice."

"How do you know what Billy's really like?"

Evelyn lowered her eyes.

"Well. . .?"

"I told you. He calls. . .and we talk."

"How often does he call?"

"Lots of times."

"What do you talk about?"

"Nice things, Dad," Evelyn replied, tears coming to her eyes. "Only nice things."

"What nice things?"

"About nature, peace in the world, love. My feelings."

"What do you mean feelings?"

"Feelings, Dad. I mean I have feelings too, you know. Just feelings. What I feel like having Mom gone all the time—how sometimes I want to go live with her. You know, about being a divorced child."

Holmay assumed a gentler tone. "So who do you think it was in the house?"

"I think...maybe it was Mom."

He resorted to a series of one-liners to distract her while they ate, and afterward he surprised her by announcing they were going to a movie.

"Why are we going to a movie tonight?" she asked.

"I just think we should have some fun."

"On a Wednesday?"

The movie was violent and funny and absurd. Cars sped madly through city streets and the police always ended up crashing into each other's cars. In the end the bad guys, who were really good guys because they had all the funny lines, drove off a cliff in a '57 Chevy, diving, at the last second, through open windows into the safety of the waters below.

"Did you like it?" he asked on the way home.

"It was really funny," she said.

"What did you like most?"

"The one cop," she said, "the one who stood on the cliff at the end shaking his fist and saying he'd get revenge someday."

"What's so funny about that?"

"Dad," she said as if mildly shocked, "he was in almost all the scenes."

"So what?"

"Didn't you see his face?"

"Sure—so what?"

"Didn't you think his eyes were funny? One eye was blue and the other one green. How would you like it if I had eyes like that? Wouldn't you think I was funny too?"

He hadn't noticed the eyes. In fact he caught so little of the movie that he couldn't remember any of the characters' names. When the cars were not racing through the city streets he saw Billy waiting for him on his front porch, Billy pointing a finger accusing him of betrayal, and Lance and Annette walking out of class hand-in-hand, the little derisive laugh they threw his way as they left, and Annette standing at his bedroom door, tossing her hair out of her eyes. And three times—he knew it was three times because each time he caught himself in the act—he found himself turning to watch Evelyn watch the movie, each time seeing more fully the way the flickers from the screen fell on her amazed and laughing eyes.

As they approached the city limits a silence set in. Then out of the darkness on her side of the car Evelyn suddenly had a question for him: "Why do we dream, Dad?"

"Dreams are natural, Evelyn. They're nothing to be afraid of."

"But *why* do we dream?"

"Well...because. Because when we're asleep there's another part of ourselves that's awake."

Evelyn gave a little laugh. "How can I be awake and asleep at the same time?"

"Not all of you is awake when you sleep—just part of you."

"Which part?"

"The part of you that's afraid of things."

"What do you mean, Dad? I don't understand what you mean."

"Our dark side, Evelyn. We have a light side and a dark side, and they're like the waking and sleeping parts of ourselves."

Evelyn's eyes narrowed. "Do you mean I have a bad side?"

With his free hand he reached over and pulled her under his arm. "No, my little sweet. Nothing about you is bad, not even that part of you that's awake when you're asleep. Because there are a lot of things that are awake when you're asleep. For example, owls are awake while you sleep, and the moon is sometimes out, and the stars. And everybody on the other side of the world—everybody in China and places like that. And I'm awake while you sleep, just to make sure that everything is safe and sound for you. So would you call all these things that are awake while you're asleep bad?"

"There's no real reason to be afraid of the dark, is there Dad?"

"No, no real reason at all."

She gave a little laugh. "I never thought of it that way before. I mean—that there's a me that's awake and a me that's asleep. That there's two Evelyns. Do you think, Dad, that they trade places? I mean—when one wakes up the other falls asleep?"

"Yes, it could work that way," he said. "Maybe that's really how it works."

She broke into a laugh. "You know what would be funny, Dad? What if the waking side was making a lot of noise because it couldn't get to sleep, and the sleeping side suddenly woke up? Then they'd both be awake at the same time. I wonder what they would say to each other? Wouldn't that be funny, Dad?"

He saw it her way, expanding it into a scene from the movie. "I bet it would be a scream," he said.

It was after ten when Holmay turned into his driveway. Though his car windows were rolled up, he heard the phone ringing insistently.

"Lance!" he shouted as he tore open the back door. "Why in the hell didn't you answer the goddamned phone?"

He barged into Lance's room, resolved to give Lance three days to get out. The room was a mess and Lance was not in.

"Dad, do you want me to answer the phone?" Evelyn said as she walked into the kitchen.

He cut off her path to the phone. "No, you go upstairs right away. It's very late. I'll take care of the phone."

For the first time Billy raised his voice. "Why did you leave right after getting my note? Do you think I'm blind?" He paused, as if to give Holmay a chance to defend himself. Holmay held the receiver away from his ear and stared at the wall.

"What kind of professor are you? I am your student and I called for help, and you did not respond. That is called irresponsibility. Do you understand the implications of that?"

He waited again before going on. "I didn't get the job. I went to the post office, handed them your letter personally, and went home and waited for them to call. But they didn't call. I waited and waited. I knew they wouldn't call, because I knew they didn't want me to have the job. Because they're afraid of me. They know I can see right into them, and they don't want me around knowing all I know. So when they didn't call I went there in person and I stood right in the doorway of the postmaster's office, and I didn't say one word until he called the police. Then I asked him why. Why? That's the only word I used. And when the policemen came I told them too. I told them they had no right to persecute me, that I knew they didn't want me to have the job either but I was a public citizen and they had no right to affect my attempts to get employment as a public servant."

Billy is crazy, Holmay said to himself.

"You think I'm crazy, don't you?" Billy went on. "But I happen to know who got the job, and what would you think if I told you it was the nephew of one of the police officers who came to the postmaster's office? Coincidence? You call that coincidence? I call it unfair treatment, corruption of public trust, decadence. I left peaceably enough, but as I left I gave the postmaster more than a piece of my mind. I personally handed him a copy of the letter of recommendation you wrote for me. I said, 'Read this again. See what this professor of literature says about me. Know that this man does not lie, and then ask yourself who really deserves the job.'"

"Daddy, who's on the phone?" Evelyn called from upstairs.

"And do you know what else they did?" Billy paused as if fully expecting Holmay to say yes. "When I got home to Mrs. Lupinski's—I call her Mom now, you know, because she's just like a mother to me—they had her on the phone. The Department of Social Services. They asked if she had anyone living in the house, and she told them yes. And they said that if she derived income from me she would have to report it to them. And she told them I paid no rent but they told her that any work I did around the house could be counted as rent. So they were keeping an eye on us, and we'd better be careful or else they could cut off her monthly checks. She was crying when I walked in the house, and I grabbed the phone and started giving them a piece of my mind, but they just hung up on me. And Mrs. Lupinski just cried and cried. I told her I had a theory, and when she stopped crying I checked the theory out. And do you know what I found out in less than a half-hour of checking around?"

"No," Holmay said weakly.

"That the postmaster, Clarence Curren is his name, has a brother named Ronald. And do you know what?"

"What?"

"Ronald Curren is County Director of the Department of Social Services."

"Maybe, just maybe, Billy, it's a coincidence."

"Oh, you think so too. I was beginning to think you might. I do not think so, Dr. Holmay. I suppose you also believe that we will some day not be visited by creatures from another world. Some day, you know, we will."

Billy hung up the phone, his words suddenly lost behind the buzz of the receiver Holmay still held to his ear.

"Who was that on the phone?" Evelyn asked again as he was coming up the stairs.

"No one," he said, "no one at all. Nothing to concern yourself with."

"Was it Mom?"

"No, it was just business."

"Would you read me a story tonight?"

"No, not tonight. I'm tired and it's late. Besides, you had a story tonight."

"You mean the movie? The movie's not a real story, Dad."

"No story tonight. Now hop into bed so I can tuck you in."

"I was hoping for a story with a happy ending," she said as he pulled the blanket under her chin, "because I want to have a good dream tonight."

He sat on the edge of his bed long after he was sure she was asleep. He was tired, confused, unsure of what to do about Billy and Lance, disgusted at the thought of facing his students in the morning. "Fuck it," he said aloud. "Fuck everything. And I should have fucked that young thing too—just for the hell of it." As he stood to undress himself he heard a car door slam on the street and small quick footsteps on the sidewalk hurrying toward his front porch.

"It's Billy," said Wendy Corrigan as she stepped just inside the door, her eyes swollen with tears. "I hate to barge in on you like this, but you've got to do something about Billy."

"It's midnight," he snapped. "Don't you know it's almost midnight?"

"I know, I know, but I'm afraid for Billy. I'm afraid he's going to hurt himself. He just called me and screamed. I told him again I wasn't in love with him any more. Then he didn't say anything at all, and when I tried to talk to him he told me nothing mattered any more, that he was tired of living."

"We all get that way sometimes, and then we lie down until the feeling passes."

"Please, Dr. Holmay, please. I'm afraid he's going to hurt himself. He talked about it before—when we were together. He always said that Jesus Christ committed suicide, so why should anybody be afraid of death."

"What do you expect me to do? Why don't you call the police?"

"Because he thinks they're after him. He said something about the postmaster. When he screamed at me over the phone—he said he had guns. He kept saying he had guns, three of them. You're the only one who can talk to him, reason with him. You're the only one he really respects. You're the only one."

Wendy's car was an old Ford with a noisy muffler. As they pulled up to the curb in front of Mrs. Lupinski's house, Holmay was suddenly terrified by the blank silence of the neighborhood. In a small house halfway down the block a yellow light shone through a bedroom window, and at the corner the streetlight glowed against the night. But Mrs. Lupinski's house was completely dark, almost invisible from the street.

"Looks quiet enough to me," Holmay said.

"But there's no way to be sure he's okay," Wendy said. "Please, just knock on the door and let him see you. Let him know you care about him."

"I'm insane for doing this," Holmay said as he found himself standing at the front door. "Why in the hell am I doing this?"

He waited for a sound as his eyes tried to penetrate the dark. "Billy," he said softly. "Billy, it's Dr. Holmay."

He strained to hear any movement within. "Billy," he called again, "Billy." He found a doorbell and pressed hard, but it made no sound. He cursed his luck and was about to return to the car when an impulse led him to rap on the door. He rapped softly and only twice, but the door gave under the weight of his hand, opening a crack big enough for him to see in.

"Billy," he called again. With the back of his hand he gave the door a little push and it opened the whole living room to him. "Billy," he said again as he carefully stepped forward.

The floorboards did not creak as he took small steps toward the kitchen, but as he inched past he snagged his pocket on the arm of Mrs. Lupinski's rocking chair. "Billy," he said more loudly this time. "Billy, are you all right?"

From the window on the west side of the house a three-quarters moon sent a pale light onto the blanket covering the bed. Mrs. Lupinski's gray hair looked silvery in the light, and her face, though ashen and weary, seemed lost in the peacefulness of deep sleep. Next to her on the bed, his arm lovingly thrown over her and his body conformed to the contours of the old lady's, was Billy, his face serene.

Holmay held his breath, then carefully backed out of the room.

"Billy's fine," he assured Wendy. "He's sleeping like a baby now."

Fifteen

HOLMAY HAD TO wait out a sleepless night for his apology. By nine the next morning the note was already under his office door.

> *Dear Dr. Holmay:*
>   *I offer only deepest apologies for the events that transpired yesterday. Please take into consideration the inordinate passion that overwhelmed me on my discovering the injustice that accrued when my job opportunity was so conspiratorially denied. I could have killed someone I was so mad. However, I now have regained the prudent equilibrium necessary to pursue justice by taking my appeal to a higher authority.*
>   *Again I ask your forgiveness for my untoward outburst, my loss of cool, as "they" say.*
>
>

Love,
Billy
>

Love. The four letter word he did his best to avoid in class. Because it was forbidden, except when the handsome man was finally alone with the beautiful girl. "They make love," Holmay thought he recalled Annette saying one day when he asked her why Hester and Dimmesdale met in the woods. "They just do it."

As he avoided looking them in the eye in any way suggesting a special intimacy, he had a perverse urge to have Lance and Annette hear him use the word out loud. After crumbling Billy's note into a ball and throwing it away, he marched, full of new resolve, into the classroom.

"Is there any love in Hemingway?" he asked even before he put his book down on the desk.

The class, accustomed to easing into chairs, stiffened as if expecting a slap in the face. A few dared to glance around the room, looking for a clue as to what was suddenly wrong.

"What do you mean, sir, by *love?*" Lance finally asked, his voice diplomatically pleading innocence.

"Let's not define our terms," Holmay shot back. "I give you permission not to define your terms. And again I ask, 'Is there any love in Hemingway?'"

"He sure loves to fish," said a wise-guy sitting in the second row.

"You know damn well I don't mean that. I mean love."

"He's always alone," said Carol Munson.

"Hemingway had four wives," Lance said.

"I thought you meant the character in the story—Nick Adams. Isn't that what you meant by the question?"

Unsure about what he meant, Holmay maintained a stern silence.

Finally Carol Munson spoke again. "I think he was too depressed all the time."

"And what do you think, Miss George?"

She raised her head slightly, carefully avoiding his eyes, but she spoke calmly and immediately, as if she had prepared an answer from the very start. "He was never with a girl in the story, never once. So I didn't see any love in the story at all."

"Did he have a soul, Miss George? If there's no love in the story, no love in the man, is there any soul?"

Lance tried rescuing her. "What do you mean by 'soul,' sir? You always ask us to define our terms, so what do you mean by 'soul'?"

"Do you mean to tell me, Lance, that you don't know what 'soul' is? Is it always necessary to stop and define? Do the words 'pride' and 'freedom' and 'dignity' and 'goodness' and 'truth' and 'sincerity' and 'loveliness' and 'honesty' mean nothing to you?" He turned toward Annette again. "If in a poem you stumbled across the line, 'And may you always clothe your young beauty in humility,' would it be necessary to look up the word 'humility' in a dictionary?"

Annette, drawing her arms in as if she were pulling a shawl over her shoulders, looked down at the floor.

"Today, then, instead of a lecture you will have a little quiz, a sort of preparation for the final exam." He turned to the blackboard and wrote in large careful letters: *Is there any soul or love in Hemingway's story?*

"Please take out a sheet of paper and spend the rest of the hour answering this question for me."

❊ ❊ ❊

Four o'clock in the afternoon was no time for a department meeting. By four o'clock school was out, even for those going through the motions in late afternoon classes. Four o'clock was the time to be out for a stroll or at home sipping a bit of wine.

"The question of promotion is not to be taken lightly," Hoffstein announced, objecting to Ella Mae's motion that everyone eligible be recommended. "If we recommend everyone, we will forfeit our obligation to decide the future of our department and institution. We will give some crackerjack administrator the right to choose for us who will advance and who remain behind. It would be like allowing students to grade themselves. Would we give them that right? They would give themselves passing grades and then let someone else down the line decide their fates. I, for one, am convinced that it is our duty to sort them out, to distinguish the fit from the unfit."

"But how are we supposed to cut out people who are obviously excellent teachers and committed to their students and work?" Roger Farrington, gentleman-scholar of texts old and new on the art of catching trout, believed that it was only common sense to live and let live.

"Objectively," Hoffstein said in response. "If they are scholars, we shall know them by their fruits."

All eyes shied away from Holmay and Frances Drummond. Everyone knew that Hoffstein's logic was aimed at Holmay, unable to defend himself without losing face.

"And what is a scholarly fruit?" Farrington asked.

"A substantial scholarly achievement is a book," Hoffstein replied without missing a beat.

Frances threw a glance toward Holmay, who retreated as if he were guilty of wronging her. People squirmed in their chairs, waiting in the silence created by Hoffstein's words.

Frances looked around the room, then sat up in her chair. "I agree with Dr. Hoffstein's thinking," she said. "I think it's important that we not forfeit our right to judge the merit of a person's work. But is the simple existence of a book proof of its merit?"

Hoffstein cast his eyes on the ceiling tile. "It is not easy, Miss Drummond, to get a scholarly book published."

"But some bad ones slip through now and then?"

"Perhaps."

"Then we would have a right to decide whether your book, for example, is one that slipped through?"

"I'm not sure you're in any position to do that," Hoffstein replied.

She made a gesture including everyone in the room. Halverson, Gadjecki, Roberts, Ella Mae and the more timid members of the department shrank back, afraid that her gesture was drawing a circle around them from which they would not be able to escape. "Could we, then, as a community of scholars, judge your book?"

"If you were properly qualified."

"I'm curious, Dr. Hoffstein, how would you counter the objections to your book that I've heard whispered in academic corridors?"

Hoffstein lifted an eyebrow. "Objections, Miss Drummond?"

"Your study of the significance of vowel structures in poetry. You say that the poems of certain writers are full of *o*s, and that all these *o* sounds suggest, and I quote, 'the emptiness of pure longing.' And you say that these poems are devoid of short *a* sounds—*ah*—and that this is the sound of satisfaction. So, therefore, you conclude that these poets are homosexuals, because their vowels show they're unsatisfied, and homosexual satisfaction is extremely rare."

Farrington adjusted his cuff.

Frances pointed a finger at Hoffstein. "Do you really think that makes any sense?"

"A poet's words, Miss Drummond, do not lie. The poet's soul is expressed in the visible structuring of his own consonants and vowels." Hoffstein raised a finger to instruct. "We learn that lesson in graduate school, my dear."

She looked around for help. Holmay, his head in his hands, was gazing at the floor.

"And my data, my dear, were gathered electronically. The computer tells the tale."

Holmay lifted his head. "I think you're full of crap."

"There, there," said Richards, the department head. "Let's not get personal."

"Let's table the promotion discussion," Ella Mae said. "It's getting on toward supper time."

"So moved," said Farrington.

"Second."

"Wait a minute," Hoffstein objected. "I'd like a chance to respond."

"Sorry, Dr. Hoffstein," said Richards. "Robert's Rules of Order."

The department party was coming up right after final exams. Richards volunteered to bring two cases of soda pop, and Gadjecki said he would pick up the hot dogs and buns. Hoffstein was against any organized games, but Ella Mae said they gave the girls something to do. Richards thought there was too much emphasis on games, but Gadjecki said he personally enjoyed last year's touch football in the snow. Farrington volunteered to read some of his verse, and Gadjecki said it would be a nice thing for the people who stayed late. Richards volunteered to collect three dollars from all department members, and yes, he'd bring a football again this year. Ella Mae admitted she had poetry, but she wouldn't dare read it in front of anyone.

Richards looked at his watch a third time. "We have one other thing on the agenda," he said, "and then we can all go home. The Academic Probationary Committee has asked us to recommend on the status of a student who wants to be part of our program in English studies next term. His name is William Brand." Richards shuffled through some papers on the table in front of him. "It says here that he's failed to complete courses offered by professors Drummond and Holmay, and overall he's failed to complete more than half the courses he's taken here in the past year and a half."

"Then he flunks out," Farrington said.

"He wants another chance," Richards said. "He is one of our own, an English major, or so he says."

"I don't know the boy," Ella Mae said. "Is he nice?"

"What would you say about him?" Richards said, turning to Frances.

She faltered, as if caught in the middle of a daydream. "He's . . . a bit unusual. He doesn't seem to get things done."

"And you, Matt?"

"I recommend him. He's bright and basically . . . good. I mean . . . really *good*. True, he doesn't finish his work, but there are extenuating circumstances."

"There are, Dr. Holmay, always extenuating circumstances. They are the rule around here, it seems." Hoffstein spoke without moving his eyes, which had registered a stare on the papers in front of Richards.

Holmay went right on. "Billy is disorganized. His life right now is, and maybe his emotions are too. But he has intelligence and an enormous desire to learn. Potential. And he's full of good will." And, he thought to himself, it would be better to have Billy enroll in classes. Unless he goes somewhere else, far away. If he stays here maybe others could help keep an eye on him.

"You couldn't get him through your introductory course, Dr. Holmay, and now you recommend him?" Hoffstein scribbled some notes. "How do you justify that?"

"On a hunch, an intuition, a feeling."

"And would you, Dr. Holmay, also consider him unusual?"

Frances broke in. "I didn't mean weird."

"Then why don't you say what you mean?"

"I mean he's . . . special," Holmay replied.

"But you couldn't get him through your course? And half the professors at this venerable institution failed him?" Hoffstein did not look up from the notes he was scribbling.

"Are there any more comments?" Richards asked. "And are you ready for the vote?"

❋ ❋ ❋

Billy lost five to four, with Frances voting with the majority. "I did it for two reasons," she told Holmay afterwards. "In one sense it was strictly a professional decision. I couldn't justify an exception in his case."

"What do you know about his case?"

She went right on. "Secondly, maybe he's not ready for college just now. Maybe he'd be better off away from here—somewhere he can get his head together, maybe at home on the farm for a while, or maybe working a real job somewhere."

"Maybe in the army," Holmay said as he parted company with her. Frances had stood by him, risked her advantage over him by challenging Hoffstein, but he

99

felt betrayed by her vote against Billy. If her challenge to Hoffstein was a sign of her devotion to him, so was his defense of Billy devotion of sorts. They should have had him, as it were, in common, the three of them—Billy, Frances, and himself—bound into a circle of solidarity. Somehow Frances did not feel the force, broke out of the circle, stood outside examining with a cold and critical eye.

"Well, piss on her," he said to himself as he walked home.

It was well after five when he mounted the steps to his front porch, half-expecting Evelyn to greet him with a leaping hug. The front door was open but he heard no sounds. He shuffled through the mail, tucked it under his arm, and entered the house.

"Evelyn," he called, "I'm home."

There was no response.

"Evelyn."

He sat on the front porch, opened the mail, read through some of it twice. A citizen's group needed money to continue its public information campaign against nuclear war. His electric bill had increased by another eight dollars. A legal defense fund was being established on behalf of an eighteen-year-old indicted for refusing to register for the draft. Some lucky person would be eligible to win a new house and car if he mailed in the enclosed form which allowed him to subscribe to three magazines of his choice at once.

Evelyn danced around the corner and up the steps.

"Where have you been?"

"Now Dad," she said, "I tried to call. You said if I was ever going to be late I was supposed to call."

"You mean you're just now getting home?"

"Yup. But I called, like you said."

He gave her a hug. "Where have you been?"

"I was with Billy," she said. "We went down by the river."

"You weren't supposed to do that."

"Why not?"

"I told you that you are not to leave the house without my knowing where you are."

"I tried to call."

"You weren't supposed to leave the house."

"I didn't leave the house."

"Then where were you all this time?"

"I was at school, Dad. I was just going to come home right after school, and then I saw Billy. He said he hadn't seen me for a long, long time and he wondered if it was okay for me to take a walk down by the river with him."

"You should have said no."

"But I tried to call, Dad," she said stiffening. "And he said he was waiting in the playground especially for me."

"You shouldn't have gone with him."

"I'll go with him wherever I want."

Sixteen

No BEDTIME STORY for her. She would have to be in bed by eight. And no, she would not be allowed to read to herself because he would turn off the lights. In that darkness she would discover no prince entering a cave to slay a two-headed beast, no witch turning walnut shells into golden nuggets, no peasant girls carried away into palaces on mountaintops.

And Lance would have to go. Holmay tightened his fist as he made up his mind to it. Lance Walcott would have to go as soon as final exams were done.

Billy called just before ten o'clock.

"Have you ever been to Brazil?" he asked. Before Holmay had a chance to respond Billy went on. "I stayed up all last night reading about Brazil. Do you realize what a vast land is there—down under, as they say. The Amazon. I can see it . . . like it is. It coils for hundreds of miles inland toward the heart of the continent, and its mouth opens wide to the sea. Do you think there are jobs on freighters going to Brazil? I think everyone should take a trip down the Amazon."

Billy waited, as if the pause gave Holmay time to agree.

"But I'm not sure how to get it all in. You don't think I've been doing nothing all these nights, do you? Mrs. Lupinski, you know, she goes to bed early every night, and by then I have all my chores done and have the whole night to write. I want to be the best student you ever had. You know that, don't you? That's why maybe it's a good thing I didn't get that post office job, though someday

I want you to explain how we can sue them for that. Because now I have time to write. I have twenty pages already done, and I think I maybe won't be able to get it all in. Take Brazil, for example. I know it just fits, but I'm not sure how. There's the Amazon and Brasilia with skyscrapers made of glass, and I'm not even sure if it's crocodiles or alligators that live on the Amazon. Do you know, Dr. Holmay, if it's crocodiles or alligators?"

"No, Billy, I don't know."

"There's the Iberian influence in Brazil, with its Moorish Christianity, and the Spiritualists, and then there's the most primitive tribesmen who think airplanes are strange birds sent by the gods. Everything's here. It's a place where everything seems to have a place, where everything fits in. And that's why I'm not sure how to get it all into my book. It's as if Brazil is bigger than my book, and that would mean the book is all wrong, not big enough for it all. Don't you think? Maybe that's where I need some help. For example."

He paused again, as if to make sure Holmay was still on the line.

"Take Plato. I thought about beginning my book with Plato. His Theory of Forms. What he says about beds, for example. That a particular bed isn't real. The real bed is in the mind. And I like what Socrates says when Cebes tells him that there is a child within us to whom death is a sort of hobgoblin. Do you remember Socrates' response?"

"No, Billy, no," Holmay said to himself.

"'Let the voice of the charmer be applied daily until you have charmed away the fear.' Quote-unquote. I like that, don't you?"

Billy went right on.

"Plato explains everything. If a man is a prisoner in his body, then he has no right to open the door and run away. That makes perfectly good sense to me, though I'm not sure about Brazil. There must be some vital connection. I thought maybe you could help me with this when classes begin again—in your office maybe or somewhere, the library. Because I think Brazil holds the key to everything. Of course someday I will go there to see for myself, but I can't just drop everything and just go, not with classes coming up again and Mrs. Lupinski to take care of. But someday I will go there to see for myself."

Outside his window a semi-truck, like a ponderous beast captured in a cage, groaned as it lumbered past.

Billy's voice fell to a whisper. "A lot of things, you know, worry me."

"Like what, Billy?"

"The other night I was in bed, you know. And I know I'm not making this up. It was a real bed, in Plato's sense of the word, because I could see the bed and I could see myself in it. So therefore I know I heard the front door open and I saw a shadow, a presence of some sort, make its way past Mrs. Lupinski's rocking chair until he stood in the doorway of our room looking at us."

"Are you sure you weren't dreaming, Billy?"

"No, I was not asleep."

"Why didn't you do anything?"

"Because I wasn't awake either. I was thinking about things, and then there was a cold feeling like what happens when you dive into the water and then I saw the shadow of the man in our room covering both of us, Mrs. Lupinski and me, and I wanted to scream and scare him away but all I could do was run and my legs felt heavy as stones and would not let me shout anything out until five in the morning. And I know it was five because that's when I shouted something and woke Mrs. Lupinski up, and the clock said six minutes after five."

"Who do you think it was, Billy?"

"It was the postmaster," Billy whispered. "I'm sure of it now. And I'm sure of one other thing."

"What's that, Billy?"

"He came to do harm to Mrs. Lupinski."

"What kind of harm?"

"I don't know. Maybe something dirty. I don't know. But I could see fear written all over her face."

Was he worried about Mrs. Lupinski? No, Billy replied, because things were looking up for him even though he didn't get the post office job. He called because he wanted to ask about Brazil. He thought maybe it would be a good idea to write his book under a new name. Maybe Billy Brazil. What would people think of that? But he didn't know how to make all of Brazil fit into his book. So for now maybe he should begin the book with Plato on one end, write the last chapter about Brazil, and then write from the end toward the middle, with the middle chapter being like the middle stone on a Gothic arch where everything came together, balanced, converged. He wanted to ask if it would be okay to write his book this way. And he wanted to ask about what had come of his petition to be readmitted to the university.

"I voted for you, Billy," Holmay said, "though our departmental vote counts only as a recommendation."

"Oh good," Billy said, "good, good. Then I won't worry about it."

Holmay heard the back door close. "I have to go, because there's someone at the door."

"You should be careful, Dr. Holmay, to lock your doors every night. I don't read the papers but I know the world is full of trouble these days. And that daughter of yours, that Evelyn, is such a lovely, beautiful human being, you would never want anything to happen to her."

"Yes, I wanted to talk to you about her, but I can't right now."

"Yes, thank you, Dr. Holmay. You just come right over any time, or do you want me to come over there?"

"I'll call."

* * *

Annette George sat on the edge of Lance's bed, her eyes bloodshot. Her upper lip quivered whenever she tried to speak.

"So you haven't seen him all night?" she asked Holmay.

"He comes and goes, but I'm sure he hasn't been here since late this afternoon." Holmay could not pass up the chance. "Lance and I don't communicate very well, you know."

"He's a lot different than you think," she said.

"I have my doubts."

"And there's more to him than you think."

"I can imagine that."

"You never really tried to get to know him."

"I'm not sure it would be wise for me to get to know each of my students personally."

She glared at him until he backed off. "You're never going to let me forget that night, are you?"

"Not until after final exams."

She looked up at him, her eyes filling again with tears. "I know you well enough," she said. "I don't think you're the type who would try to get revenge. I think you will be fair."

"I will proceed strictly by the book."

"Because if you knew all the facts you would take a completely different view of things—of why I came to your room that night."

"What are the facts? Why did you come to my room that night?"

She put her head into her hands and stared at the floor. Then she began shaking her head, no, no, as if refusing to believe that she was not in the middle of a terrible dream.

He looked down at her. "What's wrong?" he asked, softening.

She kept shaking her head.

"Is he with another girl?"

"No, no. I only wish he was."

"Then. . .what?"

She cringed, hunched her shoulders.

"Is he in trouble?"

She gave a short ironic laugh. "You could say that."

"With the law?"

"No."

"Then what is wrong?"

"I can't tell you," she said, lifting her head. "It's strange."

"Then tell me about that night, why you came to my room."

She began shaking her head again, her eyes all the while retreating from his as if unable to believe what she remembered of the night. "I came to your room because he encouraged me."

"You were both in on it?"

"You really won't give me a chance, will you? He asked me to come because he was trying to get rid of me."

"And you just went along with him because you thought it would be good clean fun?"

"He was trying to get rid of me."

She looked away and fumbled with her handbag.

"I don't think I understand," he said. "Why would he want to get rid of you?"

"You don't understand. And there's one other thing you don't know."

"Now what?"

"When I came to your room that night, it wasn't really for the grade. I came. . . because I respect you. . . as a professor." She turned and looked directly at him. "You're the most intelligent man I've ever known—I mean the way you can see hidden meanings everywhere. And I wanted to make love to you."

She pulled a brush out of her handbag and rearranged her hair. When she stood, running her hands down the sides of her hips, he was too bewildered to respond. She glanced over her shoulder as she walked toward the door and gave him a soft smile.

"You may wait here for him if you'd like."

"No, I don't think he'll be back tonight. Thanks anyway."

Evelyn's door was half-opened when he mounted the steps toward his room. She was fast asleep, her head turned toward the wall and her legs tucked in tight beneath her chest. He bent down and kissed her lightly on the forehead, and as he drew away he saw her eyelids flutter as if something in her mind had taken her by surprise. He went to her window, looked out at the spot where Billy had stood beneath the streetlight, and pulled down the shade.

In his room he opened Evelyn's thick volume of folktales. "Once there were three peasant girls who fell into a dragon's pit hidden beneath the root of a huge chickory plant," he began. When the dragon had them in his power, he required the three sisters to eat a human hand, arm and foot, but because the two oldest tried to fool the dragon by hiding the hand and arm, he cut off their heads. The third, because she ground the human foot into a powder which she placed in a bag on her stomach, became the dragon's wife. When the dragon, delirious from a drunken spree, revealed the secret of his charmed egg, Mariuzza, the youngest and most beautiful of the three, killed her new husband the dragon by breaking the egg over his head. Then, finding the secret room where he had hid the heads of her sisters, she restored the sisters to life and returned to the world where kings and princes played cards to see who would have the right to marry the three sisters.

After he closed the book he turned off the light . "It makes no sense," he said to himself. "It's a crazy story that makes no sense at all. And maybe all stories make no sense." He visualized Annette George looking up at him with eyes expecting him to explain everything to her. "I'm sorry," he whispered in the darkened room, "but I'm not nearly as smart as you think."

Seventeen

HOFFSTEIN PASSED Holmay the next morning in the hall. "Cheerio," Hoffstein said, smiling as he nodded.

Frances Drummond could hardly believe her eyes. "What's wrong with him today? Do you think he's had a conversion experience?"

"More likely it's all the powdered sugar going to his brain. One too many donuts today."

"I'd still beware."

Annette George's note, written in a neat, clear hand, was under his office door.

> For the sake of our mutual respect, I have decided to drop your course. Thank you for everything, almost.

He carefully refolded the note and put it in the top right-hand drawer of his desk, faintly imagining that one day it would become useful as a way of proving his innocence.

Jason Kerns, one of the three college counselors, put on his omniscient smile when Holmay entered his office. Kerns always wore a dress shirt and tie, always loose at the collar as if to signal that he was open enough to everyone's secrets, that he cared more about people than they did about themselves.

"Matt," he said as he showed Holmay to a chair. "It's so nice to see you again."

"I saw you in the cafeteria yesterday at noon."

"Yes, but we didn't get a chance to communicate, did we?"

Holmay suddenly recalled a report that Kerns had written for the faculty. It was full of sentence fragments and dangling modifiers.

"I wonder if you could help me," Holmay said.

"Certainly. You know that's what I'm here for."

"I have a student who seems to need help."

"Counseling?"

"Yes. He seems...confused, somewhat lost."

"Depressed?"

"Yes, but now and then too high."

"Drugs?"

"I don't think so."

"Having trouble with grades?"

"He's very bright—very bright. Perhaps too bright."

"Troubles at home?"

"I suppose so, but I'm not really sure how bad they are."

"What makes you think he needs help?" Kerns' question quietly accused Holmay of being all wrong.

"He is, you might say, a lost and wandering soul."

Kerns smiled. "I like your words. I was an English major myself for a time, and I still read English literature whenever I get a chance."

"He fails to connect."

"His thoughts?"

"Thoughts, beliefs, dreams, ideals, impressions. His mind is sometimes lucid and sharp, but then again it's a loose ball of strings, all the ends lost in the middle somewhere."

"What's his name?"

"William Allan Brand."

Kerns tried to remember, then opened his filing cabinet. "Nope," he said, "no one by that name. Can you get him to come in for a session with me? I'm free from four to four-thirty this afternoon."

"He's not a student any more, not officially enrolled."

"Then what do you expect me to do?"

They would have to get together some night for a few drinks, Kerns said as Holmay made his way toward the door. It was too bad they had gotten so far out of touch. It was bad for faculty morale, and he did still read English literature in his spare time, and he hoped Holmay would have a nice day.

✳ ✳ ✳

Holmay was sure he had found the place even before he saw the name "Brand" painted in thick white letters on the mailbox tilting up away from the culvert. Two dogs, both of them lean short-haired mongrels, had ambushed his car from underneath an old wagon piled high with used lumber, and they made mad leaps at him as he eased his car up the driveway toward the house. The house was big and broken, the white paint on its boards streaks of dry flecks. The front porch, propped on cinder blocks, seemed to be sinking under the load of old furniture and junk piled high even against the front entrance of the house. Gray shades pulled down over the two upper windows gave the impression that the house had closed its eyes and gone to sleep.

He stopped his car within ten yards of the back door, the dogs standing shoulder-to-shoulder growling at him. To his right was an old barn tilting precariously close to an abandoned chicken coop with a caved-in roof, and to the left of the barn was a garage with the skeleton of an antique tractor visible inside. Two goats, tethered to a clothesline, strained their lines to get at grass just beyond their reach, and scattered all over the yard chickens, ducks, and geese wandered about look-ing for a morsel in the gravel and patches of snow.

He saw a shuffling inside the darkened screen door and waited for someone to come out. When he made a move to open his car door the dogs backed off and sent up a new howl. He honked his horn and waited. "God dammit," he said beneath his breath. "Why in the hell doesn't someone come out and shoot these goddamned dogs?"

The dogs put their tails between their legs and sulked away when Billy's mother appeared on the back porch step.

"We ain't got no eggs today," she said.

"I don't want eggs," Holmay said as he got out of the car.

She was a short thick woman of fifty enclosed within a gray apron on which she kept wiping her hands. Her left eye curled up in suspicion as he approached the porch.

"I said we ain't got eggs."

"I'm Professor Matthew Holmay, Billy's teacher. I wonder if you and your hus-band could take a few minutes to talk about Billy."

She looked over her shoulder into the house.

"He hasn't done anything wrong," Holmay said.

A voice, low and slow, came from inside the house. "Ellen? Who is that man?"

"I don't know," she said over her shoulder.

"I used to be Billy's teacher, and I just wonder..."

"Ellen, you tell him this is private property and he ain't got no right to come trespassin' here."

She wiped her hands on her apron again. "You heard what William said."

"Is there a chance we could sit down and talk a few minutes—the three of us?"

"What do you want to talk about?"

"I want to talk to you about Billy. He's not in trouble with the law or anything like that, but he's a very confused young man who maybe needs some help."

"Ellen," said the voice from inside, "you never let me have my way with him. Now they say there's something wrong with the boy."

"What's wrong with Billy?" she asked.

"He's acting strange."

Again the voice from inside. "Strange. That's the word all the smart-alecks use when they're so smart they can't figure something out."

"Now William," she chided, "you let the man talk."

"I think, Mrs. Brand, that Billy needs professional help."

"A doctor?"

"A head doctor," said the voice from inside. "Over my dead body."

"Do you mind if we go inside?" Holmay said.

"Oh no, you can't go in there." She moved back a few steps to a position in front of the door.

"They can get Jesus for free," said the voice, "but they want us to pay big money for one of those witch-doctors of the mind."

"What's Billy done?" she asked.

"He has not done well as a student. He's not sleeping properly and he seems distraught."

"What does the man mean?" Billy's mother asked over her shoulder to the figure inside.

The voice: "The professor thinks Billy's mixed-up, like I told you he would be the minute he left home."

"Do you think, mister, you could make Billy come back home to us?" Her voice was plaintive, weak.

"If he knows what's good for him, he'll come back soon enough," the voice said. "I figured he'd get his fill of books soon enough."

"Is he okay?" she said as she wiped her hands again.

Holmay dared to take a few steps closer to the porch, angling his way toward Mrs. Brand so he could catch more of the shadow lurking behind the blackened screen door. As he approached, Mrs. Brand turned to place herself between him and the door.

"No, Mrs. Brand, I don't think your son is okay. If I thought everything was fine, I wouldn't be here. Your son needs help. He has dropped classes and can't get a job. His behavior is. . .irregular. It is irregular enough that he may get himself into trouble some day soon, but I'm mainly afraid that he may do harm either to himself or to someone else."

"Where's he staying?" she asked.

"I'm not at liberty to tell you that, under the circumstances."

"He's covering up, Ellen, that's what he's doing. The boy goes away and he don't want anything to do with his folks any more. You ask him if he reads his Bible and he answers you back, says there's other books. So I figure he's learning, all right. Do you professors believe in the devil and sin?"

Billy's mother stood wide-eyed, waiting for an answer.

The voice repeated the question deliberately, as if delivering an ultimatum. "Do you believe in the devil and sin?"

"Yes, Mr. Brand, I believe in sin."

"But you don't believe in the devil, do you? You didn't say you believed in the devil, did you? It's just like I told you, Ellen, and like I told Billy all the time.

Now you tell Ellen, Mr. Professor, so she can hear it herself. Do you believe in the devil or do you not believe in the devil?"

Holmay put his hands on his hips and glared at the shadow behind the screen door.

"I asked you a question, Mr. Professor."

He turned, half-resolved to leave without saying another word, but a chicken crossed his path, its head bobbing indifferently as it waddled by. "Goats," he said, "I believe in goats. I like those two goats you have over there."

Mrs. Brand turned to look at the goats.

"No, I do not believe in the devil, Mr. Brand, any more than I disbelieve in goats."

"Did you hear, Ellen, did you hear?" The screen door opened just wide enough for Mrs. Brand to squeeze sideways through. For a moment she was a shadow, but then she disappeared to one side. Holmay quickly fumbled in his pocket for his car keys, his heart skipping a beat until he recalled he had left them in the ignition. The dogs, lying under the old tractor in the garage, suddenly stood up and glared at him.

"Mr. Professor," said Billy's father from inside the door, "you'd better get out of here now. We raised Billy to be a God-fearing boy. So Billy knows that Jesus is the truth and the light. And Billy believes in the devil, Mr. Professor—he knows about the devil because he saw the devil right in that barn over there, not once but twice. And the devil spoke to Billy, said things right out loud to him. And Billy never lies, Mr. Professor, never, never lies. So I want you to get out of here. I want you to go back to that college of yours and tell Billy to come back home where he belongs. You tell him it's milking time. You tell him his mother is tired of doing the milking for him. You tell him that. You tell him, mister, to come on right back home."

Holmay stared at the shadow inside the house.

"And now, Mr. Professor, you better get on your way. I'm going to give you one minute to get in your car and get out of here. If you ain't gone in one minute from now, I'm going to turn them dogs loose. And I got a twelve-gauge shotgun right here in my hand that's been telling me to make you mind your own business from now on."

Eighteen

AS HE RACED down the county road toward home, Holmay kept glancing at the rearview mirror, expecting to see the faceless Mr. Brand running after him. It was ten minutes to three when he parked his car two blocks east of Evelyn's school and walked slowly toward the door where she usually appeared.

When he was a half-block away he stopped on the sidewalk and looked back, a fear leaping out at him: Billy was waiting for Evelyn too. So he had to see Billy before Billy saw him. And if Billy was anywhere near the school, he would no longer hesitate: he would call the police and file a formal complaint. But it would be best to catch Billy in the act, to see him suddenly appearing a half-block from the school, offering Evelyn his hand, leading her only God knows where. Then he could spring like a tiger, make his words sink in like claws, tear away any tie between himself and the mad boy. And he would pronounce the words clearly to Billy's face: "I'm calling the police. You have no business lurking near elementary schools and picking up little girls. I want you arrested and put in jail."

A dead elm at the far end of the playground. From there he could watch for her, the streets leading to the playground, the sidewalk leading home. As he came to the elm he was suddenly uncertain of himself. Billy was no fool. Maybe Billy was watching him. He leaned uncomfortably against the shredding bark of the tree, not knowing what to do with his hands. He kept checking his watch, afraid he was already too late.

At two minutes past three children began streaming out. He sorted them immediately, dismissing from view all but the few who could have been Evelyn. He tried to remember what she had worn—was it lavender jeans and the brown winter coat? Or was it the red wool coat with the hood? One little blond girl in the doorway looked around as if perplexed, then picked up some snow. He had an urge to run toward her, take her hand, but he checked himself when he saw that her face was too round to be his Evelyn's face. He looked at his watch again. Four minutes past three.

Evelyn opened the door half-way, waved at someone inside the building, and then stepped into the sun. She paused a moment, looking both ways, then skipped down the steps. Without breaking stride she mounted the monkey-bars, twirled herself around twice, and landed on her feet. She wandered next to the swings, chatted with a smaller girl, helped her get going high. Then she turned, waved, and walked toward the sidewalk leading home.

He followed from a distance, his eyes looking ahead, trying to see behind every bush and tree.

Lance was waiting for him on the front porch, a troubled look on his face. "I was wondering if we could talk."

"What's on your mind today?"

Lance looked away. Holmay had never seen him falter before. "I wonder what you really think of me?"

"What do you mean? You're a student. You rent a room in my house."

"That's all there is to it? No more than that?"

"What am I supposed to say?"

"Did Annette talk to you today?"

"No, but she left me a note. She's no longer with us."

"I'm not dropping out. The final's only one week off."

"I don't think she did it because she was worried about her grade."

"I am worried about my grade. I want to do better than a C."

Holmay lifted an eyebrow. "Try studying harder."

"I've read everything, studied all my lecture notes, and for the past two weeks I've done extra reading in the library. All the stuff you said we should do. I'm aiming for a B or an A."

"Heading for law school?"

"No."

"Trying to impress Annette?"

"Let's forget about her. We're not even friends any more. The truth, Dr. Holmay, is that I don't think you like me at all. You don't think there's any. . .*depth* to me."

Holmay smirked as he repeated his own words to himself: Lance was a student. Lance was renting a room in his house. "I think, Lance, that you have a quick and clever mind."

"I had a talk with Dr. Hoffstein. I want to take his poetry writing class next term. I need at least a B to get into the course."

"I didn't know you liked poetry, Lance."

"You don't know a lot of things about me."

Lance looked shyly away, as if ready to confess some sin. Holmay twisted Lance's words his way. "You can't help being impertinent, can you?"

"I'm not being impertinent. I respect—admire you as a teacher. I'm grateful to you for letting me live in your house. I know you've put up with a lot of crap from me. I think you and your daughter are both really nice."

"I've been considering asking you to move out at the end of the term."

"I was afraid of that too." He put his hands in his pockets and looked at the floor. "I like it here, want to stay. I could do things around here for you, could help more around the house."

"What kind of things do you propose to do?"

"You sometimes forget to lock your doors. Someone could just walk in and rob you blind. I could do more around the house. Shovel the snow. Things like that."

"Maybe we can work something out. Maybe I could put you in charge of keeping an eye on Evelyn. . .during certain times."

For the first time he invited Lance to dinner. Lance seemed timid and shy, reluctant to speak until spoken to, unsure of himself. Evelyn noticed the change and kept looking at him. She had kept a distance, he the intruder who had taken Billy's place in the house, and Lance had gotten his revenge by sustaining an indifference toward her. But the dinner table scene forced them to look at each other close-up, and Holmay did his best to bridge the gap.

"Lance is trying to get an A in my course," he said, "and next term he's taking poetry writing."

"I hate poetry," she announced as she turned toward Lance, trying to suppress a smile, "and I bet you can't think of a word that rhymes with orange."

"Scrounge," he said.

"Nope."

"Forage."

"Nope."

"I'm stumped," Lance said.

"Do you surrender?"

"I do. I guess you're smarter than me."

When Lance offered to help Evelyn clear the table, she smiled and let him pass. He washed the dishes and she dried, Holmay slipping out of the kitchen to his favorite chair, undisturbed by the laughing in the other room.

Then Wendy appeared at the door. "Have you seen Billy?" she asked. Her hair was disheveled and her eye makeup smeared.

"I'm glad to say I haven't," Holmay said. "What's the trouble this time?"

"He's been calling me every other hour for the past three days. He's been saying weird things, telling me all sorts of strange stories."

"What sort of stories?"

"He says there's a voice telling him to finish his work here because he's got to move on to another plane. That's what he says over and over again."

"What is this work?"

"He won't say. He won't tell me."

"Where is he now?"

"I don't know. I don't know. But I'm afraid. I think he's going crazy, and he's driving me crazy too. I can't stay in my room because he calls me there, and I'm afraid to go anywhere alone. I don't know what to do."

"Did you call the police?"

"I called his parents—I talked to his mother. She wants him home. She told me to make him go home."

"And what did Billy say?"

"He keeps saying his mother is dead. The first time he called—three nights ago—he said his mother was dead. Then he kept saying that *I* am his mother."

"When did you see him last?"

"A week, two weeks ago, but whenever I go anywhere I expect him to be there waiting for me."

Evelyn, standing rigid in the kitchen doorway with a dishtowel draped over her arm, showed no emotion as she listened. When Wendy saw her, Evelyn turned and disappeared into the kitchen again.

"I think you should call the police," Holmay said.

"I couldn't bring myself to that. I'm leaving town tonight, going to my parents' house. I want you to do something for Billy. You're the only one who really cares about him."

He walked to her car, saw to it that she was composed enough to drive. He made her promise that she would drive straight to her parents' house. Then he went back into the house and locked all the doors. A gun, he thought. Everyone else has a gun these days, and Billy has three, and I don't believe in guns.

It was almost midnight when the phone broke the silence like a scream, the ringing shrill, the sound of Billy's voice gone insane. He picked up the receiver and held it close, but for twenty seconds a silence so deep waited for him that he felt as if he was staring into the bottomless pit of space. He was about to hang up when Billy spoke:

"I am deeply sorrowful to inform you, Professor Holmay, that Mrs. Lupinski has passed on, peacefully in her sleep. I want you to be the first to know, for maybe it is time now to consult the proper local authorities, your sometime friends the police. Be aware, moreover, that I am not unaware of your visitations with my mother. And despite your signs of unfaithfulness to me, it is an enduring sign of my devotion that I include you among those to whom I announce my departure from these parts."

"Where are you going?"

"Neither here nor there. Everywhere and nowhere. I leave with a profound regret that I must for now abandon our lovely Evelyn. Convey to her that my promise to her still holds, that someday I will return for her."

"Where are you, Billy? Where are you going?"

The phone died in Holmay's hand. "Farewell," Holmay said to the darkened room. "Fare you well, Billy, and please, please keep going, all the way to Brazil."

Nineteen

BILLY WAS GONE.

Holmay stretched himself out on his bed, turned off the light, and stared into the darkness of the room. He saw himself behind the wheel of a car floating westward on a smooth country road, the level cornfields reflecting the autumn colors of the setting sun. The car, big and wide, seemed to hum at an even pace, reassuring him that nothing would interrupt his journey away from home. In the rearview mirror the road narrowed, its converging lines losing themselves in a dusk encroaching too slowly ever to catch up with him. The road went on and on, gliding past distant mountain ranges and over desert sands until it faced a vast ocean. He closed his eyes. There he saw a small boat, its sails made of paper or sheets, dancing on the waves rippling up to the shore. As he approached he saw a dark form on the boat, and when he looked again he saw that it was himself. He smiled, waved a farewell, then watched it drift away from himself until it disappeared on the horizon.

Billy was gone. Thank God Billy was gone.

Mrs. Lupinski's funeral took place within forty-eight hours.

"I want to go too," Evelyn complained. "She was my friend too, and I've never been to a funeral."

"When I say no, I mean no," he replied. "You have school. You're behind in math."

She gave him a sullen sneer. "I hate school."

Besides the priest, only seven people were present at the Hillside Cemetery. Four were older women, weighty peasant types on whose faces the lines of grief had left their permanent marks, one of them accompanied by a short crew-cut man in a black suit who kept turning his hat in his hand. Wendy, shooting confused glances at Holmay, stood apart from the huddled group as if its age and sadness were contagious. The sun, askew in the cloudless sky, threw a lambent light on the gray tombstones standing like squat human forms along the surrounding hills, and the trees, their dark boughs weighed down by breezeless air, stood perfectly still.

The priest, himself an aging Polish refugee, was slow and deliberate. He spoke kindly of Mrs. Lupinski, praising her dedication to her husband, himself passed on fourteen years ago, and to five nameless children "scattered," the priest said, "like seeds in the wind." His words, spoken as if he were talking to himself, gave dignity to the common credit due Mrs. Lupinski. "She was an honest woman," he concluded, "who intended no harm to anyone. And she was generous the way some people are—willing to share her small riches with someone in need. It is people like her who are at the heart of the unwritten chapters of the history of peace."

Holmay lifted his eyes before the conclusion of the final prayer, not aware of anything but the words stirring memories of Mrs. Lupinski. But when the priest stopped a shadow suddenly crossed the silence. Holmay looked again and saw it once more, this time leaping from tombstone to tombstone away from the huddled group, up toward the tree-covered ridge overlooking the cemetery. He looked away a moment, distracted by the sudden wail of one of the old women, and when he looked again he saw nothing but the trees standing silent against a serene blue sky. He scanned the tombstones one by one, his eyes sweeping over a hundred of them and then returning to double-check more systematically. The old man with the hat slid past him to comfort the wailing woman, causing Holmay to lose track of his place among the tombstones. He stood to one side of Mrs. Lupinski's friends, all of them in tears, and began doubting his eyes.

"She is gone now," the priest said to him, "to be with God in heaven. God bless you too, my son, for coming on this day to share with us the loss of a dear, dear friend."

As the priest moved away Holmay saw the shadow again. It was two-thirds up the hillside, only a dim gray head visible, the rest hidden behind a tombstone rounded like the shoulders of a man. As Holmay's eyes found the form, it slowly ducked down until it was completely hidden behind the stone.

Billy, he thought as a shiver ran through him. Billy isn't really gone.

He lingered behind as the others took slow steps down the hillside path to their cars. Wendy, ahead of the rest, waited by her car a while, then waved goodbye and drove away. As Holmay found himself standing alone, a cold fear went through his mind. If indeed the form was Billy, why hide behind tombstones? If it was not Billy, then who? Above him and to his left the form rose up again, paused as if to fix him in a stare, and floated away behind a large monument twenty yards below the treeline on the ridge. Holmay, his shoes slipping on the grass, started up the hillside.

He saw nothing until he was almost directly in front of the monument. Then suddenly he saw the form leap out from behind a bush near one of the tombstones higher up.

"Billy!" he called out.

The form dashed to another monument, this one further down the hill. Holmay saw it more clearly this time: the figure was dark-haired, Billy's height, with blue jeans and a gray jacket.

"Billy!" he called out again. "Billy!"

His voice resounded off the silent hillsides like the echo of a hunter's gun. He waited in the silence for some movement or word. Glancing over his shoulder, he could see that all the cars in the parking lot were gone, that he was alone in the cemetery. He fumbled in his pocket for his keys, remembering that he had locked his car door. He took a deep breath, then approached the tombstone cautiously.

"Billy, is that you?"

"Leave me alone."

Sprawled on the grass was a boy about sixteen. He smiled as Holmay approached, revealing a mouthful of browned oversized teeth. His hair fell incoherently over his face, and his eyes, half-closed, failed to focus. His smile broadened as they found Holmay's face. Then he reached into his belt and pulled out a pint of brandy.

"You wanna drink, mister? I gotta few swigs left."

"You're drunk."

"I ain't nothing."

"How old are you?"

"Too old for you."

"How come you're not in school?"

The boy opened the bottle and finished it off. "School ain't shit, man. It ain't nothin'."

"What's your name?"

The boy broke into a wide coy grin. "Billy," he said.

"You're lying."

"What you gonna do about it?" The boy curled up closer to the tombstone and put his head in his hands.

"How come you ran away from me? Are you afraid of something?"

"What are *you* afraid of? You're the one who started chasing me."

"I chased you because you've got no business in a cemetery."

"You're right, man. I ain't gonna make no livin' in a place like this."

"Then what are you doing here?"

"I do what I do, man. So why not do it here? The world's fucked up, man. You ever watch the news, man? So it's a nice day and I come here. It's nice and quiet here until you come along. This is where all the action is, man."

Holmay extended a hand toward him. "Come on, I'll give you a ride home."

The boy tried a smile. "No, man, I don't want no ride to your home. I don't want nothing from nobody."

Holmay, his hand still extended, forced the words from himself. "Come on, I'll buy you a cup of coffee. We'll get you sobered up, something to eat."

The boy gave him another big brown smile. "Hey thanks, man, but fuck off."

Billy was gone. Holmay's sense of relief returned as he walked down the hill. He glanced over his shoulder at the canopy still standing over Mrs. Lupinski's grave. Mrs. Lupinski was gone, so maybe Billy was also really gone. "Maybe for good," he said out loud to himself.

He reviewed his decision to extend his hand to the drunken boy. An unthinking act. His hand had gone out to the boy before he thought to stop himself. He had offered to take the boy home. Fool that he was. He stood at his car door, gazing up at the hillside, trying in vain to find the tombstone behind which the drunken boy sprawled. All the tombstones looked alike. Finally he got into his car and started his engine. "I did what I could," he said to himself. "I let him choose. And maybe, maybe, the boy has a good point. Maybe he's better off just where he is."

"I don't want a story tonight," Evelyn announced as soon as she arrived home from school. She threw her knapsack down in a corner and marched upstairs to change her clothes. Lance, standing by the door, shrugged his shoulders. He didn't know what was wrong with her.

"Do you want me to read you a story tonight?" Lance called up to her.

"No," she answered sharply.

Holmay went to her that night, sitting on the edge of her bed. She had pulled the blanket up to her chin and smoothed it down the length of the bed. At first she refused to look at him, but when this tactic failed to move him she fixed him in an uncompromising stare.

"I'm tired," she finally said, "and I want to go to sleep."

"We usually have a story before you go to sleep."

"Not tonight."

"Why not?"

"I just want to go to sleep."

"Were you tired in school today?"

"School is boring. I wasn't nothing in school today. I don't want to go to school any more."

"Why not?"

"School's where you go to get smart, right?"

He nodded.

"Well then I don't see any reason to go *there*."

"Why not?"

"Because I had a friend once and he doesn't go to school any more."

"If you don't go to school, what will you do with your life?"

"I'll go away—away somewhere far."

"Where?"

"Brazil."

"And who will take care of you there?"

She suddenly sat up and lifted one eyebrow intellectually. "Maybe I have a friend there who will take care of me."

"Maybe your friend isn't really in Brazil."

"How do you know where he is?"

"I want a kiss goodnight."

"I thought you said you were going to read me a story."

"You said you didn't want one tonight."

"I don't. I just want to know which one you were going to try to read to me."

"I was going to let you choose."

"I don't have a say in anything."

"I was going to read the story about the man with two hats."

"You already read that one to me."

"You said you liked it a lot."

"I don't like it at all. How does it start?"

"'Once upon a time.'"

"And then what happened?"

"There was a young shepherd named John who always wore two hats, because one hat was given to him by his mother and the other by his father and he didn't want to disappoint either one by taking one off."

"That's stupid."

"Then over the years he found he couldn't take either hat off. It didn't bother him at first, except a little bit at night when he had to sleep with his hats on, and during hot days when the sun beat down on him. But he learned how to sleep with his head propped up and to live in the shade."

"Then what?"

"He saw a lovely princess and wanted to marry her, but he was ashamed to talk to her because of his two hats. And do you remember what happened after that?"

"Probably something really stupid."

"He met a wizard in the woods who told him he was wearing an ancient curse. There was a serpent coiled inside the hats and the serpent refused to let go."

"I don't like that story," she said as she turned her head away.

"Why not?"

"Because I know just exactly how it ends. I know how all stories like that always end."

"How's that?"

"The shepherd boy kills the snake. Something happens and he kills the snake. Then he marries the princess and goes and lives in the palace with her."

"And they live happily ever after."

"Bullshit!"

"Evelyn! Where did you learn language like that?"

"In school."

"Are you lying to me?"

"The story is full of lies."

"What lies?"

"The story says the snake had to be killed. I don't believe that at all. A snake has just as much right to live as anybody else."

"What would you have done?"

"Don't you think the shepherd could have gone to the mayor of the town and asked him to call all the mothers together in the city hall? They could have talked to the shepherd boy, maybe helped him out somehow. The people in the town could have talked to the boy. The people could have done something for him if they really wanted to."

"How would that get rid of the serpent?"

"I wouldn't. I just told you that. He'd have to learn to live with it, and maybe the mayor and the mothers could help him with that."

"What about the princess? Would he get to marry her?"

Evelyn wiped her eyes on the sheet. "If she really really loved him and didn't marry him, it would be her fault."

He bent down and kissed her on the cheek, but she did not stir. As he left he was careful to leave her door halfway open. He was already in bed when she spoke clearly from her room.

"Good night, Dad."

"Good night, Evelyn."

And he had a good night until after three A.M. He found himself in his car again, gliding away over the same smooth highway leading west, when the phone next to his bed suddenly rang and rang and rang.

Twenty

"WILL YOU ACCEPT the charges?" the operator asked.

"Yes," Holmay said, suddenly aware of the clock.

"I owe you no small debt, professor, for troubling yourself on my behalf. One may hope hereinafter not only to repay the debt in kind but to multiply the grace you have extended toward me."

"Where are you, Billy?"

"I am nowhere and everywhere. I am on my way, which is where we all are at any moment in time."

"On your way where?"

"Brazil," Billy said. "I was sure you knew that."

Two thoughts elbowed their way forward. Brazil. Good. Billy was on his way—away—and Brazil seemed far enough away. But the long distance call—he was taking it. How many calls would there be?

"Where exactly are you, Billy—by the map?"

"By the map?" Billy gave a short sharp laugh. "I always liked the way you always want to put things in their proper logical perspective. Where am I, then, by the map? Let's say I'm in Iowa. It's a small town—you know how they all have names— and they say Nebraska is only an hour's drive ahead."

"You have a car?"

"I have thumbs. Someday I'll have my own car. But for now I have thumbs, digits proving I am no ape. But don't get me wrong: I am not trying to say I'm any better than the apes." Again he gave a short laugh.

"Why did you leave the way you did?"

Billy lapsed into a silence. Holmay visualized him edging his way toward the end of a high platform, then pausing the way divers do to collect their balance before making their sudden leap.

Billy broke the silence solemnly. "An inside narrative," he said in a low voice, "is not an easy thing. Because it would be too hard for me to keep from screaming throughout. And that would be no good because it would seem like I was losing control. Do you know what I mean?'

"I'm not sure."

"When in the course of my life I take the time to consider, I often conclude that silence is the only proper response. But for someone like you who understands I will make exception. Do you understand?"

"Yes, Billy, I think I do."

"I have much injustice to scream about, good reason to be out of control. I now see my father for what he is, a lost pathetic soul. He began using the strap on me before I was five, but nothing hurt the way it did when he locked me in the chicken coop. And why? Because he caught me reading a book named *Gulliver's Travels* when I was supposed to be asleep. And yet I cannot hate the man. And what would you do, Dr. Holmay, if everyone but one person in all of God's teeming wonderful creation had hurt or abandoned you? You know my Wendy, how she was lured away from my love by some voice that broke in on her dream in the middle of the night, and how her leaving left behind no more than a shadow of herself who still loved me enough to keep whispering to me. Do you know what it's like to have a broken heart?"

Holmay remembered his wife pulling away from the house, the picture crossed by the image of Annette George standing just inside his bedroom door. No, not since he was a teenager had he suffered a broken heart.

"You know what it's like," Billy went on, "to have a sick feeling in your stomach and head, and after a while you don't know what to do because. . . because you want to vomit but you're afraid you'll lose your mind. And then you apply for a job and the man in the post office calls the police on you. And you know, as soon as you see that man in the post office looking at you, that somehow they're going to keep you from getting the job, and you just try to pretend you're not hearing the truth when your mind keeps telling you the man in the post office is saving that job for one of his friends."

Holmay took a deep breath and let it out slowly.

"And then you can't get back into college, even though you tell me I'm one of the best students you ever had and voted for me. So you and I we both know there's something definitely rotten in Denmark there, there's somebody working against us."

He paused, as if a new idea had suddenly occurred to him. "Maybe you know who it is. Do you know who he is?"

"I have no idea, Billy."

"That really confuses me. Because I was sure you would know."

"Tell me about Mrs. Lupinski, Billy."

He fell silent. Holmay could hear the hum of traffic on the other side of the line.

"What do you want to know?"

"Tell me everything. What happened, why you left the way you did."

"I didn't leave her. She's the one. I woke up one morning and she was gone. I asked her if she wanted her coffee and she did not respond. Not yes or no. She was there with her eyes looking at me, but she didn't move or say one word."

"Then what happened?"

"I was scared and I went out for a long, long time."

"Why were you scared?"

"I don't know."

"When was she like that for the first time?"

"I don't know."

"Why did you get scared?"

"I don't know why I got scared. I came back later and she was still there with her eyes open, and she didn't move. Then I told her again to get up and she still didn't move."

"Then what did you do?"

"I went to the porch and I began working on my book."

"Your book?"

"My book. You know, the book I'm writing about my life."

"And then?"

"Then I went back in and looked at her, and then I was really scared."

"Because she was dead?"

"Because I was afraid she was. . .leaving me—like Wendy did."

"But she was already dead?"

"That's when I talked to her, asked her if she was leaving me too."

"Then she wasn't dead?"

"She said, 'No, no, I would never do a thing like that.'"

"What else did she say?"

"She didn't say anything else. She just kept looking at me, and that's when I got scared."

"What were you scared of?"

"Nothing."

"How can you be scared of 'nothing'?"

"She kept looking at me, and then I saw she was accusing me."

"Of what?"

"Nothing."

"Tell me, Billy."

"Of poisoning her."

Holmay pulled the receiver away from his ear, as if Billy's words were a rare disease.

"Did you poison her?"

Billy said nothing for a long, long time. "I looked everywhere," he said, "in the basement, under the sink, in the cupboards, everywhere—but I couldn't find any poison anywhere in the house."

"Then you didn't poison her?"

"No," he whispered, "I'm sure I did not poison her."

"Then why did you think you may have poisoned her?"

Billy's answer was sharp and fast. "I never said I thought I poisoned her. I said she accused me of poisoning her."

"Why would she do that?"

"I don't know, I don't know. Unless she was afraid she was abandoning me and wanted me to stay with her to a ripe old age."

Billy's words, turning back on themselves like a snake coiling on the ground, had the logic of a strange symmetry that Holmay did not try to appreciate. He rushed on to get the fact he was looking for.

"How long did you stay with her?"

"Three days."

"And then you hit the road?"

"Yes. I'm in Iowa now. There's a town here and it has one of those Iowa town names. I'm not far from Nebraska now."

"How long have you known about Mrs. Lupinski's death?"

Another pause, a big truck, this one approaching Billy's telephone booth like a distant storm gathering strength, then rushing past, leaving in its wake a silence like the memory of a scream.

"She is not, you know, in any literal sense deceased. Her present state of mortification is metaphorical."

Holmay said nothing.

"Her death is fictive," Billy went on, "the way the characters in a novel are fictively alive. Surely, Professor Holmay, you understand this mode of translation."

Only too well, Holmay thought, aware that he had not bothered to turn on the light, that he had been speaking into the telephone receiver with his head resting on his pillow the way lovers do in the middle of the night. Billy, still a soul-mate of sorts, aware of how characters in a novel are fictively alive.

"When did you know for sure she was dead?"

Billy answered in a weak wavering voice. "Even before I saw that she couldn't close her eyes. She died in the middle of the night. I know because I heard her whisper something to me, and then she didn't move any more in the bed."

"What did she say, Billy?"

"She said I have to go to Brazil. She said I had to take the two hundred dollars in the coffee can and go to Brazil right away. She said she had saved the money for me."

"Why Brazil, Billy?"

"Sometimes, Professor Holmay, you require me to belabor the obvious. Surely you know why she requires my passage to Brazil. Brazil, as you well know, is the wonderland of the world. Next to the Soviet Union, it is one of the largest nations on earth, but its significance is not its size. What we cannot see from a map of Brazil is the variety and depth of its culture. . . its widely differing social composition in its various regions, its south urban and industrialized, its politics and social ideas more progressive than in the north. It's like there are two Brazils— that's what all the writers say—and everybody can find a place in Brazil. The Portuguese, and other whites there from Spain and Italy and Germany. And they live right next door to Negroes and Indians and the yellow races from the Orient. And the two sides can mix and get married and it's the normal thing. And people have the freedom to think and freedom of belief. It's mainly full of Catholics, but there are Methodists and Lutherans and those of the Islamic persuasion, but most importantly there's the Spiritualists. The Spiritualists have almost three thousand churches in Brazil. Did you know that?"

Billy did not wait for an answer.

"The Spiritualists, I think, are Brazil, because they're the ones who are making the two Brazils into one. That's really why I'm going there."

"Have you thought this through?"

"Oh, yes, a long, long time. I want to go there to study Melville's works. I want to study the relationsip between Melville and the Spiritualists. I really think I can help Brazil, and I think it would be a good topic for a doctoral dissertation."

"Billy, do you really think it sensible to go to Brazil to study Melville's works?"

The silence lengthened beyond the darkness of Holmay's room until it occured to him that Billy maybe had hung up on him.

"No," Billy said in a clear voice. "I would like to stay with you, but you say your house is full."

He moved quickly to close the door Billy was opening for himself.

"How will you get to Brazil on two hundred dollars?"

"I have my thumbs and my own mind. And I need only a bed of grass."

"What will you eat when your money runs out?"

"You forget, Dr. Holmay, that I know how to hunt."

Holmay's mind reeled again. Billy and his guns.

"And now I have to get to the point," Billy said. "I have a favor to ask. I need you to write the Brazilian consulate in Chicago. I know it's in Chicago. I want you to tell them I'm going to Brazil. I will want to go immediately to Brasilia, to the university there, and I will need some sort of assistance once I arrive. Tell them I was a student of yours. Inform them of my intention to pursue the connection between Melville and the Spiritualist movement there, set up a humble room and library privileges, *et cetera*. If you will do that much for me I will be most grateful to you. Will you do that for me?"

Holmay saw Billy drifting away, diminishing into a dot somewhere on a lonely highway disappearing in the jungles of Brazil.

"I'll see what I can do, Billy."

"Good. It's decided then. And now it's time to pop the biggest question of all."

Holmay waited.

"Wouldn't you like to start all over again with your life? Wouldn't you like to join me—the three of us: you, me, and Evelyn?"

Twenty-one

CRAZY.

The word that had passed through his mind so many times, hiding in a dark doorway or room whenever he approached, suddenly stood still, like a thing he could really see.

"No," he said in a firm, clear voice, "I have no desire to join you in Brazil, and you must understand that Evelyn is only a nine-year-old girl who will not be free to go wherever she wishes until she is eighteen. Do you understand?"

Billy had no more to say. He hung up, and within minutes Holmay was almost asleep, secure in the knowledge that Billy was hundreds of miles away.

The next morning he saw his colleagues smirking and whispering. He ducked into Frances Drummond's office and quickly closed the door.

"What am I missing out on?"

Frances cupped her hand over her mouth. "You mean you haven't heard about the new member of our department?"

The old malaise descended on him again. He had not even begun to think about writing a book.

"I guess I've been in the dark for some time now."

Frances moved in close and whispered. "Hoffstein has been born again."

"Well, I'm not surprised. He's always been a crypto-Bible-banger, so what's new?"

"He's had a spiritual renewal."

"We could all use one of those. Did he buy it on sale?"

"No, but maybe he got a deal on his new little hat."

"What little hat?"

"His round little black hat. Didn't you see him wearing it today—in the halls, in his classroom, everywhere?"

"He's wearing a *yarmulka?*"

"Dr. Hoffstein announced today that he is heretofore and evermore a born-again member of the Jewish faith."

"Jewish?"

"A sudden conversion experience he's been keeping under his hat. That's what he said right to my face. Now he seems anxious to tell the whole world."

"Even me?" Holmay asked with a sneer.

✳ ✳ ✳

"Even you," Hoffstein said as he approached Holmay in the hall, "must be wondering about why I'm now a Jew. Care to join me for a cup of coffee in the faculty lounge?"

Before settling down in a chair next to Holmay, Hoffstein carefully sealed the end of the plastic bag containing three untouched donuts. He looked heavier than ever, his stomach, once high and proud, beginning to sag. Not quite covering a monkish bald spot was his little black skullcap, held in place by a bobby pin. He smiled apologetically toward Holmay as he filled his own coffee cup again.

"I deeply believe," Hoffstein began, "that you and I have entered a new phase."

"No doubt in my mind," Holmay said, groping for words.

"There's no doubt, is there? You read my book, you understood it, came to see how my mind works—and the barrier between us began to fall. That's what books are all about, isn't it? That's the magic books have."

"Your conversion to Judaism certainly surprised everyone."

"In a certain sense my conversion was perfectly natural, perfectly predictable. Anyone with any wits about him at all can see from my book my more than latent interest in Freud. My use of the computer, rather than standing apart as a dialectical antithesis to my Freudian inclination, validates it. The computer, you know, gives us only hard facts, and it's hard to argue with facts that prove Freud right. And Freud, of course, was a Jew."

"So Freud, then, more or less inspired your desire to convert?"

"Yes, he was the catalyst, the—as you would say—inspiration. Not one that struck me blind as Paul was struck dumb on the road to Damascus, but one that—how shall I say?—insinuated itself right along. Freud gave me a creeping suspicion, an intuition, that he was right, and from there it was all a natural result. No, I won't say I had a vision or transcendental dream like those of the childish Romantic poets, but when I suddenly knew I was a Jew my hair stood on end and I felt the numinousness along my spine. Luckily Gloria—did you ever meet my wife Gloria?—has been beside me all the time. Then we found a good therapist, and, frankly, to facilitate the transition I've been doing psychotherapy ever since."

He shook his head and gave a little laugh as he stuffed the donut bag into the pocket of his sport coat. "You know what's really funny?" He waited for a reply before going on. "My psychoanalyst is Jewish too. We're really very lucky about that, Gloria and I."

"What's it like—the psychotherapy?"

"Expensive," he said, shaking his head. "They want a wheelbarrow full of money every hour. I'm having big fights with my insurance company, because I have to call my therapist five times a week. There are many zeroes involved. And would you believe that the administration here is on the company's side? Mallory wrote a letter to the insurance company affirming that I am not dysfunctional. Can you imagine that, the college president trying to destroy one of his own faculty members financially?"

"Well Lance Walcott thinks you're a remarkable teacher."

"Ah yes, Lance. A nice sweet lad. But the point, you know, is that I haven't completed the program yet. It'll take another few years. And I know for a fact that most who don't complete the whole program backslide."

"What would you backslide into?" Holmay asked with innocent eyes.

Hoffstein stiffened. "I would certainly never return to the Cross."

He stood up and abruptly turned away as if he had suddenly made up his mind to boycott a group gathered to whisper behind his back. For a moment Holmay thought he was leaving the room, but Hoffstein stopped instead at the coffee urn, refilled his cup, glanced back over his shoulder toward Holmay and returned to his chair.

"It's been a real process of self-discovery," he began. "I've finally opened my eyes. First I've come to realize who my real friends are. I thought I could count on the administration here. Now I know the truth about our dear President Mallory—Gloria and I both know. He won't pay a dime. And I know who my real friends and enemies are—right here."

"But you don't really think you have enemies?"

"You're projecting," Hoffstein snapped. "The fact that you don't have enemies doesn't mean that there are not people here who are my enemies."

"But who?"

Hoffstein smiled, looked around the room to assure himself that the two were alone, and whispered. "Your comments say something about your feelings."

Holmay shifted uneasily in his chair.

"Don't be embarrassed. Take my words for what they are. You fail to imagine I have any enemies because you are not my enemy."

"Who, then?"

"Don't you see them in the halls, how they whisper and laugh when I walk by? Then they close their office doors on me."

"Everyone?"

"Some are much worse."

"Who?"

He smiled again. "Your ingenuousness is positively charming at times. You see no evil at all, do you? You especially don't see evil in a pretty face."

"What do you mean?"

"Frances Drummond, that's who I mean. She's the one who hates me the most. She has a way of smiling, you know, the way all women smile. That pretty face, that voluptuous body that she advertises in front of us. I understand perfectly well how she has tried to lure you away. You end up in her office, the door closed. Then she tries to turn you against me."

Holmay looked around for a way out, but Hoffstein would not give him an opening.

"When the question of promotion came up, wasn't she the one who put herself in direct competition with you? She's the one who has a book almost done, and what do you have? But of course the real question is whether a book is worthy of being read. Isn't that so? Do you think she would ever encourage a genuine comparison of your teaching performance with her performance as a writer?" He raised a finger to instruct. "I assure you it would not be in her best interest to try something like that."

"I've never really worried about my job," Holmay lied, "and I've never seen myself as being in direct competition with Frances."

"And you need not worry about your job. You can be certain of all my support."

Holmay stood up, thrusting out his hand. "I appreciate that."

"Wait a minute. I feel as if we're just getting to know each other after all these years of passing each other in the halls. Have another cup of coffee. I want to tell you more about how I decided to convert."

Hoffstein took long steps toward the coffee urn and poured, splashing some on the carpet as he handed the cup to Holmay and motioned for him to sit.

"It has a lot to do with the discovery of my own self-centeredness." He looked quickly around, as if to make sure he was not being overheard. "That's the real trouble with Christianity, you know. The preoccupation with salvation. I had it. As you know, I was saved—we both were, Gloria and I. I became a deacon in our church and gave my entire life to Christ. Then one day it occurred to me that I was only trying to save myself, that my salvation was no more or less than an obsession with my future personal safety, a fundamental self-centeredness. That realization confirmed the uneasiness I'd been feeling all along about being saved. Because I kept thinking I'd somehow mess it up."

He heaved a deep sigh. "Do you know what saved me during those troubled times?"

Holmay stared into his coffee cup, suddenly fascinated by the steam swirling its way out of the cup before disappearing into the atmosphere.

"My book. That's what saved me in those days. I poured myself into that book. I gave it my best shot. And when I was done I had to look some things squarely in the eye. I had the book in hand and I had to face some things."

"What did you decide?"

He sighed, as if the memory weighed him down. "It was all crap. Crap. I mean *crap*."

Holmay turned away. Hoffstein's eyes were filling with tears.

"My whole life was nothing but crap."

"So what did you do?"

"I started thinking more seriously about Freud. Then one night—it was three A.M. and I was in bed with a small paperback copy of *Civilization and Its Discontents*—I suddenly saw the order he was talking about. I knew about his Jewishness then, but it still hadn't occurred to me to convert. That revelation came later, and in the strangest way. What mainly struck me then was all the law and order in the man's mind, how everything makes sense. That's what I fell in love with at first sight—the law and order of that man's mind.

"So I kept tying things together, tying this thing to that, trying to make sense of everything. Gloria was involved, you see, in the deepest way. I secretly wasn't saved any more, but I kept going to church and I kept showing up here as if nothing was wrong. One of the deacons in the church picked up the hints, said I had a troubled face. I lied to him again and again, and I lied to Gloria a hundred thousand times. She said I didn't love her any more. Then I started doing research for my second book. I spent months in the library, had thousands of notecards stacked in my room. But I couldn't write a word. My computer just sat there in my bedroom, staring at me with its big blank face. Then one February night I threw all the notecards into boxes and lugged them downstairs. I didn't know Gloria was pretending to be asleep, but she was watching my every move. And while I stood there throwing the stacks of cards into the furnace she was standing on the staircase watching me. And when I finished she looked me straight in the eye and came right out with the words: 'Are you having an affair with a student maybe?'

"And then I said the stupidest thing."

"What was that?"

"Yes. I said yes."

"Why did you say *that?*"

"It's what I felt like saying. She slapped my face and I couldn't move or talk. I couldn't take the words back. Then she started screaming and beating me with her fists and she called me a filthy pig and swine and whore, and she scratched my arms and back and tore off my shirt. When she stopped I came right out with the words. 'I'm no longer saved,' I said. 'Christianity is crap.' And she said right back to me, 'Do you think that's news to me?' She slapped me one more time hard across the face, then we sat on the stairs and wept."

His eyes had cleared, but his coffee cup quivered in his hand. He cleared his throat, pulled his hanky out, and wiped his beard with it. Then he took a deep breath and sat back, his knees almost touching Holmay's. Outside the room students were filling the hall, as classes were letting out.

Holmay waited for Hoffstein, his eyes and face drooping with sadness, to conclude. He looked fat and soft, too weary to lift himself out of his chair.

"I must go," Holmay said as he got up again.

Hoffstein snapped to attention. "That's transference."

"It's what?"

"Transference. You're displacing your real desire to stay. It's simple and obvious."

Holmay eased himself back down into his seat.

"The revelation I finally had, the one that triggered my desire to convert. I haven't explained it to you yet, and your natural desire to know is what egged you on to leave just now. But I'll be brief. It was a Friday. I had just picked up my paycheck here and was on my way to the bank. But I knew I hadn't explained anything to anyone yet, and in fact I was still a deacon in the church. I had the check in my shirt pocket and I decided to drive by the church instead, but when I got there I couldn't get out of my car because I didn't know what I'd say. You see, there was nothing I could tell the people in the church. I had no faith. I had nothing to take its place, so what could I say? I sat in the car a long, long time trying to think of something to say. I was right across the street from the church, afraid someone would see me there. Then something made me look up—a bird, or maybe a fly on the windshield—and I saw the sign on the church. JESUS SAVES. And suddenly the right word came. It had never occurred to me before, and it made everything add up—my loss of faith, my book, the troubles with Gloria, Freud, why I couldn't write my second book—everything. A little word came to me and suddenly everything added up."

"Yes?"

"Jew. Everything in that one small word, even our dear Methodist President Mallory."

Twenty-two

Holmay spent the rest of the afternoon in his office, the lights out and door closed. For the first half-hour he stared blankly out the window, making no response when two students knocked on his door and giggled while they waited. His trance ended when he saw a file folder slide under the door and heard footsteps stealing quickly away. He stared at the folder a long time, as if it contained some secret surprise he wanted to avoid. Finally he picked it up and looked inside. A late freshman theme— "Why Cars Should Have Airbags."

He began clearing his desk, half-filling the wastebasket with notes, old letters, book catalogs, the red tape of his trade that lost its importance the moment he swept it all away. He reduced his essentials to three file folders, two paperback books and a red ballpoint pen, then stacked them neatly on the corner of his desk. The blank surface in front of him gave him a vague sense of accomplishment. He began reorganizing the books on his shelves, plugging holes here and there but unsure about whether to arrange them topically or chronologically. He sat down again after ten minutes of this, bewildered by the rows of books.

When he arrived home Lance was in the kitchen frying a hamburger.

"Is Evelyn here?"

"Yes, she came right home after school," Lance said. "She's upstairs in her room— probably up to no good. She's been awfully quiet today."

The door was closed. He debated about whether to knock, then opted to make sure she heard him clearing his throat. He heard some shuffling inside, but Evelyn did not come to the door.

"Evelyn."

No answer.

"Evelyn. Can I talk to you a minute? Can I come in?"

No answer.

"Evelyn."

He waited, then finally leaned on the door until it opened. She sat in front of her mirror, her back to him.

"Leave me alone," she said without facing him.

"What are you doing?"

"Nothing. Leave me alone."

As he approached he saw in the mirror what she was trying to hide. She had completely covered her face with white powder. Over the powder she had painted her eyes with purple eye shadow and daubed her cheeks in heavy rouge. He suppressed a laugh as she turned toward him. She looked like a little whore. "What are you doing?"

"Nothing."

"Where did you get all the makeup?"

"From an old purse." She stood up, as if suddenly unashamed of herself. She was wearing a skirt three years old that barely reached beyond her underpants.

He looked away. "Why are you wearing one of your old skirts? Isn't it too small?"

"I'm not just a kid any more."

"You tell me, then. When does a kid stop being a kid?"

"When a kid is grown up."

"And when is a kid grown up?"

She turned toward the window and gazed far away into the western sky where the sun was just beginning to slant low over the tops of distant trees. Then she put her nose in the air and looked him straight in the eye. "A kid is grown up when she's in love."

"And are you in love?"

"Maybe."

"And who are you in love with?"

"That's my business, not yours."

"Is it somebody I know?"

"Oh you know, you know."

"Is it somebody who's gone?"

"Oh he's not gone," she said. "I've got him here, all the time." She put her hand over her heart.

"Billy is gone."

"We'll just see about that," she said, looking at him hard all the time. "Maybe he'll be back."

"Well, wash up. We'll be having dinner soon. I thought you could help me with the dishes afterward and then the two of us could watch a TV show. Then you can do your homework before I read your story for the night."

"I don't want any stories any more. Besides," she said, "something came in the mail for us today. I want you to read me that."

* * *

He found it on the dining room table, a large plain envelope under a mail order catalog. It was addressed to "Professor Holmay + Evelyn." In the upper left hand corner the words "Somewhere in this world" were handwritten. The postmark was faint, showing only the date.

"Read it now," Evelyn said after the dishes were done. "I don't want to watch TV."

All the arguments raced through his mind. It was none of her business. He had forbidden Billy to have anything to do with her. She was nine years old and he had a perfect right to tell her what she could and could not read. He had her welfare in mind and a responsibility to do as he saw fit. What was in the envelope was none of her business at all. He was her father, the boss.

"I don't think the contents of that envelope are really intended for you."

"It's Billy's handwriting, and my name is on the envelope too."

"We can't do everything your way."

"Would you try to keep your students from reading a book?"

"If I knew the words would hurt them, yes."

"Books are made of words, Dad, and thoughts are made of words. I'm just try-ing," she said as her eyes began filling with tears, "to understand what in the world is going on."

He saw his own eyes racing ahead over Billy's words, sorting, editing the ones appropriate to give to Evelyn's eager heart. It is better this way, he told himself, better that she know whatever truths or fictions there are to know, better that she hear them all while she is safely at home. That way they could talk, set every-thing straight.

"All right," he said, "but get your homework done first, then get your pajamas on. I'll read to you upstairs in your bed where I can keep an eye on you."

While Evelyn brushed her teeth he opened the envelope and took out twenty pages ripped from a spiral notebook pad. There was no letter, no note. The top page had Billy's Book, Part I printed on it.

* * *

"So this is really the beginning of Billy's book?" Evelyn asked as she curled around her pillow on the bed. "Read it to me."

Holmay kicked his shoes off and propped a pillow behind his back before he heard himself begin:

> The fulsomeness of life, its whole round plenitude, seems by destiny or design (or perchance both) to be crossed, perhaps bisected, by itself. Con-

sider the vertebrate embryo, how in its origins it conforms to its full roundeur but then as it fulfills itself distinguishes itself into head and tail. Such is the destiny, the condition, of man.

Holmay glanced at Evelyn before going on, relieved that Billy's book was perhaps meaningless. Still she had settled back, repose on her face.

As creatures swimming in the moil of existence, we no more can fail to think big than we can shrug off our minds with a shake of our heads. We are of necessity metaphysical, existential beings. We are in time and space and maybe somewhere and somehow in another dimension between, of, or around the two. We have many identities, calling ourselves students, citizens of a city, state or country, and we have our social roles created by peer group pressure plus environment. But on all the forms we fill out there is no line asking us if we are members of the planet earth, the galaxy Milky Way, or some existence even more far out. These far out ones are our greatest identities, even though we close our deepest philosophical being off like a cloud keeping out the sun.

Thus bisected we are fundamentally in the deepest, highest sense. Maybe because we're really afraid to face it. Maybe because we're really afraid to die. But there's no denying death as the factor of life. I don't even have to back this statement up on paper.

So where do we go from here?

We go outward and onward into consciousness. We are cursed, blessed by our own minds, not able like pure animals to accept existence in its natural (i.e. meaningless) state. Our minds nag us to know. My own won't leave me alone, pulls me away, beyond myself, hears voices trying to break through to tell us all the truth. In our lives we've all had one professor like that, a great teacher, a Michelangelo, a sage who made us see things in a new way. We always respected that man, loved him because he is the one who showed us how the ordinary mind could be equal to the greatest among men. But there are other sources of the light. We hear them at night when the windows are open, when the town sleeps. They sing for us and ask us to come out of our sleep. We have all left our beds in the middle of the night, sat alone looking out the window, walked alone in empty city streets.

Our thoughts follow us then. We can see them watching us from the windows of buildings across the street, and they lurk in doorways waiting for us. We try to quicken our pace to escape, but they're always ahead of us, waiting for us to turn our backs. I don't know why they keep trying to catch up with us.

Don't they understand that this is America? Don't they know that here a man has a right to his own opinion, a right to privacy and a right to be left alone? Sometimes I want to turn around and scream at them, tell them to leave me alone. Don't they understand that a citizen of the United States of America has a right to defend himself? I for one am not against the right to bear arms.

Undaunted, the honor of consciousness struggles forth. Turning its back on its foes, it travels ineluctably toward brave new worlds. There is foremost the realm of poetry, literature and philosophy, the Holy Trinity of Knowledge. And on this base the human sciences are formed, even physics and chemistry and biology, the Mother of Sciences. We read books, one day plunge into our own, try to see ourselves through page by page as worthy seamen did through uncharted perilous seas. We compile lists of words, memorize many every day so we can better communicate the nature of things. We come to understand that there are many brave new worlds—the body and mind itself, the world of our peers plus environment and societal-sociological influence, the planet earth itself swimming in space, and other places—faraway, wonderful, down under, never studied by the likes of us—places like Brazil and Antarctica.

We seek the origins of the problem. We glance at the daily newspaper. Everywhere we see man's inhumanity to man. A man murders his brother here, and there parents conspire to poison their son, and there again a desolate youth commits an outrage on an innocent girl. The evils grow into national giants. Here and there a war and desolate terrorist act and everywhere the deliberate blank grind of government boots on the face of the poor. In the sky where once there were birds and sweet air and butterflies we now look with horror for the mushroom of holocaust. It swirls upward in our minds, boiling gray. 'It is finished,' we say in wonder and despair at the work we have wrought, and then we see clearly the true nature of the mushroom cloud: it is humanity's own brain going up in ashes and smoke.

Of course it will happen someday. Of course it will. In the winter of our discontent.

To discover origins we must go back and rediscover our depths. Therefore to Brazil, eventually Antarctica. Before and beneath Europe was Brazil, upon whose dire marshes the cities and castles and dukedoms were built. And beneath Brazil is the polar wonderland. And is there anyone alive who has proven, beyond all reasonable doubt, that the poles indeed are not open, that the oceans do not indeed flow into and out of them?

A logical preview of factors and conditions is imperative. The embryological devolution dynamic may be stated thus:

1. Proposition One: In the beginning all things are one. God is Genius, a circle lacking radius or diameter, an ovum that is neither male nor female, yet both. God is pure wonder and longing without end, the boundless passion of the soul for knowledge and being.
2. Proposition Two: Therefore is God dis-eased. Pure wonder and longing infinitely, endlessly, strive to overreach their source. (It is like a lonely man, alone on a street at night, who watches his shadow grow as he walks away from a streetlight.)
3. Proposition Three: Therefore does rebellion in the Heavenly Kingdom occur. As wonder and longing strain the soul, the heart of the Heavenly Kingdom eventually breaks.
4. Proposition Four: Mankind is born.

Evelyn stirred under Holmay's arm, then with a heavy sigh threw her arm over her pillow and turned away from him. Seeing that her eyes were closed, her face

face radiating a warm complacency, he leaned in closer to her. The power of words. They did not need to make sense, did not need to pull the mind toward some conclusion carefully constructed for its unavoidability. It was enough for them to sing a strange lullaby, enough for them simply to babble on.

Billy was not back, but he was not entirely gone.

He saw himself—a father on a bed next to his daughter, the beast and the sleeping beauty—and suddenly glanced over his shoulder to make sure the neighbors could not see into the room. With his left hand he drew the shade all the way down just to be sure, then he lay quietly next to her until he was sure she was asleep. He was careful not to make noise as he got up, covering her shoulder with the blanket, then kissing her lightly on the cheek. He wondered about what dream she was wandering in, certain that the little girl had Billy in her dream. And as he tiptoed out of her room he was certain too that Billy still had her in his.

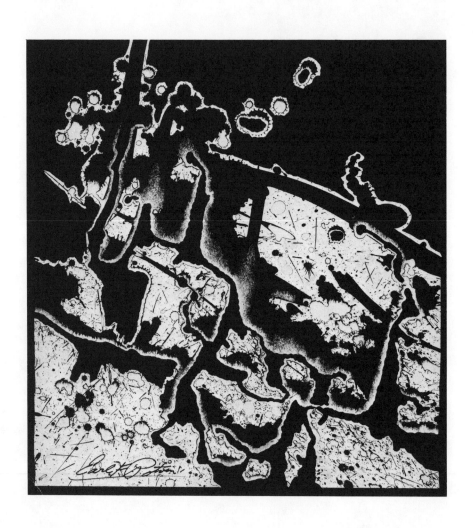

Twenty-three

HE PULLED THE shades down and crawled into bed. On the table next to him Billy's Book waited. Proposition Four. Mankind had just been born. Out of God, genius, ovum, perfect circle longing beyond itself and therefore diseased. Dis-eased. Billy had broken the word apart, given it new sense. If God was by nature diseased, He was not simply and crudely deformed, a hump-backed white monster doling out an incomprehensible mix of love and hate on souls arbitrarily crossing His path. God too was a troubled pathetic soul, afflicted by no more than a cosmic neurotic discomfiture while groping toward food, shelter, love. And this God, Billy's God, was of course no more than an invention of Billy's mind, a mind dis-eased rather than hopelessly deformed.

Merely diseased. For there were moments of clear, simple level-headedness: "Our minds nag us to know. . . .We have all left our beds in the middle of the night, sat alone looking out the window, walked alone in empty city streets." And steady-ing this melancholia, giving it a firm footing in normality, was the wholesome American citizen-soldier, the one who would go to his grave insisting on the right to bear arms.

Billy was crazy: that was a conclusion he could not take back. It was clear that Billy would never entirely fit in, would be doomed to wander on the outskirts of normal society, in the dim region of poets, artists, prophets, outcasts. There was a Billy in every school, perhaps one in every classroom. And at every party,

143

where people gathered to display their foolishness, a Billy was present too, sulking in a corner, brooding, analyzing, dreaming. There were thousands of Billys, more and more of them without a place to stay, many of them youths but some grown old in their solitudes, shooting strange glances at ordinary people passing by. Billy was in the parks, the elevators, the movie theaters, barrooms, churches, and factories. He was walking the streets.

Holmay turned the word "mad" over in his mind again. Angry, infuriated, not only touched but overwhelmed by incoherent fury. Therefore dangerous. The madman in the tower sniping at people walking by. The madman who dresses in military fatigues, walks into a hamburger joint with a semi-automatic and shoots everyone in sight. Billy, the boy who owns three guns and insists on the right of every citizen to bear arms.

Or Billy the mad artist. Theseus wrestling with his Minotaur. Saint Teresa making love to God. Dante wandering in his circles of hell. Blake's imagination blazing like the fire in his tiger's eyes. Shelley floating in the poetic delirium of his drunken boats. Poe, unable to rid himself of Pym's absurd trip to the bottom of the world, crying out Reynolds's name hour after hour as he lay dying in his bed. Melville, Ahab to his own Ishmael. Ambrose Bierce. Hart Crane. Delmore Schwartz. Jack Kerouac. Allen Ginsberg. Theodore Roethke. John Berryman.

Mad writers all.

And Billy. A young man, still a boy. His heart full of passionate desire, his mind on fire, his fingers compelled to push the pen shaping the barbaric yawp within his soul into words on a white sheet of paper. And he, Matthew Holmay, the boy's master-teacher, his Michelangelo, introducing him to his task, unveiling a huge marble block to the boy and instructing him: Here it is, life. Have at it, boy. Chip away at it until things take shape in it, until the prisoner, man, agonizing inside of it, is liberated from the earth, his body, the stone itself. Follow my instruction and the passionate genius within your own soul. Now and then I will take your hand, the one with the chisel in it, and I will guide it over the rough spots on the rock. I will help see you through the ordeal of the creative act of living your life.

On the table next to Billy's manuscript was the red pen he always kept there for marking up freshman themes. Without thinking he put it in his hand as he picked up the remaining pages of Billy's Book.

> We might best begin this phase and aspect by consideration of the shape of the world mankind is born in.

Holmay lifted his pen, compulsively prepared to draw blood, strike out the word "aspect" and scrawl the word "awkward" in the margin. He caught himself in time, gazed a moment at the pen as if it were an object with a mind of its own, and put it back on the table. Suddenly at ease, he read on:

Emanation One: The first emanation of the dis-ease of God is the separation of heaven and earth. Our spiritual place (for now) is characterized by mass, weight, and things like that, and as we move away from earth into the atmosphere these things dissipate into purer and rarer substances. To call space a vacuum is wrong. Space is spirit, with planets and their moons and all the stars. Heaven, pure heaven, is beyond all them.

Emanation Two: There are, consequently, two Kingdoms of Force, the Evil and the Good. These are Repulsion and Attraction and are called (merely ethnocentrically) Satan and God. Satan or Evil is that which pulls away from, draws away from or alienates from. It is hate. That which is Good (and God) is that which unites, ties together, binds, make things one again. It is Love. Evil and Good wage perpetual war on the earth, where God's dis-ease is furthest afield from its source.

Emanation Three: Predicated is separation between heaven and earth and the forces of Evil and Good. The corollary to predicate is the division between body and soul. 'I think, therefore I am,' says it all, as we behold man, the centipede, pondering the eternal question of what leg he first moves. Do we not wonder why man is so often paralyzed by thought? The body is of earth and clay. It is Repulsion, denying the free expression of love to the soul. This is the source of all the suffering in the world.

Emanation Four: The human mind serves both body and soul. Therefore is it afflicted by the conflict between the two Kingdoms of Force. In it we find things that attract and repel (e.g. the serpent and the dove), and the battle rages from morning all night. "Perchance to dream. There's the rub." For how can we know ourselves but by our instruments? We know only that small-minded people are full of hate, for that is the force of Repulsion hardening and closing them. We know too that the mind reaching for God is expanding its love almost to a breaking point.

Holmay glanced ahead at the pages still unread. No emanation five, thank God. He had a sudden urge to call Frances. Dr. Holmay, Doctor of Philosophy, was finding his faculties failing him. He did not know what to make of Billy's words, at once so full of nonsense and faintly familiar sense. He wanted a second opinion.

It was nine twenty-two. Too early and too late. Wouldn't Frances be delighted to come over to see Billy's Book? Loneliness could make all nights seem young. And if he called her at this hour, would she want to talk about other things? Annette George. The name suddenly came to him, along with the flash of her auburn hair. If he knew Annette's number. He would ask her to come over, show her Billy's words, ask Annette what she thought. Frances had gained more weight, it seemed, and it wasn't his fault. There were some things for which he was not responsible. Maybe Annette's opinion would be better, more simple and straight. Honest. And he loved the sound of Annette George's name. Her name exactly right. He waited for a car on the street to turn the corner and disappear, the room to be perfectly silent and still. Into the silence he whispered Annette George's name.

Then he began reading the final few pages of Billy's Book:

The emanations of God are the web in which the spider, man, is caught. But there are windows, open doors, portals glorious in space and time. A clear delineation of alternative projections is not precluded in this introductory discourse. We pick up the telephone and a man's voice comes through as clear as real words. We turn on the radio and with a turn of the dial we may have words, music or the news of the world. We wonder how words spoken hundreds, thousands of miles away can enter wires and wander the skies, twisted and turned by clouds, only to find us as we stand in front of the radio. And it doesn't end there. Now we stand before the TV by the millions, transfixed.

There are, therefore, spaces between the emanations through which we may escape. The Deity is an inflection, innuendo, or glimpse. We need but listen to the sounds at night. To stronger souls are available the visions and voices of poets and prophets.

Does the soul live on after death? Listen to the voice of a beloved one long passed away.

Are there spirits living on other worlds? Look into the sky at night.

Therefore, the words of the strong-souled are also beyond dispute. There is something pulling us away, evermore hinting that we are walking wonderlands full of mind, soul, eternity, space, time, truth, love and God. Why let Repulsion dominate? We look into space and time, seeing and feeling that the seasons revolve around a pause in the infinite Now toward which galaxies gravitate. What can we do? We enter the stream, give ourselves up to it while it carries us away. It makes the mind spin and confuses me. I listen for the sound of it and hear it rushing like a cataract below, the strong sea surge. A voice says, "Her love is honest and pure. She is the virgin of the entire world." Another cautions me: "She too is God and therefore she is disease." I see bright green and red and white, the swirl of a dance at carnival time. There all humanity comes together in a new wild land, everyone with everyone else in the streets. There we find the Negro and white and brown and all religions are one. A brother in heaven revealed this to me. We are a reed adrift on the river of life, and what is the greatest river in the world? How unexplored, how ageless and yet young, untouched! When we open the window we hear the river calling us out. Amazon. Brazil. Can there be any mistaking of its metaphysical and historical import? Brazil. The real Brave New World, cradle of poetry and spiritual technology. I heard a voice crying in the wilderness. Am I not bound to repair myself thither?

Is it possible that an imagined thing has no sort of reality at all? If not, what gave rise to the imagined thing?

Therefore do I heed the call. And beyond Brazil far to the south I see the vast region of white, the endless expanse of frozen salt sea milk, a current I feel in my bones. No one has explored deep below the surface of things.

Therefore one day onward to Antarctica too.

Will you be left behind?

Twenty-four

OUT OF SIGHT, out of mind. No word, no call, for nine weeks. Billy's Book, shoved to the far side of the nightstand, an envelope stained with the imprint of coffee cups, lost entirely under a stack of freshman themes. Freshman themes welcome for the first time in years, proof that the normal still amounted to something in the world. Welcome the way soldiers come home to no sound of artillery in their ears, then walk in the streets of their towns, happy enough to work in their garages and factories, eat a hamburger in the corner joint, pay their bills and taxes again. A career—fifteen years worth of freshman themes, the vast majority nonlinear, inarticulate, incoherent and dull. Proof of the human brain's incapacities, perhaps of its natural, if not total, depravity. As Billy's absence lengthened itself out like an evening sky dimming in the west, freshman themes, so full of ordinary human nature, were peace.

Even Hoffstein was peace. His ponderous body, carrying new dignity through the corridors of Laurel Hall, he walking with gravity, looking down as if lost in ancient thought, a man suddenly indifferent to the politics of promotion and tenure. Those who at one time had gathered in groups to snicker at him discussing football instead, their indifference their way of saying they had resigned themselves to living with him.

Then on a Tuesday, in the middle of Billy's silence, Hoffstein entered Holmay's office and closed the door. "They're not talking about me in the halls any more," he said. "Do you think they're up to anything?"

"Like what?"

"Do you think they're scheming of some way to get at my job?"

"Why would they want to do that? And how could they, even if they wanted to?"

"I don't know, I don't know. But they might think of a way. They can get you if they want, you know. There's always some way."

"But why would anyone want to *get* you?"

"I don't know. Maybe because they're jealous. Nobody else here, you know, has published a book." He leaned in close. "Maybe it's political and religious grounds. You know what I mean? And maybe it's because they don't like what my book has to say."

"I haven't heard anything like that."

"So I'm going to write another book."

"I figured that," Holmay said. "You seem to be lost in thought these days."

Hoffstein twisted his blush into a frown. "Yes, it certainly appears that way."

"It seems that your book can call forth only one possible response."

"What's that?" Hoffstein said nervously.

"Another book, what else?"

"And so I am—writing one in my mind. There's much ground yet to be broken there. Cybernetics and poetry, you know, have barely begun touching each other in a significant way. There is really only my book so far—if you don't mind my saying so. Someone needs to bring these two worlds together."

"Your book shows how the computer illuminates the meaning of poetry," said Holmay, the edge of his irony smooth, "so maybe in your next one you can show how poetry can make sense of the computer."

"No, actually I wasn't thinking of that. Actually I was thinking of something else."

"You going to let me in on it?"

"I want to write a novel—a spiritual autobiography. Are you familiar with that sort of thing?"

"Oh yes, it's the very best sort of book."

"Naturally," Hoffstein said as he got up to leave.

Later Holmay couldn't help asking Lance about Hoffstein's class. "Are you enjoying it—the poetry class?"

"Yup," Lance said. "It's really interesting. He really has interesting things to say."

"Like what?"

"He makes us look inside words and find all the hidden meanings there. I'm just amazed at all the hidden meanings he finds. That's stuff I just couldn't get on my own. It would just be too hard."

"Maybe it's a good thing," Holmay said, "that he's there to explain."

"But he doesn't explain everything. He talks a lot about the Germans and Jews. It's really interesting stuff."

Interesting stuff. Poetry and computers—the secret significance of orbicular vowels. Germans and Jews—the maddest episode in the history of mankind.

148

Interesting stuff, all so small and big. Students wide-eyed with wonder. What more could a teacher ask for? What more could a teacher do than keep his students wide-eyed with wonder?

Billy. Wide-eyed with wonder.

"Hoffstein's the best teacher I ever had," Lance said, "except maybe you."

Holmay escaped. "That Annette girl, the one I used to see you with."

"Annie George?"

"Yes, is she still around?"

"She's taking classes."

"She's very pretty, isn't she?"

"Yes," he said, turning away. "I haven't been seeing her lately. The chemistry wasn't right."

The chemistry again. Everywhere the chemistry—atoms, molecules floating, within the space defined by the table, like dense particles of dust. The solar system itself—a sort of atom, one particle in a universe made up of the endless dust of stars? The brain, the human mind? How many electrons, neutrons, swirling in there? What was the molecular configuration of a human thought? What was added to or subtracted from a thought gone wrong, an evil thought? What did one have to eat or fail to eat to make the thought a virtuous one? What about the time of day or year, humidity, room temperature, barometric pressure? Pressure. Alias anxiety, stress. The force resulting when a material is strained, maybe small and strong enough to tear the human spirit apart. Repulsion, an implosion of sorts. A headache, sore shoulders and back, jittery hands, a stomach tied in knots. A crisis triggered by pressure a hair too intense.

He was certain the phone would ring that night. Midnight passed as the premonition approached, a thin silver streak like an impulse carried by electric wires. Billy's voice already riding on that streak, though not a word had been spoken yet, nothing accomplished other than a decision, an act of will, made by Billy to get through to him, the premonition proving itself to be the thin leading edge of a fact accomplishing itself. At two-thirty in the middle of the night Holmay was awake, waiting for the phone to ring.

"I'm in Shenandoah," Billy said.

"What state is that in?"

"It's a state of mind. It's in the heartland of America, the center of the universe."

"Iowa?"

"Iowa."

"I'm in a Country Kitchen. It's a restaurant, and it's snowing outside. That's where I am. That's what I wanted to talk to you about."

"Where have you been?"

The silence was long and void. "I've been to the border, but now I'm halfway back."

"Are you coming back here?"

"I've been to the moon. Have you ever been to Oklahoma? I spent a night in Oklahoma. The place where I slept—the soil was rocky and dry. And it was red.

I began shivering and couldn't stop. It was cold, oh so cold, and then I felt light and the coldness went away. Did you know that the gravity of the moon is only one-sixth that of the earth? I was floating and then I saw myself. I looked down and saw myself asleep on the floor of a crater. It was incredible, because there I was floating with nothing to hold me up. Then I wasn't cold any more and I fell asleep."

"Why were you in Oklahoma, Billy?"

"On my way to Brazil."

"Why did you turn back?"

"They were waiting for me at the border. It was the truck driver, the one who picked me up in Texas. He was laughing all the time. He thought I didn't know he was laughing at me. Now I know he was the one who called the border patrol and told them I was on my way to Brazil. I got to Brownsville, Texas, at three in the morning and I was tired because I had to keep an eye out for him all the way. No sleep for three nights. Did you know that? So when I showed up at the border they knew it was me. They asked me where I was going, as if they didn't know."

"What did you tell them?"

"I told them I was going to Brazil."

"But did you tell them why you wanted to go to Brazil?"

"I told them. I told them. I explained that the Spiritualist Church in Brazil was growing faster than any church in the world. It was waiting for its prophet to come. I told them I wasn't just a tourist. I had a reason for going to Brazil."

"Then what?"

"They asked me how much money I had. Can you imagine that? Materialism on guard at the gates."

"Did you have a passport, Billy, a visa?"

"You and I know, Dr. Holmay, that the mind is the only passport required of anyone."

"So they wouldn't let you cross the border into Mexico?"

Billy fell silent before speaking again. "They put me in jail, Dr. Holmay. They took everything away from me but my twenty dollars before they let me go again. And they think I don't know it was the truck driver who took everything away from me. The policeman was the truck driver. They can't fool me. They thought they could fool me by changing the color of his hair and eyes."

"So you hitchhiked back?"

"I've been in this town for three days. This is the second night I've come here to the Country Kitchen."

Billy fell into a silence again.

"Why do you go there, Billy?"

"Tell me you don't know," Billy said sarcastically. "It's on the highway, isn't it?"

"I don't know."

"It's where the truck drivers stop. And right now, sitting at the counter are two policemen. They don't know I'm watching them right now. They don't know I'm aware of what they're doing."

"What are they doing?"

"They're looking for me."

"Why?"

"Because I know."

"What do you know?"

"They're eating ribs—both of them. They're laughing and talking while they're eating, as if there's nothing wrong in the world and nobody knows."

"What's wrong, Billy?"

"I don't have to explain to you, do I? Haven't you ever been to Iowa? There's pig farms everywhere, but they never let the pigs out. You can go for miles and miles and never see the pigs. Do you know why? Certainly you know why Jews never eat pork."

"I don't understand."

Billy whispered the words. "Those two policemen at the counter are not eating pork. That is human flesh and bones they're feasting on. And they're looking for me. I've got to get out of here."

The dial tone make it clear that Billy was gone. As soon as he put the receiver down, Holmay went downstairs to lock the doors.

The next day he waited for Evelyn at school and escorted her home. "I don't see why you have to walk me all the way home," she complained. "I'm not a baby and nobody else has a father waiting after school."

Billy's letter was waiting in the mailbox when they got home. The postmark was clear this time: Shenandoah, Iowa. The letter had been mailed two days before.

Dear Dr. Holmay:

Once you asked your class what peace was really like. I arrived here in Shenandoah (Iowa) two days ago. I had just had a bad experience hitchhiking in Texas. I was depressed and a little ashamed, but it was a beautiful evening when I arrived, the sun setting in a beautiful sky, a huge silvery moon rising through the branches of a maple tree standing alone in the field, the town just sitting there solitary in the snow. The wonder of it all! I felt privileged to be alive. And all I could do was stand apart and marvel at it.

I had only $4.61 and no place to stay. I hadn't shaved in six days and all I had was an old overcoat. One of the Texas truckers had driven off with my suitcase—and in there I had the second chapter of my book. So I had nothing going for me.

It must have been near midnight when the good feeling came over me. I was alone on a bench in the park, and the night, I knew, would be long and cold. Still I wasn't worried or afraid. The trees were calm and there was a gentle snow. Everything was beautiful.

I can't describe the feeling exactly to you. I'd had it before—once especially when I was swimming alone in a lake far from the shore, and I was afraid suddenly that I would never make it back. But then a voice in me said don't worry, what is there to fear, give yourself up to the water and she will take care of you. So I gave myself up, turned over on my back and with slow regular strokes made my way to the shore.

That was exactly the feeling I had in the park. The feeling lifted me up off the park bench and I started floating through the streets of the town. There were lights on in most of the houses and I said to myself, That is good, everyone's happy here, and where the lights are out the people are asleep in their own beds with somebody nearby. There are hundreds of people in this town—mothers, husbands, babies, teenagers, carpenters, lawyers, waitresses and people with no jobs at all. They get by. Some of them never read a good serious book, but they go to church and sing and they do other things.

I thought, this would be the way to be. Shenandoah would be the place for me. Not too big, not too small. I could get a job here, a room, maybe a small apartment, and neighbors after a while. I would say hello like everyone else, and maybe, maybe I would meet someone special here. I think you would like it here but I know you're well settled with your job, your house and Evelyn (oh do give her a hug for me!). But I could see myself spending the rest of my life here.

What do you think? Don't be surprised if I write to you again. And thanks. As I sit here writing this, a half-dozen people walked by and looked at me. I was from out of town but they all smiled when I said hello. No one bothers me here. This is peace and quiet here. Is that too much for one person to ask for in life?

> *Deeply I miss you and Evelyn.*
> *Love,*
> *Billy*

Twenty-five

THREE DAYS LATER Lance showed up with a diamond stud in his nose.

"Hey, what's that?" Evelyn asked.

"Do you like it?"

"Sure do. Where'd you get it?"

"From a friend."

"It looks pretty silly on you," Holmay said.

"Oh Dad!"

"What I mean," Holmay went on, "is that it doesn't seem like you. It seems out of character."

"Oh I'm a character," Lance said, opening into a smile. "Everyone says I'm quite a character."

"It's nice, Dad. It's different."

"Are you wearing it for a particular reason?"

"Reason? I just wanted to try something new, get out of my rut."

"Did you get your ears pierced too, Lance?" Evelyn asked.

"Yup."

"Did it hurt?"

"A little bit. But you know what they say: No pain, no gain. Say, Dr. Holmay, why don't you get one too? Add a little excitement to your life. Try something new. You know, get out of your rut."

"Yes, Dad, why don't you? That would be really funny, Dad."

He took Lance's words with him to his favorite chair, turning them over in his mind as he passed his eyes over the pages of a book. Add a little excitement to your life. Try something new. Get out of your rut.

Upstairs Evelyn had turned the radio up too loud. Holmay threw his book aside and stormed up to her room.

"Turn it down!" he yelled. "How many times do I have to tell you to turn it down?"

"Why do I have to turn it down? You play your music as loud as you want."

"Because I listen to real music, that's why."

"Mine's music," she replied. "It's my music. Maybe you should try listening to it just once."

"That's not music, it's junk. So you keep it turned down low. Besides, it's getting late. I want you to get ready for bed."

"I don't want to go to bed."

"I'll let you read until you fall asleep."

"I don't want to read. I want to listen to my music."

"You brush your teeth and get ready for bed," he said, pointing a finger at her.

He returned to his chair and opened his book, an anger searing its way into his gut. What nerve. Lance accusing him of being in a rut. And Evelyn siding with him, turning her music up, slapping him in the face with it.

He stared at the ceiling until Evelyn closed the door to her room, then he tossed the book to one side again and slowly made his way up the stairs. He paused to listen outside her door. Hearing nothing, he knocked.

"Evelyn," he said softly.

No response.

"Evelyn?"

No response.

He opened the door and looked in. She was curled to one side of her bed, her pillow over her head.

"Do you want me to read to you?"

No response.

"Do you want me to read?"

"No," she said turning toward him. "I don't like books any more. That's all you ever do is read to me. We never go anywhere different or new. We never do anything. Sometimes I wish I was living with Mom."

"I don't just read to you."

"What else do you do?"

"I take care of you."

"Oh thrill. Mom would do that. Or Billy. I could go live with Billy in Brazil. He would take care of me. All you ever want to do is read."

"So you don't want me to read?"

"No."

He returned to his chair and flicked off the light, staring into the darkness.

Maybe they were right, both Lance and Evelyn. Maybe he was in a rut, had grown dull, had been dull for many years. Sane or insane, Billy deserved credit for venturing. Billy did not borrow his dreams. He invented them, trying to make them real. And Billy, like a true adventurer, was risking everything.

What, Holmay asked himself, have I ever risked? When it comes to risk I'm one of the elect chosen to spend my days on high level ground immune from tidal waves that wash entire Oriental nations away. And I can afford to pity those, Californians all, dancing on a fault destined to shudder under a weight of foolishness so heavy that all of them, one bluest day, will be buried alive. Nor will it be likely that the body politic in which I live so resentfully will ever unbalance the terror holding the world in its indelicate grip. And the odds aren't good that I will suffer any singular fate. No meteorite will single out my skull for any particular doom, and, having no firm control over events, I will inspire no assassin to target me. My enemies are all friends armed with words too dull to kill. Besides, I am earning my fate, for I believe in air bags, and I religiously fasten my safety belt, and I always stop when asked merely to yield, and, wingless, I never try to fly. Therefore I will be privileged to suffer no special wounds, God's blessings, and will take my place among the ordinary, perhaps concluding my life as just another drowsy cancerous soul laid to rest when a finalist cell has finished in its marathon run through my flesh.

No pain, no gain.

He could try putting a diamond stud in his nose. Evelyn would approve.

He could ask Frances Drummond to marry him. Maybe Evelyn would approve.

Then he could ask Billy to move into the house, for Evelyn would approve.

There was a commandment inscribed somewhere in stone: He, divorced, should do only what Evelyn approved.

He went to the window and looked out at the streetlight under which Billy had stood. No Billy there, nobody anywhere in sight. Billy was faraway, in Iowa, a state of mind, searching in some Shenandoah for the peace that passeth understanding, the chance to be like everyone else, anonymous and dull, left alone at least one hour per day to enjoy the peace that was searing a hole in his mentor's gut.

The conclusion was inescapable. Billy was in retreat. He had tried his wings and failed, and the quiet anonymity he sought in Shenandoah was the fallback position of the weak. Gathering his strength, Billy would relive or reinvent his crazy dreams. Then he would be off again—to Brazil, Antarctica, who knows where. Billy knew that you can't go home again. Billy had dreams. Crazy Billy had the courage to be.

Holmay put his book down and went to the front door. Why did he keep forgetting to lock the door? He turned the deadbolt and checked to see if it was properly set. When he returned to his chair he swept his book to the floor.

Too many books. Too many dreams. Hoffstein had a book and Frances Drummond, childless, was having a book. And Billy was working on a book, a fantastic romance about a spiritual pilgrimage. Anybody could write a book and though the libraries were filling up Holmay also had to write a book. What would it come to, this book? Frances Drummond had figured it out for him: "The promotion will be worth $3150 the first year and $4730 the next. You figure out what it comes to over ten years, plus interest. And you've got twenty years before you retire."

Twenty more years of teaching people how to read.

All those books and no credible dream of his own. Did he for one minute believe that in writing a book he would be lifting a finger to make the world a better, safer, more humane place? And if he did lift a finger would it amount to anything more than a polite protest against overwhelming political wrongs? The book would merely whisper its inquietude into a few minds.

Upstairs Evelyn was by now sound asleep, her dreams full of the inquietudes he had conveyed to her through his stories each night. How well had the words in those stories armed her to deal with the world? The insane music on the radio already had silenced the story for this night, was beginning to win her over to its noisy senselessness.

He saw himself standing in front of his class and heard the words come forth: You have to love books. You'll fall in love with them if they're good and you really know how to read.

Why, the skeptical faces asked, What good would that do?

Because that's how we learn right from wrong. They lead to proper action, that's why.

Oh, the faces said, confused but half-convinced.

It was then, when he saw them half-convinced, that he could imagine caring about them.

A good teacher loves his students.

All of them? Billy said, looking up.

No, just a few. The ones that are willing to live and learn.

Annette.

Holmay got up from his chair and went to the window again.

Annette had been willing to live and learn, and he had turned her out. Could he have learned something from her? No, no, he had already made that mistake before, had had his little fling with a seventeen-year-old. What could they talk about, what would they learn? And the risk, the risk, particularly now when his promotion was up for grabs. It would be insane.

Yes, insane.

Annette was maybe not as clever, imaginative, or even as good with words as Evelyn. So he should sleep with Frances Drummond instead, let her satisfy his mind in every way. Or perhaps continue to carry on his little romance with Evelyn, contenting himself with telling bedtime stories until some sensible Billy came along for her.

He went to the door and checked the deadbolt once again. Yes, he was locked in, all right. The little girl upstairs had locked him in from the moment her mother had driven away from the house. And now, suddenly, he wanted out. He wanted action, a little insanity.

He unlocked the door and opened it. The night air, cold and sharp, flowed in.
Annette. Why not?

But you can't just leave. Evelyn is asleep in her room and heaven only knows when Lance will get home tonight. You can't just leave her alone in the house.

I refuse to be locked in. Why not just go?

Insanity.

Then at least close the door, lock her safely in.

"Ah Billy, my boy, you've taught me something, you have."

He wandered out to the sidewalk, leaving the door unlocked.

Twenty-six

INSANE, YES, and calculating every move.

First he would have to find out where she lived, her dormitory room, then find a way to get her out of it. And he did not have much time.

He went straight to his office, his hands shaking as he thumbed through the student directory. Annette George. The name—feminine but firm, and regal like the beauty that required him to keep his distance from her. But not tonight if he had anything to do with it, if he could get close enough to get one hand on her.

She lived on the third floor of Dausman Hall. Room 212. Phone 5234.

He looked up and down the darkened corridors to make sure no one was burning midnight oil, then closed the office door and picked up the phone. He could not keep his hand from shaking as he began to dial.

And if she said yes, she would like to see him tonight, where would they go? For a walk down some secluded street where suddenly, up against some tree, he would begin easing his hands inside her coat. Or for a little drive out of town, somewhere at the end of some lane, the two of them falling into the car seat without saying a word, the windows frosting over in the cold. But he wanted her naked, spread out on a bed, or better yet on some floor, the lights on, him looking down at her face and eyes. "Then why don't we go to your place?" she would ask, and he would say no, no, we can't go there, I couldn't do that. Then why not here, right here in the office itself? Right here on the floor next to your desk, with all the books on the shelves looking down on us. Here where it's never been done before, where we could laugh at our moans and nakedness and at the professors in general, the Drummonds and Hoffsteins, who never would be able to guess what had been done under their noses in their sacred hall. "Why not in your office?" she would ask, and he, vaguely aware of the symbolic victories each could achieve naked on the floor next to his desk, would agree, "Yes, why not?"

He held his breath as her phone rang.

"Yes?" said a lively voice on the other end.

"Annette?"

"Do I sound like Annette?"

He did not respond.

"You want to talk to Annette?"

"Yes."

"Annette," said the voice sarcastically as it walked away from the phone, "somebody *wants* you."

"Who is it?"

"Some *man*."

He heard her approach.

"Hello."

"Annette?"

"Yes, who is this?"

"A secret admirer."

"Oh?" she said coyly. "Do I know you?"

"Yes."

"Well then, there's no secret, is there?"

"I'd like to see you tonight."

"Who is this?"

"A secret admirer."

"Why do you want to see me?"

"Oh, you know, the usual sort of thing. You might say I'd like to make something up to you."

"Like what?"

"Something I owe you."

"Then why don't you leave it at the desk downstairs?"

"I can't do that."

"Then come up to my room and leave it here."

"I prefer not to."

"What do you want to do, Mr. Secret Admirer?"

"I want you to meet me somewhere tonight."

"Where?"

"Anywhere."

"I don't meet strange boys just anywhere."

"You name the place."

She said nothing, but he could hear laughter in the background.

"Well, Mr. Secret, are you handsome, intelligent, and rich?"

"You'll just have to see for yourself."

"What makes you think I'd be interested in you?"

"You were...once...when I was...preoccupied with someone else."

"Oh?"

"You wanted me."

"Well maybe I've developed my tastes since then."

"Then maybe you'll want me more."

"Or not at all."

He said nothing, letting a silence drag on.

"Well, it just so happens that I am going out tonight," she said.

"Where should I meet you?"

"The Stein."

"That's the bar?"

"Right on, Mr. Secret. If you want to see me you just start looking there about eleven o'clock."

"Fine."

"How will I know you?"

"You'll know me as soon as I walk in the door."

"Ha!" she said, "I think I already know who you are."

"Who am I then?"

"You'll know when I walk up to you tonight."

Would she dare lie to him, send him on a wild-goose chase, leave him stranded in some raucous downtown bar known as the most popular hangout for the student crowd? Would she try to humiliate him?

He hurried down the stairs of Laurel Hall. Her dormitory was halfway across campus, a quarter of a mile, and already it was twelve after ten. And it was cold, beginning to snow. He began running across the lawn, his heart racing as he passed behind the library.

"Hi, Dr. Holmay," said a girl walking hand-in-hand with her boyfriend. "You in a hurry tonight?"

He waved, not able to see her face, and slowed to a walk. As Dausman Hall came into view on his left the moon, small and high in the sky, looked down on him from behind the branches of an elm. He kept to the sidewalk surrounding the dormitory, his eyes zeroing in on the second-floor windows.

So many windows, six levels in all. Some entirely blank, the lights turned off, some with shades drawn. He saw a movement in a third-floor window to his right, a form walking to the center of the room, glancing toward the window, then disappearing from view. On the fifth floor someone turned off a light.

Room 212. How would he find her room?

He circled to the other side of the dormitory, making his way between cars in the parking lot. In four of the second-floor rooms the shades had not been drawn. He paused before each one and strained to see in, but he saw no movement in any of them. He circled back to the other side. Room 212. Eighteen windows on each floor. He counted twice to be sure, rubbing his hands to get them warm. Seven windows with the shades not drawn. Then he counted the windows from left to right. One to twelve.

Yes, he had it now. Annette's room. 212. Lit up, the shade not drawn. He circled to his right, retreating to the shadows of the trees. Someone walked past the window, a blond-haired girl he did not recognize. She stood partially out of view, talking to someone else. Not bad, Holmay thought, though a bit on the heavy side.

On his right two forms emerged from the dorm. As they passed under a streetlight he saw that neither was Annette. In the window the blond-haired girl came into view again, adjusting her hair, laughing, pointing her finger at someone else, laughing again. He circled to his left toward a thick tree. From behind it he could see her—Annette, facing a mirror, brushing her hair in long even strokes.

"Yes," he whispered to himself, "you brush your hair, and then later tonight when you return to your room it'll be all undone, wild, and you won't give a damn."

She came to the window, still brushing her hair, and looked down to her left as a group of three girls emerged from the entrance of the dorm.

Holmay shrank behind the oak, not taking his eyes from Annette who undid the two top buttons on her blouse and drew down the shade.

He looked at his watch. 10:37. It would take her another five minutes to change clothes and that would leave her only eighteen minutes to walk downtown. She would never get there on time. In the window the shadows were dim, any sign of Annette lost in them. Suddenly he was infuriated at her. Why was she playing with him? Why unbutton her blouse and then draw the shade? Did she think she could just toy with him, lure him on, then keep him waiting forever under a tree? Did she think she could be as late as she wanted any time? There were some things he wouldn't stand for. He pulled her in close, and when she whimpered he tightened his grip. Now you just listen to me, you little brat, why don't you just grow up?

Another couple walked out the front entrance of the dorm, then suddenly the light in Room 212 went out.

He kept as close to the trees as possible, searching for a spot from which to get a better view of the dorm, finding himself under a streetlight, not knowing which way to turn. He could hide behind parked cars or the bushes between two houses across from the dorm. He ducked behind a car just as Annette and her friend emerged.

He held his breath, trying to hear their talk. She laughed, a loud sassy laugh, the kind of laughter he hated in the young. Her friend the blond walked without taking her eyes off the sidewalk at her feet. Damn her, he said, damn the blond one to hell. Damn them for traveling in packs. If Annette had been alone, he could appear at the sidewalk at the end of the block. She would walk straight up to him and without saying a word take hold of his hand and lead him away.

They walked past his hiding place. He let them go, let them cross the street before coming out from behind the bushes, his eyes searching for another place to hide. He stood still, watching them diminish before he ducked behind a fence from where he could keep them in view. His mind raced ahead. They had to cross High and then Jackson streets before getting to the edge of downtown. From there they would turn right on Brighton Street before getting to The Stein.

Would she dare double-cross me, he asked himself, go somewhere else?

He ran between two houses and followed the alley to High. From behind a garage he heard Annette's voice, then stepped back into the shadows for a car to pass. He did not move until he was sure the girls were across the street. Then he raced on ahead, cutting through two yards behind Brighton Street. At the end of an alley was a used car lot. From there he would be able to see them walk into or past The Stein.

He looked at his watch. 10:57. Damn her. More than anything she needed a lesson or two.

He approached the used car lot and found a dark place next to a fence. In front of him a row of cars showed chrome smiles, their headlights like empty eyes, their grilles arrogant sneers. On the windshield of a big Buick the words "ONE OWNER, LOW MILEAGE, GREAT BUY" were written in yellow paint. Used cars everywhere. One-owner, two-owner deals. All of them great deals, used. Divorced.

Annette would know. They had already seen each other on the kitchen floor, and then later she came to his room asking for it. And when he called she seemed willing enough to play along. Why did she play with the buttons on her blouse? All these little things had their obvious meanings, like words in a book. So she would only be a few minutes late. He would walk into the bar a few minutes after her, and without looking his way she would signal with her eyes to meet him outside.

Annette too was a used car. She too had been around the block more than once.

She and her blond-haired friend appeared at the corner of Brighton Street. Four minutes after eleven. Together they walked to the door of The Stein where An- nette, glancing over her shoulder at the used car lot, tossed her hair before entering.

✳ ✳ ✳

He looked at himself as he stood at the door. Gray cotton slacks. Light blue oxford shirt. Blue wool parka. He ran his fingers through his hair, feeling the percussive pulse of music reverberating through the door.

As he stepped inside he braced himself against the blast of sound overwhelm- ing the quiet in the darkness outside. Bewildered, he stood still, his impulse to leave checked by the fascination of the chaos all around. Quickly he scanned the room for a sign of Annette. On a small platform people were dancing in their strange free-style way, their gyrations flickering and fragmented by pulsing lights.

To the left of the platform stood a boy in a black jacket and tight pants, his shoulders hunched, a cigarette dangling from his lips, his face impassive as he glanced at the dials of the amplifier on the table next to him. The music man, the one in charge of the sounds, the one turning the volume up or down for no good reason at all. The bar was to the right of the platform, high stools on each side, people bent over their drinks. And hovering over the scene was a bluish smoke made lurid by the flashing lights.

"Hey Doc, you coming in?" a boy shouted at him from his left.

"All right!" said another voice. "The Doc's gonna party tonight!"

He ventured a weak smile and walked to the bar, pausing when he saw no empty seat. He began scanning the room for Annette, his gaze carefully nonchalant, examining the peripheral tables one by one from left to right. He eliminated them all except for two in the darkness by the side of the platform. Then he turned his eyes to the platform itself, the forms of the dancers there jagged in the lights cutting their movements to shreds.

"Hey Doc, you gonna dance tonight?" another jeering voice shouted at him. He smiled, turned toward the voice, and flashed the two-fingered Victory sign.

"All right!" said the voice.

A girl he had never seen before pushed a bottle of beer into his hand.

"Have a beer, Doc, courtesy of the senior class," she said as she turned and marched away.

He saw an opening at the end of the bar, an empty stool. A lucky opening. From here he could see faces crowding the bar, the dancers, most of the tables, and, by swinging his seat to the right, the front door. He settled onto the stool, took a sip of beer, and started scanning the faces at the bar.

"You get a freebie, Prof," said the long-haired bartender as he slid another beer in front of him.

"To whom do I owe this precious gift?" Holmay asked.

"Somebody who wants a good grade, Prof," said the bartender emotionlessly.

"No deals," Holmay said with a smile.

He circled the room once again for a sign of her. She had to be on the lookout for him, watching for her caller to come through the door. Should he go stand by the door, wait there for her, make it easy for them to slip out without having to wade past the faces in the room? Surely she had seen him come in, stand in front of the door before advancing toward the bar. She had to be at one of the dark tables, trying to work up her nerve.

At the opposite end of the bar a dark form, hunched over a beer, was staring at him. Holmay's heart leaped. Billy? He strained a moment to see into the shadows covering the form, averting his eyes, convinced only of the fact that the form was fixing him in a steady stare. No, not Billy. Billy was gone. Billy would not come to a place like this. Billy would not drink beer. No Billy here.

He turned in his chair, showing his back to the staring form.

"Hey Doc, you wanna dance?"

The voice belonged to a short, pert blond, her face sassy and childlike. The girl in Annette's room.

"Come on, Doc," she said, extending her hand, "loosen up."

She led the way, pushing her way through the crowd.

"Hey Doc," said a voice to his left. "Hey! The Doctor-Man's gonna dance!"

She let go of his hand as they got to the platform, her form dissolving into the sharp shreds cut by the flickering lights. He, the Doctor-Man, was about to dance, the music a huge siren in his ears, his bones vibrating inside his frame, the thump, thump, thump of heartbeat drums stirring his blood.

"Aren't you gonna dance, Doc?" the blond screamed over the music, even as he felt his legs begin to move under him.

"Come on, Doc! *Groove* a little!"

He saw himself from the quiet of his living room, the solid comfort of his favorite chair, his feet moving of their own accord over the floor, his trunk twisting forward and back, and his arms, his arms, he didn't know what to do with his arms, flailing outward with them, or pumping out a rhythm, or high overhead in a hallelujah Praise the Lord, or yet just limp at his sides, they too not involved in the dance, at once ashamed, alarmed, amused by the head jerking back and forth, the arms as helpless as the rest of his body being swept away by the blast of music stronger than any thought in the room. Carried away, he stood apart from the wild motions of his body on the floor, his gyrating form separate from his curiosity about what it was doing or why. This is wild, he thought. What am I doing here? He reached out toward the blond turning within inches of him, his arms hungry to draw her in toward his chest so he could feel the wild beating of her birdlike heart next to himself.

"Do it, Doc! Do it!" she screamed, her face turned away from him as if she were addressing someone else far gone.

The music ended and she walked away without looking back, he hurrying to keep up with her.

"Hey!" he screamed above the new music starting up. "To whom do I owe the honor of sharing that last dance?"

"What?" she replied, turning.

"What's your name?"

She gave him a contemptuous look.

"Is Annette here?"

She shrugged and stalked off.

He looked in vain for his bottle of beer, not knowing what to do with his hands. For a moment he stood hip-cocked next to the bar, looking indifferently away from the noisy crowd next to him. At the far end of the bar the staring form had disappeared. The Billy who was not Billy was gone. Two girls, sexy and pretty, were laughing with a sweat-shirted boy who had taken the seat of the staring form. Normal. All normal. Everyone having normal, All-American fun.

He wanted out and turned toward the door.

"You leaving so soon?"

Annette, a smile half-smirk on her face, had him by the sleeve.

"You're a pretty good dancer, for an older guy. Where you going so fast?"

"Just out."

"Aren't you going to ask me to dance?"

"Sure, let's go outside and dance."

"There's no music out there."

"We'll make our own."

"Where?"

"Anywhere you want. In my office."

"Tonight?"

"Sure. Why not? Maybe you'd really like it there."

"No, that would be too much like church."

"Are you expecting to meet someone tonight?"

She lifted an eyebrow. "Maybe I am. But everybody I meet in this place is only interested in one thing, Dr. Holmay."

"What's that?"

"I think you're old enough to know. And you should know that a girl wants someone who really cares."

"A secret admirer?"

The words took her by surprise. She turned away to rethink them apart from him. When she looked at him again she had a smile of triumph on her face.

"You?"

"Should we try my office now, or a little drive?"

"Oh no," she said, backing away. "Oh no. You've got me all wrong. I was expecting somebody else. What kind of girl do you think I am?"

❋ ❋ ❋

He took the alleys all the way back, keeping to the shadows as he ran. What a fool he had been to show his face, and what a fool Annette had made of him. With good reason she—they—could laugh now. And he had left Evelyn alone in the house, the door deliberately unlocked.

His legs went limp when he saw the lights in the house—all of them, upstairs and down, blazing in the darkness at the end of the street. Something was wrong, something was terribly wrong.

He came in from the back door, quietly like a man sneaking back to his bed. Lance's door was still closed and there was no light on in his room. He walked to the living room, listening for some sign.

"Evelyn," he called out quietly.

The front door was still unlocked.

"Evelyn," he called again, looking up the stairs.

He found her on his bed, her eyes fixed on his as he entered. She had wrapped her teddy bear in her blue blanket and was hugging it close.

"Evelyn, are you okay?"

She did not respond.

"Why are all the lights on in the house?"

She looked away, out the window to her left.

"Where did you go, Dad? Why did you leave me all alone?"

He sat next to her and took her hand, but she did not turn toward him.

"I just stepped out for a minute, and then something came up. Are you okay?"

"But where did you go?"

"I was with a student. . .who had some troubles that needed talking through."

"Billy?"

"No."

She took her hand away from his.

"Were you scared when you saw I wasn't here? Is that it? Is that why you turned on all the lights?"

"I was scared at first, but not after a while."

"You're getting to be a big girl, aren't you? You're not scared of the dark any more."

"The phone scared me. That's when I woke up and I thought you would answer it. But it just rang and rang."

"And you answered it?"

"When I answered it I wasn't scared any more."

"Who was it?"

"Billy."

"Billy?"

"He knew I was all alone, and that's why he called."

"Where is he? Where did he call from?"

"He says he's close by. He told me not to be afraid because he'd be nearby to take care of me."

"What did he say?"

"We talked a long, long time. I can't remember all the things, but I wasn't afraid any more."

"Why did he call? What did he want from you?"

"He just wanted to talk. He just asked me to do one thing for him."

"What's that?"

"Leave a light on in the house tonight so he would know for sure I'm waiting for him."

Twenty-seven

HE CALLED IN sick the next day, glad that the sky was overcast and the temperature below zero. He shuddered as he pulled the covers over his head, lying still long after all need to sleep had passed. They could all go to hell. Annette and her little blond friend, students in his classes, Hoffstein and Drummond. He had nothing more to say to any of them. They could all go to hell.

It was almost noon when he threw the blanket to one side. Once upon a time he had a wife who brought coffee to the side of his bed. His head ached and there was no coffee now. He put his robe and slippers on and went downstairs. Lance, hurrying through the kitchen to his room, stopped to look him up and down.

"You sick?" he asked. "Somebody said you're sick today. I sent Evelyn off to school this morning full of Cheerios."

"I'm fine. I'm just sick today."

"Anything I can do?"

"No, thanks. I'll take care of myself."

The letter had been mailed in a large used envelope, with the return address crossed out in ink. Holmay knew immediately, even before he saw the postmark covering the stamps. Billy. Shenandoah, Iowa.

He sat in his chair, tore the envelope open, and put his cup of coffee on it as he began to read.

168

Dear Dr. Holmay:

I've been in Shenandoah now for almost a week and already it's beginning to feel like home. People are very friendly here. Or most of them are. They know everyone makes fun of Iowa, all the jokes about Iowa, etc., but they don't let it get to them. Because they know we've got something here the rest of the world doesn't have. Here people are normal and decent to each other day by day. Not many drug cults, far-out ideas, and such. On the edge of town we can look out at the land going on and on, all flat and level, all white. It's plains, but as they say (ha, ha) it's also great.

I don't have a job yet but three places have told me to try try back again. I have conveyed to prospective employers my career inclinations and professional aptitudes, impressing upon them also my extreme adaptability to their particular circumstances. There may be a job at the grain elevator next week. I don't know what I'm going to do.

When you think about it this might be the perfect place for me. I've heard a little about the world—Detroit, for example, take a place like that. Trouble everywhere. I haven't been there, but I know. I read the newspapers too. Did you know that the main streets in Detroit are shaped like the spokes of a wheel, with the hub centered in the downtown? The streets used to bring people in, but now they just let people get away, far out. So now everybody wants out, lives on the edge, far out from the true center of things. Hence we see our Age of Technology and Analysis, the advent of the dissociated society, disintegrating as it mushrooms out from its center of consciousness. Uninhibited growth, like a cancer. I say 'disintegration' with conscious intent. For what do we conjure when the word 'Detroit,' metaphorically-speaking, is spoken. Black versus white. Race riots. The failure of integration. Contrast this with Brazil, where four distinct components live in spiritual richness, however impoverished they may be in matters of the world.

Detroit is nowhere. It's a monster huge and immobile (note the irony of this— all those automobiles it daily spawns) rendering defunct the very fields which gave it life. In Shenandoah we can count for something. That's why I want to settle down, establish my career, then volunteer my talents and energies for public service. Do you see what I mean?

I chanced upon the lobby of the hotel here two days ago, a quaint edifice recalling a yesteryear. But one anomaly took possession of my soul in that scene, the TV with its endless flickerings. I watched a story or two with some interest, but as the hours moved on the stories all began to look insane. I began hating them and I wanted to smash it right in front of everyone. And then there are the cars everywhere. I don't trust any of them. Hence it is that our society drives itself to distraction. This leads to drugs, Satanic cults, pornography, then violence, the various self-suicides. Have you ever noticed how insanely some people drive these days?

Do you agree with my analysis of the state of the contemporary psyche? I would be interested in your critical response. Can you help me think these things through?

They would not let me remain in the lobby of the hotel, despite my vehement protestations. Their claim that I am not a genuine preservationist is absurd. First, they have no right to doubt their new mayor, given my commitment to values deemed traditional. Secondly, one does not normally bear his credentials on his person. Third, the television set was clearly out of order in that particular hotel. Anyone with eyes can see it. If Shenandoah is to progress, it will have to do without. So I left peacefully.

And the lovely Evelyn? Hardly a night passes when she does not visit my dreams. You and Evelyn belong here with me. I've given the matter much thought, a small business publishing books of importance to the world, not novels and trash, but real books. Why Boston and New York? Why not Heartland Books, Shenandoah, Iowa? Give it more thought.

If television belongs in any place, don't you think it's the bars? In Shenandoah there are thirty-four bars, and only fourteen churches. That says something, doesn't it?

As I walked in the park late yesterday afternoon, everybody was looking at me again. When I looked around I sensed that they were hiding again. I don't mean the ordinary people at all. There was a girl walking past who was Wendy, and there were two little boys with a sled. And on the ice not far away was a man leaning on his cane. No, they weren't the ones bothering me. It took a while. In the parking lot and all along the street, the cars. Dozens of them staring at me, some of them showing their actual teeth. For the life of me I don't know why they let them into the park. Isn't a park where we go to be free? I think that'll have to be made into an ordinance as soon as possible, for too soon there will be televisions everywhere, here too in the park, unless you, me, Evelyn, all of us, join forces to prevent that eventuality.

They just won't leave me alone. Yesterday I was out looking for a job again. I have only nine cents left in my pocket. I went to the park with my book under my coat. At first I thought it was the cars, twisting the words in my book until they were a tangle of worms. But then there were three of them standing by one of the cars. Looking at me, laughing and drinking beer, throwing the cans right in the snow, and my eyes told them to stop. They swore at me, used some very dirty words. I turned away but they knew I could still see. I was afraid of them, but I'm very good at concealing things, so don't worry about me. I got up to go away but they began following me. "Queer," they said. They kept calling me queer and one threw a can at me. Can you help me? I didn't know what to do. I just kept walking away, but they began chasing me. I have a right to defend myself, didn't I? It's a God-given American right, and I thought about just getting it out. But then I thought better of it, thinking I didn't want to hurt anyone. It would be like shooting at cars passing by on the highway below. They caught up to me and what they did was all wrong. They

*hit me and called me names. Later when I reported it to the police they asked
me why I wanted to be mayor. I told them the truth. I love their town and
was looking for a decent place to stay.*

*So now I'm convinced that it's always important to keep in mind the ideal.
Shenandoah would be ideal if you and Evelyn were here and we had our little
book business in place, but I'm not sure what really to call home yet. Process
for now perhaps, not product yet. So maybe I'll be heading south again toward
Mexico, and eventually Brazil.*

Would that all of us could come together there one fine day.

Love,
Billy

❋ ❋ ❋

Evelyn said he had to read the story to her. "And don't try telling me I'm not
old enough to understand the words. I'm not going to let you get out of it, Dad."

The copy she had found at the public library was tattered and worn, its print
small on the yellowing pages.

"Why do you want to hear this story?" he asked again.

"I told you why. Just because. Because Mrs. Fromson read one to us like that
yesterday. She told us to go out and look up some more. She said he was one
of the greatest writers in America."

"This is a scary story, Evelyn."

"I like being scared. Everyone in class was scared yesterday. Just read, will you
please."

" 'The Pit and the Pendulum' is really scary. Let me read that one to you."

"No, Dad. I found this one in the book all by myself. I want you to read this
one to me. If I get too scared I'll let you hold my hand until I fall asleep."

He read—flatly, dully, blurring all rhythms and tones, now and then pausing
to see if his monotone had worked its effect, only to find that her eyes were alert,
searching the ceiling as if the story's words were written there. Once, toward the
middle of the story, she shifted her position in the bed, half-turning away from
him while he read on and on. And she did not interrupt. As he approached the
end, the story's last paragraph, alone in italics at the top of the page, blared at
him like an alarm. He was determined to slide over the words as if he were wiping them away with a cloth, yet his heartbeat quickened as he came near:

*"You have conquered, and I yield. Yet, henceforward art thou also dead—dead to
the World, to Heaven, and to Hope! In me didst thou exist—and, in my death, see
by this image, which is thine own, how utterly thou hast murdered thyself."*

He closed the book and pulled himself up.

"There. The End."

For a moment he thought she had fallen asleep. But she was still wide-eyed,
staring straight ahead.

"Was it scary enough for you?"

She nodded.

"Do you want me to hold your hand?"

"No."

"Do you want to talk about the story before we go to sleep?"

"No."

"It's just a story, you know. Stories aren't real."

She did not respond.

"Okay, then. Goodnight. It's later than usual. It's time to turn the light off."

Abruptly she turned toward him.

"No, leave the light on," she said.

"Why?"

"Just because."

"Are you scared?"

She shrugged.

He bent down and kissed her on the forehead. "Okay. I'll leave it on a while."

"No, leave it on all night."

"You don't have to worry, Evelyn. I'll be here all night. I won't ever be going out again in the middle of the night. Not ever again. Promise."

She turned away and pulled the blanket over her shoulder.

"I love you, Evelyn," he said from the door.

"I love you too, Dad."

He sat in bed reading for an hour and a half, his eyes passing over pages as if they were anonymous faces in a crowd. He worried: would he sleep tonight or toss and turn, reviewing his foolishness of the night before? He went to the bathroom to piss and stood over the toilet bowl, his penis limp in his hand. Pathetic, he thought as he looked down at at. Lonely, ugly, forbidden thing, powerless to speak its mind. Like a wrinkled old man in a nursing home. He stuffed it in his pants and washed his hands with soap.

The knocking on the front door began just as he was set to turn off the light in Evelyn's room. He hurried downstairs.

No, he said before he opened the door, not again.

Billy backed away as Holmay opened the door, the porchlight casting a shadow over his face.

"I thought you were in Shenandoah," Holmay said.

Billy moved forward, his face, bruised and swollen, becoming visible in the light.

"They beat me up again."

"I thought you were going south...to Brazil."

He shrugged. "Someday."

"Then what are you doing here?"

"I saw the light on in the house. In Evelyn's room. Evelyn said she would leave a light on for me."

"I don't see what that's got to do with anything."

"Dr. Holmay, sir. I need a place to stay. Can I stay here tonight?"

"I don't have any empty beds."

"Can I sleep on the floor?"

"I don't run a hotel. You'll have to be on your way."

"But where?"

"Home."

"I can't go there."

"That's your problem, Billy, not mine. Try hitchhiking. You can't stay here tonight."

After he closed the door Holmay stood still and listened for footsteps leading away. Hearing nothing, he went to the window and looked out, his eyes trying to see into the shadows of trees crossing each other on the snow.

Twenty-eight

"WOULD YOU LET him live in your house?" Dr. Altizer asked.

For some reason Holmay imagined that Dr. Altizer would be wearing a white coat, and he was surprised, on arriving at the County Mental Health Center, that there was no receptionist to show the way to Altizer's door. He was surprised too that the County Mental Health Center was on the east side just off the highway leading south. He normally shopped for groceries just a half-mile away, had passed within a hundred yards perhaps a thousand times without seeing it. It was made of yellow brick, its dimensions flat and square, its shine faded by the first year's sleet and rain. There were others like it on the outskirts of town, many of them windowless, with a dozen or more cars parked nearby, warehouses perhaps, or small factories. He knew that shoes were made in town, and canoes, recliners, bathtubs, brake drums, and screws of all sizes and shapes. But he had only been inside one building like this, and cardboard boxes were made in it.

He took the wire fence surrounding the building for granted too, driving right through the open gate to a small parking lot. From the highway he had never noticed the fence before; from the parking lot it looked as high as the building itself.

The lobby of the building was small and square, with three folding chairs lined up along the window looking over an empty flowerbox. Two old men, one with a hanky pressed to his nose, were sweeping the floor, and a pretty woman not yet twenty-five sat on the first step of a stairwell with her face in her hands.

The old men nodded when Holmay asked them where Dr. Altizer could be found. They pointed to a corridor on the left. He passed a dozen doors on each side of the hall, none of them identified by number or name. When Holmay returned to the lobby a man in cotton corduroy pants and a plaid flannel shirt was waiting for him.

"I'm Dr. Altizer," he said, "what can I do for you?"

"I want to talk to you about Billy."

"Billy?" Altizer looked confused, tried to remember someone by that name. "Billy who?"

"Billy Brand."

"Oh yes, Billy."

Altizer looked up and down the corridor before closing his office door. He was a short man, perhaps older than he looked, with stooped shoulders that caught the overflow of hair unusually long. His brown-rimmed glasses sat precariously on his nose, but he never troubled himself to push them into place. His desk was heaped high with papers, but the rest of the room was stark. Behind the desk were two steel filing cabinets and to the left of the desk was a bookcase full of uniformly bound professional journals. Across from it was a small table with an ashtray, a framed photograph of Altizer hanging slightly askew above it. Against the background of distant blue mountains Altizer was smiling at the camera, holding up high the sad-faced head of a big-antlered moose.

"So you're the English professor at the college?" he said. "I was never any good at that stuff."

"Not very good with grammar myself," Holmay replied. "Always have trouble with my dangling modifiers."

"Me, I never could figure the comma out."

"That's because we keep changing the rules."

"Why do you do that?" Altizer asked innocently.

"You know how it is. So people have to keep asking us what's right. It enhances our employment opportunities. Like footnoting. We keep changing the rules there too. Nobody knows how to footnote for sure, so they have to keep hiring us to explain."

"Yes," Altizer said as if convinced. "Are you a lawyer too?"

He caught Holmay stealing a second glance at the photograph on the wall. "That's a real beautiful thing. I just knew there'd be one waiting for me if I could get away. So one day I just made up my mind and went. I took sick leave. It took some doing to pick up and go, but I knew I'd have to go. So one night I marched in and told her I was going, and that was that."

He sat back in his swivel chair, satisfied. "You know how it is with a wife sometimes. Sometimes you've just got to come out with certain things."

"I'm divorced," Holmay said.

"Oh, then you know. So tell me one thing. What's it really like being a professor? You get three months off, right? I mean—can you do whatever you really want for three months?"

"We're supposed to do certain things, but there's no one holding a gun to our heads."

"Like what?"

"We're supposed to write books—and stuff."

"But you could get off for a few weeks now and then?"

Holmay nodded.

"Then maybe you and me should go, maybe next summer."

"Go where?"

Altizer's eyes widened. "Alaska. You ever been there?"

"I don't hunt."

"Oh," Altizer said, suddenly defeated and confused.

Yes, Dr. Altizer explained, he now knew who Dr. Holmay was. "At first I thought you were in the medical field. That night three weeks ago when the police brought Billy in he didn't say a word. You know they found him half-asleep on the library steps over at the college, and they couldn't get him to budge. They had to carry him bodily. He didn't even give us his name for more than two days. It took quite a while before he started opening up. That's when he mentioned your name."

"But he never told you what I did?"

"He said he was waiting for you to let him in the library—that's why he was waiting on the steps."

"Why would he say that?"

"They say the damndest things! Are you sure you've never been hunting in your whole life?"

"No, but Billy has."

Yes, Dr. Altizer said, he was aware that Billy was a hunter too. And yes, it was indeed a matter of some concern because Billy's actions were impossible to monitor twenty-four hours a day. Yes, he was aware that maybe Billy could walk out the front gate without being seen, and no, the gate was never locked. Billy in fact might be expected, or required, to leave someday, if he proved that he could behave himself. Yes, maybe Billy was dangerous, but then again maybe he was not. How could anyone be sure of anything these days? How could he, a professor, know that a student someday might not pull a gun and shoot him during a class?

"Then what I want to know," Holmay said, "is what's being done for him."

"That's easy enough," Altizer said. Everything in his power. Billy was being fed and he had clean bedding every three days. He had the use of a lounge and television set and a variety of games such as checkers and cards. He had a few chores to do every day. He could read, take strolls in certain corridors or just sit and do nothing at all.

"Then there is a chance he could just walk out the gate?"

There was always a chance that something might go wrong, especially in cases like his.

"What is really wrong with Billy?"

"I can't tell you that."

"Why not?"

"Because Billy's file is not open to the public."

"I'm not the public," Holmay shot back. "I've been an important part of Billy's life for a long time now."

Altizer leaned in. "In what way?"

"I'm sort of a . . . friend. A father-figure. A friend."

"Then maybe you should take care of him."

"I can't do that."

"Why not?"

Because there was no room in his house. Because the dishes were always unwashed, the dirty laundry always on the floor, toys scattered here and there, untidiness everywhere. Because he had too much to do. Because he had a book to write, a need for peace and quiet. And he had a lovely daughter named Evelyn and he remembered Evelyn walking back from the park one day hand-in-hand with Billy. There was no room in his house.

"Billy has his own parents. Why don't they take care of him?"

Altizer spoke barely audibly. "If you'd met them you wouldn't even ask."

"Before I'd ever consider having Billy live in my house I'd have to know what's wrong with him."

Altizer gave a sharp laugh. "Call my wife," he said, "call her today. Tell her we're going off to Alaska—you and me. Tell her the air there is clean and cool and tell her I just might never come back. I'd stay there the rest of my life, even when all those millions of square miles are frozen over with ice and snow. If you come to Alaska with me we'll sit down in the snow and I'll explain everything you need to know about William Brand."

"An accurate explanation might inspire me to give very serious consideration to going to Alaska with you."

"William Brand is a paranoid schizophrenic."

Altizer let the words hang in the air like a death sentence.

"Those are just words. You've got to explain that to me."

"It's a condition characterized by irrational fear and a sense of persecution. Subjects of the disease are inclined to exhibit dissociative mental processes. They sometimes have delusions and hear the voices of little green men from Mars speaking directly to them. Does this description fit your Billy Brand?"

The question, staring out at him from behind Altizer's eyeglasses, forced him to turn his gaze toward the window. "When I think of Billy," Holmay said, still looking out, "I think mainly of a very polite boy sitting in the front row of my literature class. Very polite and very bright—and very kind and good."

"Nothing unusual?"

Billy standing under the streetlight late at night. Billy with his arm thrown lovingly over Mrs. Lupinski, the two of them asleep in bed. Billy the small voice in the telephone—the voice of a little green man from Mars—calling long distance in the middle of the night from somewhere in the middle of Iowa. Billy the boy with his crazy Book, his posture too correct, his hair too neatly clipped, his white shirt. Billy Brazil.

"Unusual perhaps—but we're all unusual."

"But we're not all insane, Mr. Holmay. Your Billy's insane."

"What's the difference, Dr. Altizer? You explain it to me. I want to know what made him that way and I want to know what can be done for him. And I want to know one other thing."

"What's that?"

"Whether I have any good reason to be afraid of him."

"You'd be perfectly safe in Alaska," Altizer smiled. "Did you ever think of that?"

"There are wild beasts in Alaska. Billy is no wild beast."

"He's worse than that. A wild beast is like someone playing poker without a full deck. You can outsmart him eventually. Billy's got nothing but wild cards in his hand and nobody knows what rules he's playing by."

"What causes it?"

Altizer lifted both arms from the desk as if in surrender and defeat. "We have theories. It's maybe all genetic. There's evidence for that—it runs in families, patterns and all that."

"Original sin. I don't believe that. How do they know that it doesn't spread from one set of genes to another like the common cold? How do they know that parents don't spread the disease by the way they treat their kids?"

Altizer shrugged helplessly. "Maybe. There's evidence to show that it's triggered by environment."

"Such as the pressure we put on people to conform."

"Stress, anxiety, family trouble, sexual stuff. The symptoms often don't even appear until adolescence. A kid moves out of the house, away from mom and dad. He breaks up with a girlfriend. He tries drugs for the first time. He sees a horrible film, has a nightmare that night. Who knows?"

"So what do we do?"

Altizer fell silent and smiled. "Alaska. That's the only thing we can do. Do you want to come with me or not?"

"No, not yet. I want to know what can be done. I want to know what you're doing."

Altizer breathed deeply and composed himself. "There are some things you will have to understand. This health center has seventy-two rooms in it and right now I've got ninety-six patients here. Besides myself there are eight and one-half staff members, and one janitor. Our budget was cut twelve percent last year and twenty-one percent the year before that. We have thirty-one people officially classified as psychotic here. We have eleven manic depressives and seventeen paranoid schizophrenics. We have one-point-five suicides per year and every two years someone walks away into the winter snow and we find him thawed out the following spring. On a typical weekend night we have three women brought in. They're terrified because they're sure their boyfriends or husbands are going to beat the hell out of them again. The boyfriends usually do. We average three suicide attempts a week. The police bring us every mother or kid who overdoses on drugs. We're supposed to talk them out of doing it again."

Altizer stopped and turned his chair toward the window. "Have you ever shot a moose, Professor Holmay? It's really an incredible feeling having something that heavy and huge so entirely helpless, limp and under control."

"So what can be done?"

"Don't you see? Billy has a room here and food and we change his sheets every three days. There's a lounge with a television set and all kinds of games."

"Billy is intelligent, creative—moral. He was writing a book."

"You want to do something? Why don't you take care of him? Here—I've got papers you can sign. His parents have signed away all responsibility for him. He's not somebody's soldier, student, husband, or employee, and he's no longer even his parent's child. He's nobody's lover and you're maybe his only friend. You could take responsibility for him yourself. I'm sure you'd qualify, Professor Holmay. Should we do that?"

"How dangerous is he?"

Altizer stood up and pulled a folder from his file cabinet. Without opening it he held it up in front of Holmay's face. "William Allan Brand was arrested in Brownsville, Texas, for brandishing a handgun and threatening two guards at the Mexican border. He was extradited to this state after being jailed for vagrancy in Iowa, and he was commited to this place by his parents. He was found on the library steps of the college in the middle of the night, and he wasn't drunk or on drugs. We had him locked up in his room for six entire days, and he spent two days and nights in a straitjacket because he kept trying to smash down the door to his room. You say he's moral, do you? They're all moral, the very worst ones. They're all puritans deep down."

Altizer turned and put the file on the cabinet.

"So what will happen to him?"

"We've got him drugged up pretty good. If he stays on his medication he'll be able to stay here quite a while. But sooner or later he'll have to move out. Some half-way house. Or the State Hospital. Most of them end up there."

"And then what?"

"They die, that's what, like you and me. Like a goddamned moose. Unless you want to be the one responsible for giving him his medication every day, or if you want to be the one who tries to make him normal again, look after him, see to it that he gets and keeps a job, doesn't go haywire in the middle of a street downtown, doesn't disappear for weeks at a time. Do you want to sign the papers, Professor Holmay? Would you let him live in your house?"

Twenty-nine

It happened just before five o'clock, the only time traffic thickened on Brighton Street, and it had to happen right at the entrance to the supermarket parking lot. Holmay felt the quiver first in the gas pedal, and sat helplessly as the shudder passed into the engine itself. Then the engine light came on and the car, halfway into the street, died.

For five minutes he sat behind the wheel trying the ignition, sweat forming on his brow as he watched the cars lining up to get around.

"Get that damned heap out of the way!" some hot-shot yelled as he gunned his way past.

Holmay threw his hands up in surrender. On both sides of him cars, now jammed in tight, were blaring at him.

He opened the hood and leaned in for a look. The maze of metal and wires confounded him. He didn't know the first thing about cars. He pushed down on some of the wires, threw his hands up again in despair, and climbed back behind the wheel. The starter turned and turned, the red light dimming as the engine failed again.

"What the hell are you doing in the middle of the street?" shouted a bearded roughneck in a pickup. "Push it out of the way so people can get through!"

Holmay stood next to the open hood, angry, apologetic, embarrassed. To his left a chorus of horns began blaring again.

Fuck you, he said to himself, fuck you, fuck you, fuck you all. He slammed his fist on the fender and opened the trunk. He always carried tools in his trunk but didn't know what to do under the hood. Next to an old rag he found a tire iron. He lifted it out, clutched it tightly in his fist, and walked to the front of his car.

"Asshole," someone hissed through a window.

"Fuck you," Holmay whispered, shaking the iron in the air.

The blaring of car horns did not let up. Suddenly afraid, he retreated to his place behind the wheel again, pumping the gas pedal furiously and holding the key turned in the ignition.

"Goddammit!" he screamed at the car. "What in the hell is wrong with you?"

He threw his hands up again, slammed the car door behind him, and stalked off toward the supermarket.

He wandered the aisles, looking at nothing in particular, relieved to be free of the car, willing to abandon all claim to it, leave it to whatever fate. He was glad the aisles were crowded, glad to be lost among the people browsing slowly up and down, and offered a smile when anyone looked at him.

He asked for change at the check-out counter and found a telephone booth, dialing four numbers before getting a response. "It'll be an hour or so before we can get away," the mechanic said.

He waited inside the supermarket, wandering the aisles to pass the time, moving on when eyes found him again.

"Is there something you're looking for?" asked a white-aproned man after Holmay walked past the fruits and vegetables once more.

Holmay had seen the man watching him before, following him down one of the aisles. "Just looking," he replied as he sidled away.

At the door of the supermarket a wave of confusion came over him. Where could he go? To his left his car still stood askew in the middle of the street, its uplifted hood catching the breeze like an absurd flag. More than anything he suddenly hated that thing, wanted to be rid of it. He turned his back and began walking away, his heart leaping with fear when he heard someone shouting at him: "Hey you, that's your car, isn't it? You better do something or they're gonna haul it away."

The traffic had cleared when the mechanic arrived to find Holmay looking under the hood again.

"Any idea what's wrong with her?" the mechanic asked.

"I don't know for sure," Holmay said. "Maybe it needs an oil change."

The mechanic gave a short laugh, set his tool box down on the curb, and went to work under the hood. After a few minutes he turned to Holmay again.

"When's the last time you adjusted the points?"

"Points?"

"Your points are supposed to be set at twenty-seven hundredths. They were open to about thirty-five hundredths."

"Eight hundredths off?"

"They're a little worn. That could throw them off another hundredth or so. Try turning it over now."

The car fired up immediately, spewing a cloud of exhaust toward the parking lot. He touched the gas pedal and smiled when the engine responded, then gunned it hard. Suddenly he felt strong again, as if the engine under the hood was alive in him and everything in the world was running smoothly again.

❋ ❋ ❋

"Where were you, Dad? You said you were just going to the store."

"Ask that car of ours," he replied. "Don't ask me. I got to the middle of Brighton Street and the car decided it wasn't going to let me come home."

"You mean it just stalled?"

"In the middle of the street."

"In the middle of traffic?"

"I felt like a fool."

Evelyn laughed.

"It's not funny, Evelyn. I felt like a fool. Everyone was staring at me."

"Couldn't you do anything?"

"I don't know anything about cars."

"Then why don't you get a new one?"

"Because you can't just go out and buy a new car every time something goes wrong."

She helped him chop the celery and carrots and she set the table for three.

"Why is Lance eating with us tonight?" she asked.

"Because he's going to stay here with you tonight a couple of hours while I'm gone."

"Where are you going?"

"I've got some business tonight."

"Where?"

"Just out," he said turning away from her.

❋ ❋ ❋

It was he who had called Dr. Altizer. Even as he dialed his heart said, No, no, don't do this, don't get involved again.

Dr. Altizer seemed reluctant to talk over the phone. "No one's been here to visit Billy at all," Dr. Altizer said, "but he keeps mentioning you and a girlfriend named Evelyn. But she's never called and he won't tell us her last name. Professionally and personally-speaking it's none of my business, but I think it would be good for Billy if you paid him a little visit some evening. Someone to give him a bit of contact with the outside world. He's trying hard, being very cooperative. Just a suggestion. No strings attached."

It was a cold clear night when Holmay pulled into the parking lot of the County Mental Health Center. As he approached he saw the building in a new light: the

182

windows on all three floors, too distant to be clearly seen from the road, were barred, the light coming from them the only adornment of the dark rectangular mass of the building itself. The lobby door scraped on the vinyl floor as he pushed it open, and he had to push it shut as he came in.

"I'm here to visit William Brand," Holmay said to the gray-haired woman at the desk. She did not look up as she slid a pen and registration card his way.

"Are you a relative?" she asked as she took the card back.

"No, I'm just a friend."

She scribbled something on the back of the card before looking up at him. "Are your address and phone number correct?"

"Yes."

"Billy's in Ward Q, the lounge. Bert will take you there."

Bert was a stout black man of forty years whose mass of keys jangled when he walked. On his left forearm was emblazoned the tattoo of a dragon gripping streaks of lightning in its short front claws. On the lightning the words "FIRST AIR CAVALRY" appeared in red.

"You Billy's dad?" Bert asked through a gold-filled smile.

"No, a friend."

"I thought maybe you was his dad. You two kinda look alikes to me."

"The great non-differentiated non-familiar," Holmay muttered.

"What's that?"

"Nothing," Holmay replied. "I'm just somebody Billy knows."

Bert unlocked a thick white door and pointed Holmay down a corridor. "Billy's down there."

Ward Q was a rectangular room made of cinder blocks painted light blue. Scattered about the room were a few coffee tables, easy chairs and hassocks. At the far end of the room, in a corner where a set of four barred windows met, was a semicircular arrangement of sofas facing a television set. Next to one of the sofas sat a black youth in a wheelchair whose body seemed athletic except for a hunched right shoulder that gave him a twisted look. Next to him on the sofa sat Billy and a skinny balding man about seventy years old.

As he approached Holmay saw that plexiglass had been set over the TV screen. The colors on the screen seemed washed out and dull, the volume set so high that none of the three heard Holmay approach.

"Billy," Holmay called when he was a few feet away.

Billy did not respond.

"Billy." The old man turned first, showing a toothless grin. Then he burrowed his index finger into Billy's shoulder until Billy turned.

"Hello, Billy. I'm here to visit a while."

Billy's eyes widened as he shrank back.

The old man burrowed his finger into Billy's shoulder again. "Who's that man, William? Who's that man? You've got a visitor, William, a visitor."

The black youth rolled his eyes and stared at the floor.

"My name's George," said the old man as he stood up. "Do you want me to play for you?" He lifted a small hand-organ off the floor. It made a sound like a cat when he squeezed it together in his hands.

"No more music," the wheelchaired black youth droned, not lifting his eyes from the floor.

"I gave you two sticks of gum today," said George. "You always want more."

"You people always have more," said the black youth, rolling his eyes upward toward the old man, "so why shouldn't I get half?"

Billy stood up, his expression still scared and surprised. "Doctor Holmay, sir. You're here to see me?"

"Do you want to hear me play?" said the old man.

"No," Billy said. "No more playing. No more."

"I told you, I told you," said the black youth.

"Barry, you leave me alone," said George. "You can't tell me what to do."

"You owe me two sticks of gum," Barry said, lifting his head and pointing an accusing finger at the old man.

Billy took hold of Holmay's arm. "Here. Let's go over here."

Billy took a seat across from Holmay at a card table, his eyes glancing off Holmay as they darted about the room. Billy's neck and face seemed swollen, his boyish wiry frame unnaturally buoyant.

Holmay struggled to find words. "They must be feeding you big here. I see you've gained some weight."

Billy turned away, stared at the floor, and mumbled some words.

"What was that you said, Billy?"

"Man doth not live by bread alone. That's something, Dr. Holmay, you didn't need to hear. It's something I'm sure you know by heart."

Across the room George was taunting Barry with a stick of gum by placing the gum within the black youth's reach and yanking it away.

"Oh they feed me a steady diet all right," Billy said. "And variety too. There's Thorazine, Mellaril, Compazine, Trilafon, Stelazine, Prolixin, Elavil, Sinequan, and lithium carbonate."

"I doubt, Billy, that they have you on all those medications."

"Oh?" he said, his eyes widening, "you don't think they put it in my food, or in my veins when I'm asleep?"

"They're trying to help you, Billy. You've got to cooperate."

"Do you take drugs, Dr. Holmay?"

"No."

"Have you ever taken drugs?"

"I'll take an aspirin for a headache, Billy, but I prefer not to."

"Then you see what I mean."

"Dr. Altizer says you're coming right along."

Billy folded his hands on the table and looked up. "I am, as they say, coming right along. I've had many fruitful talks with Dr. Altizer, whom I came to deem a friend like you. He set things straight for me, many things. Those were his words. 'Set things straight.' And now I see his point of view. Yes, I've got a mental illness, a disease, like a strange terrible case of the flu I caught at birth, and it won't just go away. I've been diagnosed and my disease has a name, so therefore it exists and I am unfit to live with it in the world unless I take my medicine and live a certain way. Behold," he said with a sweep of his hand that took in the whole room, "how I am to live."

"I got it! I got it!" Barry shouted across the room, waving his fist in the air while the old man tried to pry it open.

"Stop it!" yelled Billy, throwing his chair back and stomping toward the television set. "Stop it or I'm going to turn off the TV!"

George picked up his hand-organ and shuffled off to another chair where he sat fingering the keys silently.

"And if you do it again I'm going to make you go to the Quiet Room!" Billy shouted at both of them.

Billy returned to his chair and folded his hands again.

"You know," he began, "I see now the importance of order and discipline—as the poet says, 'The blessed rage for order.' I grew up that way and for a time I thought I would break away from it—the youthful rebellion stage, you know, against my father's strict discipline. Those were the days and nights under Wendy's influence, all the longing and lust. But I see the importance of order now and I think that my life, Dr. Holmay, is coming together finally. You speak of the need to cooperate. I saw it mainly as a need to recognize I had a problem, a mental disease. I didn't want to face up to it."

"Because even though it wasn't your fault, you found it humiliating."

"Exactly. Humiliating. Degrading. Destructive of my dignity, and in a philosophic sense destructive of my perception of the human mind as created in the image of God."

"And now you're facing up to it."

"Yes, for I've revised my conception of God. If my mind is diseased and man is made in the image of God, then God isn't just diseased. He's insane. But if God is also love, then it doesn't matter if God is insane. Do you see what I mean, Dr. Holmay?"

"Yes, Billy."

Billy looked away as he spoke again. "Do you think you love me, Dr. Holmay?"

No question could have come out of a more distant blue, and none could have required as this one did a more difficult and simple response.

"Yes, Billy, I love you."

Billy relaxed his hands and let out a deep sigh. "I knew you did all along, in spite of how we failed each other."

"How did you fail me, Billy?"

"With my thoughts. There were times, Dr. Holmay, when my thoughts took possession of me, evil thoughts. Everyone's out to get someone in some way. You did things I couldn't understand. You rented the room to Lance, you kept me out of your house, wouldn't let me talk to Evelyn. You followed me everywhere, even on those nights when I had nowhere to go and you knew I couldn't sleep. You tried to keep me from getting back into the university. And you knew you were hurting me—that's what I couldn't understand or forgive. That you knew you were hurting me."

"I'm sorry, Billy."

"That's when my thoughts took possession of me. Especially when you kept following me to keep me away. And there's something, Dr. Holmay, I need to confess to you."

"Maybe not, Billy."

"Yes." He looked up at Holmay and moved his head back, his eyes narrowing into a look of contempt. "There were times when I wanted to be rid of you. Times when I wanted to get even for all those things. More than once I stood outside your house in the dark, and I had my gun. I wanted to kill you, Dr. Holmay, because I was afraid you wanted to hurt Evelyn too."

Billy's eyes filled with tears, which he wiped away on his sleeve.

"God, I'm sorry," Billy said, "but I needed to get it all said. I'm like you, Dr. Holmay. I hate lies too—and to sit here close to you without telling you what my thoughts once were would be a lie. So now you know, and you must be thinking what I thought then: He's crazy. He's insane. I remember standing on your porch one night with my gun in my hand, trying to decide whether to knock on your door. That's the first time the thought ever occurred to me: He's insane. Get out of here because he's insane. And that was the hardest thing for me to admit, and maybe that's why I ran away to Iowa—to get away from your porch. But Dr. Altizer set me straight. He said it was okay. He said the first thing I needed to admit was that there was maybe something wrong. And that's why I'm here. To look at the problem honestly and do what I have to do."

In the corner George began playing a tune. For a moment the melody, confused with the music coming from the television set, was unrecognizable, but gradually the strains of "Jeannie with the Light-Brown Hair" came through, George, his eyes closed, swaying his head back and forth in rhythm with the tune.

"No music! Billy said no music!" shouted Barry, as if suddenly awake. Twisting his head back toward Billy as if to appeal to him, he shouted again, "Billy says no music!"

Billy rolled his eyes and pushed his chair back. "Those two are really crazy," he said to Holmay, breaking into a smile as he spoke. "I should get paid for taking care of them. Be right back."

He walked over to George, who pulled a stick of gum from his shirt pocket and handed it to Billy. Then George closed his eyes and resumed his swaying back and forth, his fingers silent on the hand-organ keys. Barry, fumbling with the wrapper of the gum, grinned as he put it in his mouth.

"You see," Billy said as he resumed his place, "there is always some good we can do, no matter what place we're in, what circumstance. Now that I look back I can see that's what all those stories in your class were really trying to teach—how you tried to get that truth across. How they're all about love, bringing order into this world. And now I see what I have to do. Do you see it too?"

"Yes, Billy, I think I do."

"So I'm going to work hard at it, do everything Dr. Altizer says. There's a problem, a mental illness I can't do anything about—and I have to admit that first. Then I have to take steps, small slow ones at first, on the road to recovery. I'll have to stay here a few more weeks, get myself squared away, and then maybe go to one of those halfway houses where I can start relating to society again. I'll have to be careful at that stage and do what they say, keep on my medications and not slip up. Then maybe I'll find a sponsor, someone to relate to like in a family, like a father, someone who will help me get a job, something not too stressful at first, something that will let me use all my creative energies even if it doesn't pay too much, and then from there maybe I can try to be on my own, get my own car, a wife and family, and something more, my ultimate goal."

"What's your ultimate goal, Billy?"

He waved the question away with his hand. "First there's the practical stuff. Let's talk about those drugs. That Dr. Altizer, for example. Don't you think the soul is a pure stream coming from God? Do you think the soul wants pollutants poured into it? Have you ever looked at a glass of water recently? There's nothing fresh about fresh water any more. I want to be clean, Dr. Holmay, clean."

Bert the attendant appeared in the doorway, hands-on-hips.

Billy gave a little laugh as Holmay stood. "My ultimate dream. I think you already know, Dr. Holmay, my ultimate dream. Because some things never change. So there should be no mystery about it in your mind. You know all about Brazil. You know how badly I want to live there, how someday I'll go there and find a little place, and then you and Evelyn can come there too."

Billy fell silent when Bert came to take Holmay away. At the door Billy's face seemed strangely swollen and twisted as he strained to find his parting words.

"I will cooperate and go through the steps. I promise you that. And I know I have a mental disease, though I still don't know exactly what. Do you know what's wrong with me? But who can say? I know it can't be very much. Whatever it is has to be something really small, something just slightly off."

❊ ❊ ❊

When he returned home he found Lance sitting in a chair.

"Where's Evelyn?" Holmay asked.

Lance shrugged and pointed up the stairs. "I guess she's in her room. She wouldn't tell me what was wrong."

Holmay heard her sobbing as he approached. He knocked softly, then opened the door.

"I don't want to talk," she said.

He sat down next to her. "I'll make you a deal. You tell me what's making you cry, and I'll tell you where I was tonight."

She looked up at him, her eyes swollen and red. "Promise?"

"Promise. Nothing but the whole truth."

"You first."

"I saw Billy tonight."

"Billy? Billy's here?"

"Yes and no, Evelyn. Billy's in a hospital. He's got a mental disease."

She twisted her face up to him. "Mental disease? Is it serious? Will he be okay?"

"It is serious—and I don't think he will be able to stay here in this town very long."

"How long?"

"Maybe a year."

She brightened. "Oh that's long, Dad. Will I be able to see him sometime?"

"Maybe. Maybe not. It's not up to me. We'll have to ask his doctor when."

"Will you do that for me?"

"Yes. Now it's your turn. You have to tell me why you were crying when I came in."

"It's nothing, Dad."

"Something to do with Lance?"

"No," she said, sidling up close to him and throwing her arm over his shoulder.

"Tell me. You know you can tell me anything."

"Larry Andrews called me while you were gone. He said he didn't want to go steady with me anymore."

Holmay suppressed a smile. "That's too bad. I think it's too bad for him, even though you're almost ten years old."

She reached up and planted a kiss on his cheek. "It's maybe not so bad."

"Why not?"

"I like him a lot, Dad, but there's one person I'll always love."

"Who could that lucky person be?" he asked, waiting for her to reach up and kiss his other cheek.

"Oh you know, Dad. Billy. I'll always love Billy, Dad, more than anyone."

Thirty

"THAT LANCE," Hoffstein said immediately after stopping Holmay in the corridor, "he certainly is coming around. I've never seen a boy so intellectually raw learn to love literature so fast."

Holmay saw a chance to buy another week of Hoffstein's forbearance. "You must be doing something to him in that poetry class."

Hoffstein raised an eyebrow disapprovingly. "Actually, it's more basic than that. You should know what literature teaches. It's no accident that Lance loves literature."

Hoffstein walked away from his words with his head held high, leaving Holmay to wonder if his words had been dropped like a gauntlet or a lace hanky. Clearly Hoffstein's words concealed some knowledge of Lance that had escaped Holmay, and the presence of some intimacy not offered to him. He had been landlord to Lance, careful not to become professor, father, or priest. Still Lance, despite his conventional, if at times crudely ordinary talk and behavior, had put a diamond stud in his nose. So even though Lance had become more useful and visible around the house, and though Evelyn had warmed up to him, Holmay was taking no chances with him. One Billy was enough. One Billy was too much.

"I'll make you a deal," Lance announced one Saturday afternoon. "If you give me a lift to the supermarket, I'll shovel the snow."

"I'll help," Evelyn said.

As they stood in the parking lot loading groceries into the back seat of the car, Evelyn was the first to notice the woman standing hip-cocked next to a blue Chevrolet twenty feet away.

"Weird," Evelyn said.

"What's that?"

"Weird, that's what."

Then Holmay saw her too. She was short, well under five feet, and dressed entirely in black leather, her tall shiny boots tight against calves supporting muscular thighs. Through black sunglasses she seemed to be looking haughtily beyond the parking lot at someone visible only to her. A silver chain dangled from her waist, and embroidered in white thread in the center of her black cap was a small skull. Just under the zipper of her left jacket pocket was a medallion bearing an unmistakable swastika.

"You're right, Evelyn," Holmay said, loudly enough for the woman to hear, "weird." He closed the car door, then turned and gave her a defiant stare that the woman ignored.

"I've never seen her around town before," he said as he drove off.

"She looked really weird, didn't she, Lance?"

Lance said nothing until Holmay had turned out of the parking lot.

"She's not really so weird."

"How do you know?" Evelyn challenged him.

"I've been over to her house."

"I think she's weird."

"Why would you ever go over to the house of someone like that?" Holmay asked.

"She's Dr. Hoffstein's wife," Lance said sheepishly.

"His *wife?*"

"Yes," Lance said. "And they have an extra room in their house. They asked me to move in. I was going to tell you at the end of the week."

So this was Hoffstein's wife, the invisible one, the skeleton in his closet, woman with her own skeleton embroidered in white thread on her cap and carrying her own kind of cross. There was not only poetry but drama in Hoffstein's house, full of good guys and a very bad girl. And Lance Walcott, All-American boy, was getting in on it.

Lance offered to carry all the groceries into the house.

That evening father interrupted daughter in her room. She had gone there after supper, had turned the music loud while he read downstairs. But then he became aware that the music had stopped and that she had not been out of the room for over two hours. When he knocked on her door she didn't respond, so he opened it a crack just in time to see her stuffing a notebook into the bottom drawer of her desk.

"May I come in?"

No answer.

He eased himself into the room.

"What you been up to, kid?"

"Nothing much."

"Homework?"

"No, nothing."

"I thought you maybe were doing homework. I saw you put your notebook away."

"I was just doing stuff."

He put his arm on her shoulder and pulled her in close. "Probably good stuff," he smiled. "A letter to Mom?"

She shook her head no. "I think I'm going to bed early tonight."

"Tired?"

"No."

"Why don't you brush your teeth and get your pajamas on. Then I'll read to you."

"I don't want any more stories."

"Why not?"

"I'm too old for them now."

"What makes you think you're too old?"

"Nothing."

He laughed. "I don't think you'll ever be too old."

"Oh please, Dad, be serious."

"What's the problem, Evelyn?"

"Nothing's wrong."

"You look sad."

She looked out the window down on the street below, her stare concentrated as if she expected someone to be returning it. "Will Billy ever be back?"

The question came out of the blue. Yes, Billy would be back. It had never occurred to him that Billy, for better or worse, in sickness or health, might never be back. Billy would call in the middle of some nightmare, or be standing under the streetlight while Evelyn's eyes were concentrated on some dream. But some day the other Billy would return—the bright boy eager for the wisdom of books, the very good Billy boy. Somehow Billy would return.

"No, I wouldn't really count on it."

"Never?"

"No, never."

She let out a sad sigh. "I just wanted to be sure."

"Why's that?"

"Because."

He waited.

"Because there's Larry Andrews. He's the one in Mrs. Martin's sixth grade class."

"Yes?"

"He says he likes me again."

"Do you still like him?"

"I think I like him a lot, but I feel sad. Are you really, really sure Billy will never be back?"

"Why does it matter so much?"

"Because Billy told me we would love each other as long as we live. He said we would never, never leave each other. Even if he went away for a year or more, he said he would someday come back for me."

"Evelyn—Billy will never be back."

She was crying as he returned to his book, passing his eyes over words and turning page after page, his mind climbing over the facts of his life as if they were a high pile of scrap iron and steel. Facts that would cut his hands and knees, tear his clothes. His little girl had fallen in love, had forsaken, perhaps betrayed, Billy; and Frances Drummond still looked at him with hopeful eyes every day, as if to say, 'Here I am—bright but not beautiful, and kind, good, loving, my thick thighs my burden and sadness beyond my help and control. Any good man, like you, in time, time, time, will see my heart instead.' And Hoffstein kept whispering, told him to close the office door, warned him to beware of the department head; and there would be powdered sugar on Hoffstein's beard and he too was getting fat and his hair was falling out, and suddenly Hoffstein was Jewish and his wife, one of the best-kept secrets in town, was standing in a parking lot, Nazi-woman in black leather boots, skull embroidered on her cap; and somehow Lance was being carried away, Lance who never made it with Annette George, extraordinarily lovely and soft-skinned, Lance who maybe was Hoffstein's Billy Brand, his blessing and curse.

William Allan Brand. The name itself a curse. A name too right and therefore all wrong. A name not written on any door. All doors the same on both sides of a long corridor. Was there a door behind which Frances Drummond could acquire a new set of slim shiny legs? A room into which Dr. Altizer could usher Billy, show him to a comfortable chair, provide him with the necessary words, perhaps a pill, that would cause a spark to flicker in one cell of his brain and from there a vibration to issue forth, swell into an influence and then assume confident command like the captain of a ship? Altizer's tired eyes, forgotten behind the glasses that refused to stay in place, told a less glorious tale: Billy was an almost hopeless case.

Almost. And if Billy was an entirely hopeless case, did it provide anyone the right to give up on him? Everyone in the world was a hopeless case.

Altizer's eyes were black, not brown. There are some things nobody can control. Some things are all God's fault. Original Sin. A matter of chemistry, perhaps wayward proteins in the brain, an X or Y chromosome jiggled loose from its moorings, broken, suddenly awash, a small lump suddenly in the brain, uncalled for, unwanted like a fetus that hung on, would not allow itself to be washed down the drain.

Does anything give anyone the right to give up on him?

Would you let him live in your house? Soon there will be an empty room in your house. Will you take responsibility for him?

He choked on the word. Society. Can't Society do something for him?

Altizer laughed in his face. Billy's mother and father are Society. Your university is Society. The police station is Society. My building and my staff—the County

Mental Health Center—is Society. And you, Dr. Holmay, Professor, are Society. Soon you will have an empty room in your house. Will you let Billy live in your house? No. Because of Evelyn. But there must be a house somewhere for him. Somebody else's house.

Write a letter to the President of the United States. Maybe William Allan Brand will end up living in the White House some day.

He spends all our money on bullets and bombs. And someday, someday, the world will disappear into a mushroom cloud.

Have you ever noticed, Dr. Holmay, that a mushroom cloud resembles a human brain? Don't you think that the defect is really in the brain—that the human brain someday will fulfill its defective self once and for all?

Ashes, ashes, we all fall down. Deep in the sky that does nothing but fall we all disintegrate and drift, swirl down and down and down toward some frozen distant pole, some terrible black hole.

That doesn't give anyone the right to give up on Billy. Goddammit! Nobody has that right!

No, Dr. Altizer finally agreed. Nobody has that right.

He picked up the newspaper lying on the floor next to his chair. The sale of telescopes was booming because a certain comet was set to make another round. The hijackers of an Italian airplane demanded enough fuel for a flight to Yemen. Farmers were accusing Jews of fixing the price of corn. The lowest bid among thirty submitted for toilet seats on the largest U.S. strategic bomber was $660 per seat. Thirty more communists were killed in the Philippines, and the daughter of the vice-president of Columbia was a hostage of The Shining Path. And officials in a Moscow hospital reported no change in the condition of a fifteen-year-old girl whose development stopped at the age of two. The girl, who neither walked nor talked, had not left her bed since her father, an army officer, returned from a tour of duty when she was two.

The house was quiet, except for the hum of the furnace downstairs, a reassuring sound because the furnace had never failed in all the years he had lived in the house. He knew nothing about furnaces—not if they needed adjusting, cleaning, replacement parts.

He climbed the stairs to Evelyn's room, the door half-open but the light there out. She was asleep, her arm hugging close to her cheek a big brown teddy she had forgotten in the back of her closet for almost two years. He leaned over her, pulled the blanket over her shoulders and tucked it in tight on all sides.

So now she is acquainted with the sorrow of boyfriends. Larry Andrews. Billy Brand. And therefore she no longer will want folk or fairy tales. He bent down and kissed her lightly on the forehead, waiting, expecting some sign of gratitude. She rolled her shoulder away from him, as if the weight of his presence was disturbing her sleep.

Thirty-one

THE MIDDLE OF March brought one of those undeclared holidays. By noon the temperature hit sixty-three, no wisp of cloud in the sky. People put on holiday smiles and summer clothes, with only trees, still black and bare against a blue sky, throwing shadows in their way.

Holmay dismissed his final afternoon class fourteen minutes before the hour. "And no office hours today," he announced. "Professors also need time to play."

He would wait on the porch for Evelyn to get home from school, have a present hiding behind his back, and she would have to guess which hand it was in.

It was almost two when he turned the corner of High and Center streets, a bagful of chocolates in one hand. When he first heard the car horn he paid no attention and started across the street, and as it approached he was looking the other way. When the horn sounded a second time the car was already past. So he was not sure. It was an older sedan, maroon, perhaps a Buick or Chevrolet. One person inside, a smile on his face, twisted halfway around in his seat and waving at him.

Billy.

Holmay froze.

The car leaped forward, leaving him stranded in uncertainty, the face in the car present and gone like a life flashing before his eyes. Billy, a serene smile on his face. Billy, who one day wanted to own a car. The inmate in the mental hospital.

So why was he out, and where in the world was he going with that smile on his face?

Holmay arrived home to the ringing of the phone.

"Holmay, this is Altizer. Billy walked out of here about an hour ago. I thought maybe he'd be coming your way."

"He escaped?"

"Well, yes," Altizer said in a matter-of-fact voice. "And he's been dumping his medication. So if you see him, give us a call."

"Was he in a car?"

"He went right out the front door. And we think he stole a car. He'd been talking a lot about this girlfriend of his, about taking off with her."

"Evelyn?"

"Isn't that your daughter's name?"

His heart was beating wildly when he put the phone down. He glanced at the clock. Two-twenty-one. Evelyn would be safe in school until three. Plenty of time to get to her. And maybe enough time to do one other thing he had dreaded doing for several months.

✲ ✲ ✲

Holmay's legs trembled as he stood in front of Bernie's Pawn Shop, the little joint on the corner of First and Division streets. A dumpy-looking place with old guitars, hand-tools, and auto parts piled in the front window, Bernie's face in the window too, the high forehead, thick brows, his unmoved eyes looking out. Who is this man? Holmay asked himself as their eyes met. Is this really me standing here? He stepped back from the window, watching his reflection as he breathed deeply to slow his racing heart. Then he made up his mind.

"Yes," Holmay finally said, his voice still trembling and weak. "That one there. What is that?"

"A thirty-eight."

"How much do you have to have for it?"

"Sixty bucks. Plus tax."

"Would you load it for me?"

Bernie disappeared into the back room with the gun. Outside a train began rumbling past, Holmay calmed by the steady clacking on the rails. Above the rumble he heard a woman's angry voice. "Screw yourself!" Bernie shouted back. Holmay looked at his watch: twelve minutes to three. He paced helplessly in the narrow aisle.

Nine minutes to three. "Is anybody home?" Holmay shouted toward the back room. "I'm in a hurry here."

"Hold your horses!" the woman shouted back. "You people come in here and expect us to jump."

Bernie appeared, the gun wrapped in a paper bag. "Sixty-seven dollars and twenty-nine cents."

Holmay scribbled the figures on his check, then slowed to a crawl as he signed his name.

"Gotta see your driver's license," Bernie said as he handed Holmay the gun. It was heavier than he'd imagined. After he slipped the gun inside his jacket pocket his hand seemed to have a warm tingle the way it did when he took Evelyn on walks, or when, toward the end, he freed himself of Cynthia's grasp.

"Be careful with her," Bernie said as Holmay backed toward the door. "She's loaded like you said."

* * *

It was six after three when he finally pulled into a parking space two blocks from Evelyn's school. He stood as tall as he could, trying to get a glimpse of her among the children along the sidewalks leading home. He covered the bulge in his jacket pocket with his arm, then took long strides toward the school.

"Have you seen Evelyn?" he asked a small boy dragging a blue backpack on the ground.

The boy circled away from him.

"Do you know Evelyn?"

The boy shook his head. "I don't know, mister. I'm just going home from school."

On the playground three children were climbing the monkey bars, two others were on the swings, and a dark-haired boy was shooting baskets at the eight-foot rim next to the bike rack. Evelyn was nowhere to be seen.

Just inside the door he was met by a balding janitor leaning on his mop.

"Nice day, ain't it?" the janitor said. "You wouldn't believe. The kids, they went crazy when I opened the doors."

"Do you know the girl named Evelyn?"

"Evelyn? The little blondie in fifth grade?"

"That's the one."

"She's the nicest little girl."

"I'm her father."

"Nice to meet you," he said, thrusting out his hand.

"Is she here in the building now?"

"I dunno. Everybody's went home would be my guess."

"Do you know where the fifth-grade classroom is?"

"Second floor—down the hall, right-hand side."

He backed around the janitor, trying to hide the heavy lump inside his jacket as he squeezed past. "If you see her, please tell her to wait here for me. Tell her not to go outside."

He walked quickly down the hall. No one anywhere—only the smell of schoolrooms, dust, chalk, crayons, trapped air. To the right of the stairs silver letters spelled out the words "Fifth Grade" on the window of a door. The door was locked and there was nobody in the room.

He ran out the front door and stood for a moment on the steps.

"Is there anything wrong?" The janitor, his mop still in his hands, was leaning toward him through the open door.

"No. Nothing wrong. Nothing. I'm looking for Evelyn, my daughter Evelyn."

The boy with the basketball tried harder when he saw Holmay approach.

"You wanna see me make one, mister?"

"What grade are you in?"

"I'm in third. You wanna see me?"

"Do you know Evelyn—from the fifth grade?"

"Do you know how to make a basket, mister?"

"No, no, I don't want to play."

"What do you do, mister? What's your job?"

"I'm a professor."

"What do they do?"

"They write books, books."

"Do you write books, mister? Betcha you can't make a basket like me."

He hurried to his car and squealed to a stop in front of his house. Evelyn was not on the porch, not inside, and Lance's door was closed. "Goddammit!" he screamed at the door.

He returned to the porch, sat on the top step, and looked up and down the street for a sign of her. Two girls older than Evelyn pedaled by on their bicycles. At the corner they paused, waved goodbye to each other, and parted company. Across the street a gust of wind lifted a few leaves and swirled them into the air. Suddenly it seemed chilly and dark.

The park, he said to himself. I've got to check out the park.

He retraced the path, again saw himself following Billy and Evelyn home from the park, pausing every time they paused, hoping they would not turn and see him following them, remembering the jealous pang that surged through him when he saw them holding hands, his helplessness when they turned the corner and disappeared from view. It would be dark in another hour.

Colonel Willoughby stood unmoved on his pedestal, and the flowers, frozen all winter at his feet, had turned into a tangle of dry stems. A young couple was huddling on a park bench close to the water's edge, and a woman walking her dog was visible on the bike path at the near end of the lake. The sky, still cloudless, was dull blue, the afternoon light spreading itself like a fine film on the passing day. Only one tree, a large mountain ash standing majestically behind the statue of Willoughby, had a few leaves hanging from its branches.

He wanted to cry out her name but held himself back. To his left, where the softball diamond opened into a wide expanse of open field, two teenagers were tossing a football back and forth. Only that past summer Evelyn, nine years of innocence still on her face, stood directly on the bag at third, running her fingers along the wrinkles of his old leather mitt. It was the bottom of the ninth, and the bases were loaded everywhere in the world.

Billy will take her to his favorite place, Holmay concluded, to the rocky ledge jutting out over the river at the far end of the park. He had taken her there the first time, and there he would take her again. He was sure, terribly sure.

He ran across the field, unable to avoid the spots of soggy grass that soaked his feet ankle-high, the lump in his jacket pocket making him seem awkward and slow. A sharp ache in his side forced him to walk when he crossed the road leading to the trees.

This is crazy, he said to himself. Maybe she's at a friend's watching TV. Maybe she tried to call.

With no leaves budding the trees looked lean and black, and the path to the river seemed wide. His feet ached from the cold inside his waterlogged shoes. He wrapped his arms around himself and began making his way down the path.

What would you do, a voice said to him. *If.*

I'll kill him, he said to himself. I'll kill him without thinking twice. If he touches her, harms one ounce of her, I'll use the gun.

Billy would never do a thing like that. Billy Brand. William Allan Brand, the boy who just an hour ago drove by and waved, his meaning as ambiguous as his face was serene. God bless you, Dr. Holmay, for you have done right by me all along. God bless you, for though you have done me wrong, I forgive you anyway.

Billy would never do anyone harm.

Billy was mentally ill.

Billy was bright and good and innocent. He was writing a book.

Billy was a paranoid schizophrenic.

Billy had all the essential qualities lacking in modern man. Billy would inherit the earth.

Billy was mad.

Holmay saw him just as Evelyn ducked out of sight among the rocks along the water's edge.

"Billy!" Holmay called out.

Scrambling down the rocky ledge, Billy disappeared.

"Billy!" Holmay called out again. "I know you're down there!"

Silence.

"Come on up from there! I want to talk to you. I know Evelyn's there too."

Holmay took a few steps forward.

"Don't come any closer." Billy's voice was calm and clear.

Holmay hesitated. "I want to talk to you, Billy."

"Leave me alone. Tell him, Evelyn, tell him to leave us alone."

"Evelyn, I want you to come home with me now."

"Leave us alone," Billy said, not raising his voice. "Please don't make another move."

"Dad, Dad, please! Leave us alone for a while."

"Evelyn!" Holmay shouted. "I'm counting to three and then I'm coming to take you home. Did you hear me? One... "

Billy's face appeared above the rocky ledge.

" ...two... "

Billy, his white shirt visible against the dark background of the trees, had lifted himself halfway up the rocky ledge.

"Please, Dr. Holmay."

"This is your last chance."

"I have a gun, Dr. Holmay. They force me to have a gun."

Billy lifted his arm and pointed a handgun at the sky.

Holmay froze.

"A thirty-eight, Dr. Holmay."

"No Billy, please...not guns."

"What if you were in a jungle full of wild beasts, Dr. Holmay? And what if you hadn't eaten for a week and somebody was beating you up? Or what if somebody was trying to hurt the person you loved more than anyone in the world—then don't you think you had a perfect right to a gun?"

"No one's trying to harm you, Billy...no one..."

"No one's trying to keep Evelyn from me?"

"I just want her to come home."

"I don't want to go home," Evelyn said from below. "I want to stay with Billy."

"I want you at home with me."

"Would you let me come too?"

"We'd have to talk about that, Billy."

"Then we'll have to settle it here. Evelyn wants to stay here with me, Dr. Holmay. She doesn't believe anything you say any more."

"Why, Billy? What have I done wrong?"

Billy's hand tightened on the gun, which he pointed carelessly to the left of Holmay's feet. Holmay, his mind racing, did not move. Billy was fewer than fifty feet away.

"What have I done wrong, he asks." Billy spoke as if he were thinking out loud, his audience the trees to whose upper branches his eyes wandered as he went on. "But he really knows, and he can't fool us any more. Does he think we don't know he's been checking up on us all the time? That he's the one who keeps me from getting the post office job? That he locked me out of his house, then put me in that awful hospital and never wanted us to get out again?"

Holmay stepped forward to object.

"Stop!" Billy shouted, aiming the gun at him. "You are supposed to be an honest man, Dr. Holmay, a man of your word. Can you in all honesty say that you didn't try to keep Evelyn from me?"

Holmay looked for a way out. Just a few feet to his left was a large maple tree.

"Well...?" Billy said, lowering the gun. "Tell the whole truth. Did you or didn't you?"

"Yes."

Billy turned and looked down at Evelyn. "See. He did. I told you he did. He tried to keep me from seeing you. And tell me another thing," he said, addressing Holmay again. "Why do you hate me so much? I've never done anything wrong to you. I tried to be your very best student. I tried to write a book. Like you. I tried to do everything right."

"I don't hate you, Billy."

"And today, when I drove by, I waved at you. I thought to myself, There's Dr. Holmay, my professor of literature, one of the few who really knows about the life of the mind, the human spirit, what it's like. I waved at you—and you, you looked the other way."

"No, Billy..."

"So I knew right then. You are like the rest, all those content to get and spend. Like lawyers and Dr. Altizer and the vast superficial majority of mankind. I had to see Evelyn right away, talk to her, keep her from getting spoiled. Because I don't know about you any more. There's her goodness and innocence. She should never lose that. That should never change."

Holmay took a step toward the maple tree.

"We are good friends, aren't we, Evelyn? And we love each other, even though I'm older than you. Isn't that true?"

Evelyn, still hidden from view on the rocky ledge, said some words Holmay could not hear.

"And someday, Dr. Holmay, Evelyn and I are going to Brazil."

Holmay's mind raced through the alternatives again. He could make a dash toward Billy, zig-zagging his way, hoping to lunge at him, rip the gun away. Or he could try coaxing his way, keep smooth-talking him, lure Billy away from Evelyn and make a dash for it across the open field.

Or maybe, maybe, if he could get behind the maple tree, have just a few seconds to get his own gun free.

Billy could shoot Evelyn point blank.

"Billy, I only want what's right for Evelyn."

"But nowadays everything's all wrong. Evil and corruption in Washington, D.C. You said so yourself in class once. How can we keep Evelyn from growing up under the influence?" Billy laughed a crazy little laugh. "Unless we killed everyone in the world. And that would be pretty hard to do."

Holmay searched for words, his legs dizzy beneath him.

"I know what you're thinking. You've been thinking of ways to get rid of me. You want me to go away. You've always wanted me to go away."

"No, Billy, I want what's best for you."

"Then answer me. Why should we let Evelyn grow up in a world like this? How can you keep her safe from the influences? What does she have to look forward to in a world like this?"

"Love, Billy."

For a moment the word filled the silence, all motions of trees and wind standing still as the word disappeared into the sky. Billy relaxed his grip on the gun and let his arm down to his side. Turning halfway toward Evelyn he let out a deep sigh.

"Yes, love," he said almost inaudibly.

Evelyn said something from below.

"But your father doesn't care, Evelyn."

"I do," Holmay said. "Billy, I really do."

"You love me?"

"Yes, yes."

"You love me as much as you love Evelyn?"

Holmay reached out with his hand and began walking toward Billy.

"Yes, Billy, I do."

Suddenly Billy wheeled and aimed the gun at Holmay's head.

"Stop right there! You lied! You lied again! If you love her the way you love me, she might as well be dead! All of us might as well be dead! Why can't you, Mr. Doctor of Philosophy, just tell the truth? Can't you see that I've finally learned how to read?"

Billy ducked down and disappeared onto the rocks at the water's edge. Holmay hesitated, but his legs, insane with terror, sprang forward toward the rocks, his hands ripping the gun loose from his pocket.

"Billy! Goddammit Billy, you better listen to me!"

Holmay steadied his hand, sighting the gun toward the rocky ledge.

"Billy! You keep your hands off that girl!"

He heard nothing as Billy's form appeared on the rocky ledge. Then a sound like a sharp thunderclap reverberated off the sky, mushrooming as it went howling away through the trees.

"Evelyn!" he screamed, "Evelyn!"

He found her holding the sides of her head, her eyes wide with terror and disbelief. On the rock next to her, his head twisted away from the hand that still held the gun, lay Billy, the blood from the wound in his head already winding down the side of the rocks to the water below, where like indecipherable hieroglyphs it disappeared in the current swirling downstream.

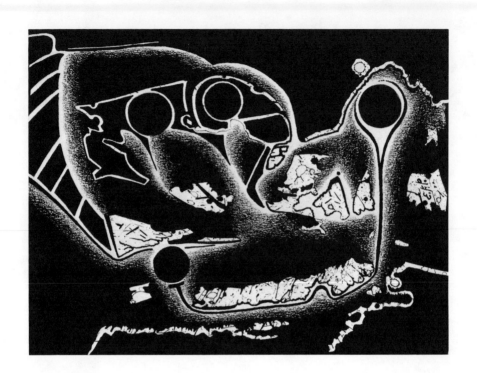

Thirty-two

SHE HELD HER hands over her ears and turned away, too stunned to comprehend. On April 16, the day she turned ten, she ran upstairs to her room just as her friends began lighting the candles on her cake. As the spring warmed she curled up against an invisible cold, her chin on her knees, her hands still over her ears. And after the first leaves appeared on trees she sat in the window staring at a silence extending far beyond the distant sky.

He watched her, guarded her, guided her by hand the way he did when she was barely able to walk, releasing her into the solitude of her own room only right before it was time for bed. He closed the door and promised not to turn off the lights, not even after she fell asleep.

One night, when he found her weeping quietly in her bed, he again tried to explain.

"No," he said, "something took hold of him, something he couldn't control. "It was as if...Billy did not kill himself."

Through trembling lips she whispered her response. "No, *you* did."

He tried staring her down. "Why do you keep blaming me?"

"Because you wouldn't let him move in."

The next morning he made pancakes for her, light-brown on both sides. He surprised her afterward with a new dress, and when he watched her walking toward school she seemed warm enough, well-insulated against a chill that seemed stalled overhead.

His students fell into their silences, their faces, even after weeks of reporting to him promptly on the hour, those of strangers lost in their privacies. Again he tried to explain to them the lives of characters he loved best, characters he knew because the printed page had privileged them to stand still long enough for him to see them complete in their strengths and weaknesses, devotions and desires, each driven and doomed by dreams grander than the paltry facts of ordinary experience that eventually did them in. Here once again for the whole world to see was Faulkner's pathetic Emily Grierson, whose love poisoned the man who tried to run off with it; and his tragic Nancy, her hands losing their grip on things because she was so 'niggerized,' out of desperation surrendering herself to the terror of Jesus' narrow-minded love; and Flaubert's Felicité, the simple heart, her Holy Ghost a lifetime of good works personified by a rotting green parrot stuffed with rags; and of course there was, again and again, Melville's Bartleby, the scrivener who preferred not to live in a Wall Street world, and therefore could live in no one's world. Ah Bartleby! Ah humanity!

"Do you see," he said, returning to the theme still one more time, "the lawyer was wrong not to take Bartleby in. He had no right to his comfort and privacy as long as another needed his help."

Again the faces in the seats in front of him said yes, yes, that seems decent and logical, a few able to contemplate the implications of taking the words seriously.

"That lady," Evelyn asked one night, "that Miss Drummond?"

"Yes?"

"Do you see her very much?"

"I see her almost every day."

"Why don't you ever go out with her? She's really nice. Remember when we went for pizza that night? I think you should go out with her."

That night Evelyn went to her room early, closing the door as if she were still holding her hands over her ears. He knocked lightly before looking in on her.

"I've got cookies and a glass of milk."

She took them and set them next to her bed.

"A penny for your thoughts."

She put a cookie on her lap and turned away.

"How are things going at school?"

"Okay."

"Do you have homework tonight?"

"No."

"What are you doing in your English class?"

"Boring stuff. Pronouns and stuff."

"That's not what English is all about."

She looked at him. "Then what's English all about, Dad?"

"Poems, stories, plays."

"Like the ones Billy told me?"

"Yes."

She trembled as she took a sip from her milk, then pulled the blanket in tight to her chest.

"Dad, I want to go live with Mom."

"You can't be serious."

"I wrote to her last week and she called again yesterday. She says it's fine with her. She says I have to ask you."

"You mean you want to live with her for good?"

"Yes."

He did not have to ask why. He sat on the edge of the bed and drew her close.

"Let's give it some thought," he said. "Do you know how much I'd miss you if you did that? Maybe you could try it for a couple weeks. Let's give it some thought before we decide."

She made room for him next to her and pulled the folktale book from the shelf. "Now read," she said, handing it to him.

He read, first the one about the little shepherd boy no bigger than a mite, and then about the widower's beautiful daughter Stellina who outwitted the king of the animals, the words carrying him into a world where magic, peril, trials, monsters, and happiness wore bright-colored clothes in the streets of old villages. Evelyn was alert as he read, following the scenes passing before her eyes. When he got to the last line of Stellina's story—her journey to India with the prince and all their treasure, their marriage and happiness forevermore—she took in the picture a long moment before picking up her cookie again.

"I wish I had been living in those days," she said, yawning. "Now read the one about the king's daughter who could never get enough figs."

Holmay stiffened. "Did I hear you say please?"

"Just read, Dad."

The little brat. What right did she have, this girl, to speak to him in the imperative? What were his, a father's rights?

Do you dare dream, his heart said as she closed her eyes, that just because I bumbled into your life—do you think you will escape your tour of duty with me? Remember, you slept in my arms all the way home, the April sun still cold that day. And it was I who took control from the start. On the fifth day, long before I took you to any park, it was I who permitted a breeze to touch your skin, and when your first autumn came, I let go of your arms, requiring first steps toward a second fall. And suddenly you are ten. So now, my little brat, I will chart your progress in Five Year Plans. First, you will begin by reading leaves of grass more closely than every other kid, and then your bones must memorize the laws of buoyancy, from the simple rule of floating face-up to the intermediate ballet of dolphin-dives. For your science and math you will put your ear to the ground and figure the sum of all small sounds, afterwards brushing your hair, as I once did, a hundred times. When I see vague longing shivering through boys bewildered by the light shimmering off that hair, I will plot all further plans in secrecy. You will learn the indoor games—the monopoly of money and place, the checkers of souls and flesh, and the religious touch, the politics of chess every damned spirit requires. When we go out I will take you to rocks, run your hand over them until you memorize their names, take you through museums made of stone, make presents of shells, chrome, agates, steel balls, show you why even the earth some day will crack. You will strengthen your arms, grow merely to endure these things, and me. And as you enter this terrible age I will let work march you clean down corridors, require you to walk on the right, smile when you come to the door of some boss. Then at night I will school you in make-up art, buy paints that cover fresh lines on your brow, demand that you practice twisting your face—until you play fully your perfect parts. And on Saturday nights when you go "just out" to fill some Ford with your perfume, I will sleep lightly in my chair, stealing upstairs as you slip in the house, turning on my light when you are in your own bed. So you will see I am awake, waiting for you and sleep to take even me until you, next morning, are gone. Only then will I have no more of you, because by then all blacks and reds will stand squared off, and the world will be sagging under its own chemical weight, stalemated eyes no longer wondering at the balance of terror losing its grip. Thus unarmed, my girl, then I will have to let you go.

He waited, again expecting her to show some sign of gratitude, hoping she would open her eyes and say, No Dad, I don't ever want to go. As she pulled the blanket over herself and rolled her shoulder toward the wall, he turned off the light, unaware that once again he had not locked the doors.

EMILIO DEGRAZIA grew up three blocks away from Detroit, Michigan, where his father worked in the Ford Rouge Plant. In 1959 he entered Albion College, and then went on to receive his Ph.D. from Ohio State University. Currently he works as a fiction editor of *Great River Review* and teaches at the state university in Winona, Minnesota, where he lives with his wife and two daughters.

DeGrazia has been writing for more than fifteen years, "for the same reason, I suppose, that serious readers read: so they can find their way out of the labyrinth by following the lines on a printed page." In addition to essays and poetry, DeGrazia has had several short stories published in literary journals, and his collection of fiction, *Enemy Country* (New Rivers Press, 1984), was selected by Anne Tyler as a Writer's Choice.